PINWHEEL

BRETT PERKINS

To my father, Randy Perkins,

philosopher of the Palouse hills

who taught me the invaluable art

of laughing at one's self.

PINWHEEL

1

After a stop at the coat check room, Exlee Ellis moved toward the heart of The Golden Goose nightclub. On the way, he greeted a waiter named Vince, then exchanged smiles with two women who walked arm in arm to the ladies' room. The club opened into a large expanse, and Exlee stopped to look down on the main floor, where tables and booths surrounded a polished dance floor. It was a Sunday night, so the crowd was thinner, but there was still plenty of eating and drinking and laughing and dancing. Silky Sherwood's orchestra was delivering the swing, but without the same pep they had the first week of their booking. The assembled didn't care; it was just background noise to their carousing, anyway. Something to enliven the lubricated conversations they wouldn't want to remember tomorrow, even if they could.

Exlee's nighttime playground was made up of places like this—the city's restaurants, nightclubs, bars, and any other venue where people drank too much and said things they wouldn't normally say. Anyone who spent time in these Stout City establishments recognized

Exlee Ellis—in all likelihood they'd had the memorable pleasure of interacting with him. He was 29 years old, tall and sort of handsome, and no one really knew how to figure him. He just didn't add up in the usual way. He was innovative, but too often toward impractical things. He had hustle, but shunned achievement. He was cynical but always optimistic. No one understood Exlee, yet everyone liked him, even his would-be enemies.

His career—if one could call it that—was just as difficult to define. The closest thing to a title would be press agent. It's what kept him entertained during the daylight hours while coincidently providing him an uneven income. Mostly, Exlee represented a bunch of low-level attorneys who inhabited the courthouse district. He embellished upon their seedier cases, turning them into salacious little stories, which he sometimes sold and sometimes gave to the newspapers. The lawyers paid him a bit for the publicity it garnered, and the newspapers gave him a bit for providing easy content. Exlee also dabbled in a few other endeavors related to publicity, which, when cobbled together, represented the semblance of a livelihood.

Not that it was an impressive livelihood. The money he received was far from noteworthy, but he made up for that by spending it with style, often in creative flurries. This compulsion for unburdening himself of money as quickly as possible was indulged during his rounds among Stout City nightlife. The laughs didn't cost much, but the women were pricey and the gambling was downright expensive. Sometimes he combined all three, like the time he bet a woman she couldn't unbutton her blouse and put it on backward in under twenty seconds. It was the reckless sort of wager that only Exlee could get away with; he'd even enticed her husband to throw money into the pot.

PINWHEEL

Tonight, Exlee surveyed the small crowd at The Golden Goose, trying to decide if he wanted to join the commotion. The majority of the assembled were happy to be out of the house, enjoying someone else's cooking, sipping on drinks and dancing to every third tune, but there was also the usual array of drunkenness, ranging from the man with his head on the table to the couple supporting each other on the dance floor. Exlee found each vignette intriguing and always wanted to know more about the people involved. He found that the best way to learn about people was to offer them engagement of the unexpected variety.

Ordinarily, after assessing the scenarios spread out before him, Exlee would wade in, seeking fun where he saw possibility, but tonight, he was preoccupied and couldn't seem to shake it.

A significant opportunity had arisen two days prior—one that might profoundly affect his "career." Whether this opportunity would be converted into a large success, however, depended on Exlee's careful handling of certain angles. They had circled his mind the entire weekend as he prepared to put things in motion Monday morning.

For the first time that Exlee could recall, his day life was encroaching upon his night life, and it was adversely affecting his carefree pursuit of fun. Even the flirtations from the new coat check girl had seemed bothersome despite her cute nose. Normally he'd have attempted to make hay with her before she discovered his reputation for self-inflicted poverty, but tonight he'd just wanted his coat checked. And right now, he just wanted to sit down, which he did at the bar.

"Hiya, Exlee, what's new?" the bartender asked.

"Not a thing, Billy, not a thing," Exlee answered without spirit. He sat turned halfway to enable further scanning of the crowd.

"Charlie G. was just lookin' for you," the bartender said as he placed a glass of beer in front of Exlee.

"Oh yeah, what did he want?" Exlee asked with mild curiosity.

"Whaddya think? He's taking action on the Carnera-Paulino fight and figured you would want in."

"I dunno. I think I've already placed a couple wagers on that. If you see him before I do, tell him probably not. Oh, and give him this." Exlee pulled a five dollar bill from his pocket and laid it on the bar. "He still returns around closing time, right?"

"Not every Sunday, but most. What kind of crazy bet did you lose this time?" Billy asked.

Exlee brightened at the memory and swung around to face the bartender. "So Charlie and I were over at the Clover Club last week, and we got to joking about a table of four we were watching. You could tell that some sort of disagreement occurred, and pretty soon they were all watching the band to avoid looking at each other. The awkwardness was heavy. Well, I couldn't help myself ... "

"You never try."

" ... and I bet Charlie I could have that table happy in six minutes. He took it, of course, and I went over to the table and pulled up a chair and spoke to one of the gals. It was two men and two women—young couples—and this one gal looked like a bit of a pistol. When you tackle an awkward scene, you always start with the most emotional—they'll usually engage in a big way and you get the worst outta the way. Anyhow, I asked her point blank why she seemed so angry. Sure enough, this only made her madder and she told me to mind my own business."

"Good advice."

"So I told her she seemed like a hothead and that she must have started the argument. Well, naturally, her date spoke up wondering who I was, but this only renewed her being annoyed at him. Back and forth they went with the other couple jumping in and catching a little venom of their own. The four of them got so heated they forgot about me. The clock was tickin' on my bet, though, so I interrupted and explained that from where I'd been sitting—removed from the picture, so to speak—there seemed to be real chemistry between the two of 'em. It's why I'd come over—because they seemed like such a fascinating couple. Well, naturally that pleased them, and then I asked the fella—the one dating the pistol—if he could imagine loving anyone else. That was a bit risky, using the word love, but I figured two people getting that emotional had to be in love, and he admitted he couldn't imagine loving anyone else. That really pleased the pistol. So now that there was a semblance of peace, I had to act fast since Charlie was up there at the bar glancing at his watch."

"Here comes the good part."

"Oh, you'll love this one, Billy. I said to the four of them, 'Speaking of chemistry, who thinks I can get a woman to dance with me using only my facial expressions? No words allowed. No hand motions. You pick any woman in here, and I bet I can get her on the dance floor in forty-five seconds.'"

"Where do you come up with these strange numbers for timing?" Billy asked.

"It creates intrigue, as though there's real calculation behind the bet. A minute is too round and obvious. And forty-three seconds sounds too specific, makes 'em wonder if it's a trick. So anyway, they accepted the bet and picked out a slightly older woman who was clearly married and looked like she hadn't attempted fun since fourth grade. I wish you could have seen her, Billy. Prim and proper. Why she was in a nightclub, I have no idea. Maybe her husband was wooing some client for his accounting firm."

"Was the husband there at the table?"

"Uh huh, along with three other men—stuffed shirts. Well, you can imagine how that worked out, me standing at their table making come-hither faces to this startled woman. I hadn't really thought it through as to what expressions would work best, so I foolishly started by hamming too much, flicking my eyebrows and winking like some pervert just released from a mental institution. I should have gone with friendly and happy; she might have thought I was shy. But it was too late. I knew I was losing this bet from the moment her eyes met mine. Oh, and the poor husband ... "

Exlee dropped his head and laughed at the memory while Billy waited eagerly for him to continue.

"The poor husband couldn't figure out what to do. Not knowing me, he wasn't sure if I was coming on to his wife or clowning with her. I could see him out the corner of my eye, and the look on his face was so funny and so distracting."

"So did the wife say anything or what?"

"Nope. She stared at me in confusion, then she looked at her husband, then she looked back at me with horror in her eyes. She couldn't decide if I was a molester or having a breakdown, but the idea of dancing with me never crossed her mind."

"So you lost the bet?"

"It was a complete failure. Cost me five bucks at the first table—the one with the pistol—but now they were laughing out loud, meaning I won the original bet easily—the one with Charlie. It was a wash from the money standpoint, but the gamble was what made it a stunt, and stunts are memorable. And people love a good memory."

"Wait a minute. Why am I delivering your five bucks if it was a wash?"

"Because I couldn't help myself. A little later I bet Charlie I could still get her to dance, using words this time. It didn't work, though. She said she didn't dance with lunatics, and the husband told me to go bother some other woman and wondered why I was so interested in her. That was his mistake."

"What do you mean, mistake?"

"Later, on a trip back from the ladies' room, she wandered past and handed me a note with her phone number. Never said a word, just handed me the note and smiled a little bit. Could be that she really does like lunatics, but I'm guessing she was just insulted that her husband wondered why I would want to dance with her, of all people."

"Well, you be careful with that one," Billy warned. "Those quiet, proper women have a lot of pent-up passion. Seriously, if you meet her at a hotel, pick one near a hospital in case she gives you heart attack."

Exlee laughed. "Don't worry, I'm taking a pass. That kind of arrangement is more trouble than it's worth. You end up climbing out of hotel windows wearing nothing but socks."

Billy chuckled then moved down the bar to take care of some other patrons before returning to Exlee.

"What's the matter with your beer?" the bartender asked, noting that Exlee had hardly touched his glass.

"Nothing. It's good stuff."

"Nah, somethin' ain't right," Billy decided. "What's goin' on with you tonight?"

Exlee continued staring out at the dance floor without answering. This was so unlike Exlee that the bartender thought he'd try one more time.

"Come on, Ex, what are you thinking?"

"Really, it's nothing," he told Billy. "I just have something happening tomorrow, and I'm running the angles through my head. Matter of fact, maybe I'll call it a night."

On the way out, he stopped by the coat check room. The new girl still had a cute nose, but she wasn't as flirty, handing over Exlee's hat with a polite smile but no comment. He was starting to leave when a glance over his shoulder explained the girl's new attitude. There was another woman sitting on a chair in the back corner of the little coat room. She could only be spotted from this angle, and even then all that could be seen were her legs—hanging coats covered the rest. Exlee didn't need to see her face to know she was having a bad night. Borrowing the coat check seat was one of those last resort tricks that females always shared with each other. You borrowed that chair when you'd had too much to drink, or needed to hide from a bad date. Females could be hard on each other, but when it came to surviving among the male animal, they were teammates.

"Who's riding in the back seat?" Exlee asked the coat check girl as he returned to her Dutch door counter.

"Just a friend."

"Well, I'm guessing your friend would be better off at home. Tell her I'll get her there."

The coat check girl wavered. She liked Exlee's face and had a good feeling about him, but she was new and wanted to protect her sister in need. She turned and looked back at the woman, trying to stall for time while gauging the risk.

Exlee appreciated the girl's concern. He walked to the club's entrance and returned with the doorman.

"Tim, tell this gal I'm all right, wouldya?"

"Depends on the definition of all right," Tim wisecracked.

"Very funny. Just tell her I can be trusted to get her friend home safely."

"He'll get her home safely," Tim declared. "It's just when he gets her there that she ain't safe."

Exlee smiled sheepishly at the coat check girl, wishing he'd explained to Tim that now was not the time for kidding. "Seriously, Tim, tell her the truth."

"All right, the truth is I've known Exlee a long time—since I worked at Five Aces—and he'll take care of your friend. On the level."

The coat check girl studied the two men with a stern expression then turned and retreated to the back corner where the woman sat. They talked softly before the woman stood up and emerged unsteadily from behind the wall of coats.

Exlee had never seen her before. He estimated she was in her late thirties. Her hair was a little disheveled, and she wore an expression of shame and sickness. If he were betting on it, he'd have wagered she was a divorcee who had tried to be fun but had wasted her effort on some bum who'd been counting on the type of fun she wasn't ready to provide.

The coat check girl mouthed "Thanks" to Exlee as he took the woman's arm in his and led her outside.

A taxi got them to the woman's apartment building near the corner of Fern Street and Montgomery. Exlee paid the driver then guided the woman up a flight of stairs to her apartment, where he waited in the hall until she was safely inside with the door locked behind her.

Exlee sauntered down the stairs, feeling satisfied, when an unsettling thought washed over him. A quick inventory of his pockets confirmed his fear: He was broker than usual. The expense of the taxi ride had reduced his holdings to forty-five cents.

He would be hoofing it home tonight.

PINWHEEL

It was September 24, 1934, and while most of Stout City slept, Exlee began the long walk homeward, thinking about his meeting with the newspaper editor tomorrow.

2

"Send someone down to the nineteenth precinct, will ya?" ordered Deacon Lowe, managing editor of the *Stout City Sun*. "They just booked some guy for stealing a car."

"That's all?" his assistant editor, Emma Beltran, asked.

"The car belonged to Bishop Harvey."

"Still ... "

"There happened to be a woman in the backseat."

"That could be bad."

"It is. She's Protestant."

"Ah. I'll get right on it," Emma promised. "By the way, who tipped you off on this?"

"Got it from Exlee Ellis, who got it from one of his shoddy lawyers. Just talked to him on the phone, and he says he has another story that's even better. Something so good he needs to tell me in person, so I'm gonna head over to Aronoff's and meet him there."

"Sounds good. Tell him he still owes me five bucks from our bet on the Iowa State-Nebraska game."

"You two are making bets now?" Deacon asked with mock suspicion.

"Oh please, Deacon, he's half my age. Then again, what single woman wouldn't wanna gamble with Exlee?"

"One with genuine hopes of marriage." The editor laughed as he unrolled his sleeves and put on his suit coat.

He walked down the hall, descended two sets of stairs and emerged from the side entrance of the *Sun's* headquarters. The brightness of the outside world caused Deacon to pause while his eyes squinted and blinked. Standing alone, he looked very small next to the eleven-story Sun building.

John Lowe was his given name, but he was known to everyone simply as Deacon. The nickname was hung on him by a long forgotten reporter who'd marveled at the editor's resemblance to half the Protestant church officials he'd known growing up in the Midwest.

The reason the nickname stuck was because it was apt in many ways. Deacon never yelled, never cursed, and his displays of tranquility among chaos were legendary. He was the only man in Stout City capable of being mugged amicably. He even looked the part of a deacon, graciously plain in appearance so as not to divert a gaze that might be used on others. His only distinguishable feature was soft, white hair that seemed to rest atop him like a gentle cloud lingering over Mount Olympus. He was 58 years old and had been his entire life.

But underneath the pastoral calm there functioned a shrewd mind. Deacon had a unique ability to absorb details and connect dots. He could tell you how the price of a hot dog on Weston Avenue was connected to Mrs. Owings losing her car keys in the Crown Heights neighborhood. Stout City was made up of thousands of moving parts, which produced a million bits of ever-changing information, and nobody was more skillful at interpreting them than Deacon. It kept him ahead of the game and allowed him to prepare for news while it was still teething.

Furthermore, for a man with such a saintly bearing, Deacon could be cunning, even by the dubious standards of the newspaper business. And while he did not condone fake news or blatant abuse of facts, he was adept at using his guile to the point of amorality, and sometimes beyond. If, for example, there were a story which refused to surface, yet would be of benefit to the readers, Deacon was wily enough to manipulate things behind the scenes for the greater good. This perfectly suited the owners of the *Sun,* who insisted on maintaining the paper's above-average reputation but otherwise didn't care how circulation was maintained—as long as the number of libel suits was kept within reason. For twenty-six years, Deacon had carefully maintained this balance of principles, not only for the *Sun*, but for the citizens of Stout City.

He understood that he was more than just a purveyor of information; he was its engineer and its masseuse. With television and computers far in the future and radios still in their infancy, newspapers were the preeminent source of civic knowledge in 1934. Thus, what Deacon Lowe deemed printable in the *Sun* was what its readers were consigned to using when forming opinions. This power bestowed on Deacon, combined with his wisdom and his caginess, made him a dangerously important man. And the funny part was that very few *Sun* readers could have identified him in person. As a matter of fact, no one offered a flicker of recognition as he strode down the sidewalk toward Aronoff's Drug Store.

Twice a day, at 11 a.m. and 3 p.m., he left the paper's downtown office for a quick glass of either orangeade or lemonade at Aronoff's Drug Store. The three-block stroll helped to refresh his mind after hours spent in an office full of cigarette smoke, typewriter clanging, and the incessant ringing of telephones. Today, Deacon was using his 11 o'clock visit to meet press agent Exlee Ellis.

Press agents were the newest trend in publicity. Representing everything from opera companies to merchant associations to racketeers seeking a better image, these agents promised to get their clients' names in newspaper articles. It was cheaper than advertising and resonated stronger with readers because seeing someone's name in an article smacked of legitimacy.

From the newspaper's perspective, press agents meant fresh information without the cost and hassle of a reporter. On the other hand, the information was slanted, and the characters who provided it were often a headache. Anybody could declare themselves an agent. There was no training required. All you needed was a lot of chutzpah and a clean suit. Many of these hustlers were fly-by-night operators who promised their clients more than they could deliver. Others were charming raconteurs or clownish hucksters, dispensing cigars and jokes as a means of gaining favor with members of the press. In fact, several press agents were ex-newspaper reporters who'd found the pay greener and the work less demanding on the other side—a boon to their already ambitious drinking schedule.

Naturally, there were many upright examples among the agents—like Buck Gordon, who represented the Stout City Stock Exchange—and it was from this established pool that Deacon took the occasional phone call. The rest of the riffraff he left to his reporters.

The one exception was Exlee Ellis. Even though Exlee promoted the tawdriest of the city's lawyers, he was an irresistible rascal whose only true ambition seemed to be entertaining himself. Others were seduced into joining this experience, often without realizing how it happened. But if Exlee had ever used this, or any of his other dubious skills, toward anything large or useful, Deacon was unaware of it.

Arriving at Aronoff's and ordering an orangeade without breaking stride, Deacon moved along the soda counter until he reached an empty stool next to Exlee Ellis.

"Mornin', Exlee. Can't say that I've ever seen you up before noon."

"Mornings are a bother, like bread crust." Exlee smiled.

The orangeade appeared in front of Deacon, and he took a large slug before gently setting his glass down and continuing. "Well, I gotta be honest, you wanting to see me this side of lunch has me awfully curious."

"Trust me, I've got something good for you. Something that could *really* help your paper."

"Good, because our paper needs some help. Lots of it, actually. Whaddya got?" Deacon asked.

"Maybe it'd be better if I told you next door. You'll understand after I explain it."

Deacon shrugged, calmly finished off his orangeade, and followed the agent outside. They entered a neighboring dry cleaning business and walked past the counter—manned by a weary looking husband and wife—around the hanging clothes, and into a back office. Deacon found a rickety chair, and Exlee sat on the edge of a desk.

As Exlee glanced around the desk to make sure he wasn't sitting on something important, Deacon took a moment to envy the young press agent. He guessed Exlee was in his late twenties, well over six feet tall. He had dark brown hair that lounged about carelessly, not exactly bothering to be curly or straight or long or short. And while he wasn't quite what you'd call handsome, Exlee had so much confidence and easy allure that observers believed him to be better looking than he was. It was beyond the editor's understanding why such a dynamic young man was content as a minor league press agent. But, all in all, Deacon was not ashamed to admit he would love to change places with the kid.

"This must be really special if we're meeting in one of your makeshift offices," Deacon said as he looked around, noting the dusty blinds and a wall calendar that was five months behind. "How'd you wangle the use of this one?"

"It's a funny story, really. I came in here to have a little laundry done, and there was this middle-aged fella roaring at the owners because his suit coat came back with a button missing. I think he was trying shake them down for a little cash, probably loosened the button at home. Anyhow, he was a mean guy, kept making all sorts of threats, and I finally got tired of hearing him and offered him the coat I was wearing in exchange for his. Mine was a nice coat, nearly brand new. My aunt had given it to me for my birthday. Well, that shut this guy up, and he didn't know what to do. Both coats were black, but mine was clearly of better quality than his. You could tell he wanted to protest some more—he was counting on that little bit of cash—but he also knew I was offering a good deal. He also knew I could throw him out on the street, so we swapped coats and he left. The owners were grateful, and I asked to use their office now and again when I was in this part of town."

"So what did you do with the lousy coat?"

"I had a button added. Only problem is that he was smaller than me, so the coat fits *real* snug and the arms are kinda short. I wear it to weddings to amuse the grooms and annoy the brides—some of whom are annoying me by getting married."

"You know what I like about you, Exlee?"

"What?"

"Nothing. You're hopeless."

The two men shared a good laugh. "Why do you suppose men enjoy insulting each other so much?" Exlee wondered aloud.

"For goodness sakes, can't you just sit back and enjoy the beautiful quirks of humanity every now and then? Now tell me why I'm in the back of a dry cleaning shop."

Exlee leaned forward for emphasis. "I've got a beauty for you, Deacon. This one is circulation gold, and you'll be thanking me for weeks. It's a case involving a married couple. Apparently she's so devoted to a certain coffee that it's wrecked their marriage. The husband will be filing a lawsuit in a couple days, and I need you to run a piece about it in your paper. It's against Pinwheel Coffee."

Deacon sighed, and his expression changed from curiosity to weariness.

"Pinwheel is the biggest fish in Stout City *and* by far the *Sun's* largest advertiser," Deacon said. "Who's the lawyer representing the couple?"

"Wickenstaff."

"Wickenstaff? I thought he was strictly collection notices. Has he even tried a case in court?" Deacon asked before waving away the question. "More importantly, is he really filing suit or is this just some public extortion trick?"

"Now you see why I brought you over here." Exlee beamed. "This one is an attention grabber, and it gets better. The husband claims that the wife can't get enough of their newest brand—Tingle. She drinks it all the time, depends on it for her good moods. And here's the kicker: He even claims that she prefers it to him when it really counts, if you get what I'm sayin'."

"In the sack, you mean?"

Exlee nodded with triumph.

"Suppose it's just that the husband is a humdrum lover," Deacon countered. "Maybe he's tryin' to shift the blame for his mediocrity to the poor coffee company."

"Would you go public with something like that unless you were genuinely convinced something else was to blame? Matter of fact, this rift between 'em is strong enough that they're living apart—separated, so to speak. I know you're used to me delivering small legal pieces, but this one is different. It has all the makings of a big deal."

"Bigger than you know. But listen, for this to be legit, you'd need proof that Pinwheel is doing something to make their coffee unusually addictive. Otherwise it's simply public blackmail. I shouldn't even touch this until it's a genuine lawsuit."

"I know, and you're gonna have to trust me when I tell you that my boy, Wickenstaff, has the goods on Pinwheel. He swears he has at least two reliable sources *and* a laboratory report that says there might be something fishy in the coffee, some sort of drug, perhaps. This is gonna make some noise, this one. And don't forget, I *could* be shopping it around to the other three papers, but you've always helped me out, Deacon, and I wanna help you out. You print this in your paper on the bottom of the front page, and I guarantee you all the exclusivity I can manage. You know in your heart this is the kind of story that moves copies. It could be big for both of us."

"So now you want this business on the front page? That's really pushing it, Exlee. We've done right by each other for a long time, but you're asking a lot from me right now."

"Just the *bottom* of the front page." Exlee grinned unabashedly. "Below the fold. That's all I'm asking." He retrieved a folded sheet of paper from inside his suit coat and handed it to Deacon. It was the item Exlee wished to see in the *Sun*.

Deacon unfolded the paper and scanned through it before setting it in his lap and rubbing the back of his neck.

"Here's the deal," Deacon explained. "If I were to do this—and that's a big if—I'd need to polish this up a bit. Also, I owe Pinwheel a chance to comment. And finally, I need the names and address of the married couple."

"Deac, you'll have the names in a few days, when the suit is filed, but right now ... "

"Listen, kid, I know you want to play it your way, but I still have owners and an editor in chief, don't I? It's bad enough that you're asking us to antagonize our biggest advertiser with innuendo, but the last thing they're gonna want is Pinwheel filing a lawsuit against us for libel. That would be a mess the *Sun* just might not survive."

"But ... "

"I won't print the names of the husband or wife, all right? I just need a little safety net to proceed—and even then, I'm giving you more room than I should."

"I don't know. Do you honestly need the names or is this just about money?"

"This is a lot about that, Exlee. Money does matter, even in the newspaper business, and it's only been exacerbated by this lousy economy. The *Sun* is in bad shape financially. Real bad. The margin for error is darn near gone. Forget the lawsuit, if we lose the Pinwheel account, lots of people would lose their jobs—people with families who give to charity and celebrate Mother's Day."

"Unlike me, I suppose you're hinting. Well, listen, maybe nightclubs aren't charities, but I spend enough most nights to keep a few people employed around town. And I've always played it straight with you, Deacon, and I'm telling you this one has home run potential. *And* just for the record, I celebrate Mother's Day, too. Matter of fact, I call her every Sunday afternoon when she gets back from church, after she's had a chance to rest."

"Probably tired from praying so hard for your questionable soul," Deacon mused. "Yes, you're right, you've always played it straight with me, but this is a different ballgame you're askin' me to play ... and one I've never seen you take an interest in. Those two things concern me because, well, like I said, the stakes have never been higher for any of us—me, you, the *Sun*, Pinwheel. This might amount to nothing, but it might be a disaster for all of us. Are you sure this is on the level, Exlee? Think long and hard before you answer."

"I can't show you the hand I'm holding, Deacon. I can only say that the choice is yours whether you want to play. Somebody like the *Daily Mercury* will if you won't."

Hearing the name of the *Sun's* archrival caused Deacon's brow to furrow. If Exlee was bluffing, he was being defiant about it. Deacon rubbed the back of his neck again as he contemplated his next move.

"Listen, I do appreciate you bringin' this item to me, even if does put my goodies in a vise," Deacon conceded. "That said, I need the names and address of the couple or I can't print it."

Now it was Exlee's turn to consider the next move. After mulling it over, he picked up a pencil stub from the desk and scrawled the names on a piece of scrap paper, which he then handed silently to Deacon.

Deacon studied the paper then looked up at Exlee. "I can't promise you anything, but I'll try and get this in tomorrow's morning edition."

"Thanks, Deacon."

The editor stood up to leave. "Oh, I'm supposed to remind you that you still owe Emma five dollars."

"For what?"

"I believe she said the Iowa State-Nebraska game."

"Damn, I forgot about that. And I even won thirty bettin' the other side. Could have paid her off right then when I had it. At the moment, though ... "

"Who bets both sides of a football game?" Deacon wondered aloud as he exited the back room.

Deacon was glad he had three blocks back to the *Sun's* headquarters. He needed to carefully consider what came next. The *Sun* was caught firmly between a bawdy story with reader appeal and its biggest advertiser. On top of that, the timing couldn't have been worse.

The *Sun's* circulation had been steadily dropping even before the depression. Once upon a time she'd been the city's flagship paper, but now she was seen as the tired paper that appealed primarily to the city's older generation. Perhaps it was the downtown headquarters that stoked this reputation. Housed in the same plain building for decades, the *Sun* had stubbornly watched as important businesses—and the other major newspapers—moved uptown, where the city's vibrancy was now centered. Admittedly, this was probably just one element being held against her, but who could know what made one enterprise enticing and another unwanted? One thing was certain: Despite putting out a quality product, the *Sun* could not seem to shake its reputation, and revenue was sliding; whispers of its demise were growing louder as the depression grew deeper.

Deacon knew that his paper could not withstand much more hardship. He'd heard the rumors from his superiors, had even peeked at the financials when the bookkeeper was at lunch. For the first time, he'd begun to see his future as clouded and uncertain. He'd even begun to imagine what he'd do should the *Sun* fold. Although Deacon figured he could land a position with another paper, he also knew that a switch at his age often meant demotion. His reputation and his years of good work would count for little against the guarded hierarchy of another staff.

His worst nightmare involved the *Sun* being bought by the *Stout City Daily Mercury*—the largest newspaper in Iowa. It was considered a sensationalist tabloid by its competitors, who both loathed and feared the giant. After the Great War, the *Daily Mercury* bought the failing *Stout City Tribune* and had continued to snare the weakest in the herd thereafter, absorbing the *Clarion*, the *Globe*, the *Times-Democrat,* and a host of other, smaller sheets. With each devouring, the *Daily Mercury* became stronger, leveraging the victim's prime assets and discarding the rest. She also became bolder by eliminating stodgy competition, thus expanding her position as the dominant progressive in a thinning landscape. By using more photos and devoting more space to stories of lurid crime, the *Daily Mercury* was not only forcing other papers to become alert to this modern agenda, she loomed as the final, ravenous cannibal for those that didn't.

If one were to poll the Stout City press corps, they'd undoubtedly identify the *Sun* as the *Daily Mercury's* next big meal. And Deacon wouldn't bother to argue it.

By the time he reached the Sun Building's side entrance, he understood what he needed to do next. He had to make a phone call to Pinwheel Coffee, Inc.

3

Pinwheel Coffee was established in Stout City not long after the Great War ended in 1918.

It was the brainchild of First Lieutenant Farrell O'Bryant, who spent months living in muddy trenches throughout France, where he and his comrades began to truly appreciate many things beyond not being shot. They delighted in rare opportunities for dry socks, the sight of a live woman, and even silence. As for simple daily pleasures, they looked forward to coffee and cigarettes for their salvation. The cigarettes were the same as those smoked at home, but the coffee was of the instant variety, a cheap imitation included in their rations. It did the trick, but they dreamed of a future overflowing with strong, genuine coffee.

Farrell O'Bryant, newly awakened to entrepreneurial possibilities, took it a step further, envisioning a coffee company that specialized in a product so robust and caffeine-laden that it would make the drinker's eyes spin like pinwheels. O'Bryant was certain he would corner the market on young ex-soldiers who were sick of drinking sad coffee and who were ready to catch up on life missed, using "pinwheel" coffee to propel them.

Having no experience in the coffee industry, however, O'Bryant was uncertain how such a dynamic brew was to be created. Thankfully, providence intervened near the end of the war. It was in the form of a British soldier whose career in the military had generated a wealth of interesting stories. And it was during the retelling of one of those tales that he unwittingly passed on the secret which would be the cornerstone of O'Bryant's success.

When the war finally ended, O'Bryant returned home and exchanged his uniform for a suit and tie. Though he'd saved all of his wartime pay, O'Bryant was far from wealthy, and he needed a few breaks to make his dream happen. His first stroke of luck was Prohibition. The law banning the production and sale of liquor in America was set to take effect in the coming months, and breweries and distilleries were scrambling to adjust. Some chose to switch over to producing new, legal products like soda pop, but many—crippled by diminished wartime sales—were forced out of business, and their production plants sold cheaply. O'Bryant snagged the former Holzapfel Brewery for little more than the back taxes owed on the property. Even then, it required all of his savings plus a loan from his Uncle Finn to swing it. He still needed some serious capital to restructure the plant for coffee making, as well as for raw product, employees, and equipment. Lacking a substantial background or high profile connections, he was blocked from bank loans. But once again, his timing was perfect.

For every venturist like O'Bryant, who was looking to profit from the pent-up spending of postwar America, there was a capitalist who had already prospered, thanks to the war. Such a capitalist was Jude Ostwald. The small belt-making business he'd inherited from his father had blossomed overnight when it received a government contract to make belts for military uniforms during the war. Without warning, Ostwald was transformed from an apathetic heir with a steady income into a wealthy plutocrat. A restless greed was released within him, one he hadn't realized existed. It seized him, and he began to dream of something bigger and bolder.

When the war ended and the government contract was completed, Ostwald could see the handwriting on the wall. His belt business would settle back into mediocrity unless he fought to build it through traditional wholesale means. His mind was ready to battle, all right, but his heart just wasn't into belts. They were so utilitarian, with little room for innovation. Ostwald wanted to sink his teeth—and his considerable funds—into something lusty and vital, so he sold the belt business while he was still flush and began looking for his new business. In a way, it found him.

Fate brought Ostwald and O'Bryant together as they stood in line at the Stout City courthouse, undertaking separate business. They chatted as they waited, and it soon became apparent that each possessed exactly what the other needed. O'Bryant had a business plan built around a lively product with a proprietary secret, and Ostwald had piles of cash in need of a bold venture. Within two weeks they had finalized a deal to become partners, and Pinwheel Coffee was born.

Both men were in their late 20s and unmarried. Their time was their own, and they invested every spare minute in the company, usually while wired on Pinwheel's special blend. Like most businesses, Pinwheel struggled to make headway in the beginning. Its first big break came when the *Stout City Sun* agreed to run full-page advertisements on the handshake promise of payment when things flourished. Some clever in-house marketing was added, and Pinwheel exploded on the local scene, instantly becoming a Stout City legend before spreading to major cities throughout the country. Their stimulating coffee grounds could be found in restaurants, cafes and businesses of all sizes, but it was the cans plucked from America's grocery shelves that provided the bulk of Pinwheel's fat profits. Just as O'Bryant had envisioned, a newly alive America was trying to burn the candle at three ends. The war had made them hungry for living, and Pinwheel Coffee fueled their restlessness using a special formula infused with prolific levels of pep.

While Pinwheel was a huge success, an inevitable sales plateau occurred when its base market became saturated. There were only so many thrill seekers, lunatics and ex-soldiers in the world. Ostwald and O'Bryant had to admit that a certain portion of the population simply didn't enjoy being buzzed to the gills every day. But they also believed there was a portion who wished to be uplifted, only they were too refined to partake. So, in 1924, the boys rolled out a new line of coffee called Gold Monocle. It was marketed as a dignified coffee with exquisite richness perfect for the man with boardroom ambition. Pinwheel played down its role as the parent company in hopes of creating the impression that Gold Monocle was its own brand, trusting that a new white collar clientele would be more willing to embrace it. And they did. Slowly but surely, freshly shaven men with a shine to their shoes began emptying the shelves and adding shine to their eyes.

Now wealthy and enjoying their time as young playboys, O'Bryant and Ostwald became less ambitious at work and more reckless away from it. Ostwald began indulging in his passion for auto racing, while O'Bryant frequented horse races, where he split his attention between fillies and rich divorcees. As with everything they undertook, their playtime was done on a relentless scale. And not surprisingly, the manic lifestyle was unsustainable, leading to inevitable consequences. O'Bryant was shot by a discarded paramour, the bullet missing its target by inches and lodging in his thigh. Ostwald crashed his Special Flyer at a race in Cleveland, shattering his ankle. He would forever walk with a limp.

Thus, by the end of their first decade in business together they were spent, even becoming tolerant to the dizzying effects of their own coffee. Ready to catch their breath and relax for a bit, they became family men.

Ostwald was the first to surrender. He married a schoolteacher named Helen he'd met on a train to Florida. Just after their first anniversary, a daughter, Annie, was born. She had barely taken her first steps when her sister, Phyllis, arrived.

O'Bryant met his bride, Maggie, while attending a friend's birthday party. She'd been hired to pop out of a large, fake cake while singing "Make Me a Wish." Maggie also proved to be quite fertile, birthing Kay a breathtaking nine months and two weeks after saying "I do."

Fully familied and suburbanized, the two men grew restless again, ready to renew their capitalistic marauding. But no sooner had they begun to roll up their sleeves than the country's economy went sour thanks, in part, to the stock market crash of 1929. The high octane lifestyle of the Roaring Twenties morphed into the austerity of the depression. The new reality for most consumers was living with less—and sometimes without. For some, this meant the end of coffee consumption altogether, while others reused their grounds in an effort to stall the expense of the next coffee purchase.

The boys' desire to conquer the marketplace was replaced by the necessity of keeping the company profitable.

At first, Pinwheel survived by cutting prices, but as the depression tightened its grip, a new strategy was needed. The portion of their sales taking the hardest hit was the grocery arena, and after studying consumer habits, they came to the conclusion that new purchasing dynamics had come into play thanks to the depression. One surprising discovery was the increased power of the wife. She had always been the primary grocery shopper, but now she was the final word. Husbands, stung by the reduction in their earning power, were ashamed to insist on their preferred brand of coffee, and the women were deciding the family brand. Too many of them were embarrassed to buy Pinwheel—a blatant buzz brew—or Gold Monocle—a pretentious choice with manly overtones and a higher price tag.

Desperate to stay profitable, O'Bryant and Ostwald poured their efforts into creating a new brand that appealed to females. It had to fit this emerging paradigm in which women didn't just make shopping trips, they called the shots. The marketing department was pushed to the limit, working long hours while constantly being reminded that Pinwheel's fortunes depended upon their brilliance. The result was Tingle. It sounded like a more delicate buzz—which every housewife secretly desired—and because it was cheap and the packaging was subtly feminine, the brain trust at Pinwheel were certain they had created a perfect brand for current conditions. So certain, in fact, that they gambled the bulk of Pinwheel's cash reserves on launching the new brand.

It had only been out a few months, but so far the sales figures had fallen short of expectations. O'Bryant and Ostwald remained confident, however. They told each other it was just a matter of patience, that wives were not accustomed to seeking pleasure for themselves; they were conditioned toward the safety of the status quo. Eventually, they would try it, and when they did, there would be no going back. Already, studies showed that women who purchased Tingle became repeat buyers at a staggeringly high rate. Competitors like Blue Checkered and Perfect Cup watched helplessly, fearing that Tingle would soon gain traction and leave them behind. Pinwheel was poised to reign supreme as America's foremost coffee peddler again.

And Stout City, Iowa, needed it. Pinwheel Coffee was the largest employer in the city, a metropolis with an unemployment rate currently just under twenty percent. If Tingle succeeded, a slew of out-of-work citizens would gain employment, and other local businesses would see increased sales as a result.

There was one thing, however, that could ruin Tingle's fragile progress toward supremacy, something that would cause wives to reconsider taking a chance on Tingle. And that thing was bad publicity. The kind caused by a lawsuit, for example.

4

"Where's Emma?" Deacon asked upon returning from his meeting with Exlee Ellis.

"Said she was going to go help cover the Mayes trial and she'd see you at your regular morning meeting tomorrow."

"All right, thanks."

Deacon sat down at his desk and collected his thoughts before pulling an address book from the top drawer. He found the phone number for Jude Ostwald's office at Pinwheel headquarters and dialed. Ostwald's secretary, Hazel Kellison, answered, and after learning it was Deacon Lowe with an urgent matter, she interrupted a meeting to make sure her boss took the call. He did, and he wasn't enjoying it.

"You're telling me that some dissatisfied wife is using *our* coffee as an excuse to ditch her dull husband, and now we're supposed to pay *him* money?" Ostwald thundered.

"I don't know if that's the whole story," Deacon cautioned with his typical brand of calm. "Perhaps there is some merit to her story but in a different ... "

"Oh, so you agree? You think we're adding drugs to our coffee?" Ostwald demanded.

"No, what I was about to say was that maybe there is more to this thing. Maybe the wife has some sort of imbalance in her brain that causes unintended reactions to your particular blend of coffee. Not that it's intentional, just that ... "

"Well, we are not paying him one cent, I'll tell you that right now. If his wife is cuckoo, then that's his problem. We all had a choice in the matter of who we hitched our wagon to. Believe me, I wonder about my choice some days, but no company is going to pay me money when my wife dislikes me."

"Listen, Jude, I understand why you're upset. But again, let me remind you, there has been no suit filed yet. At this point, it's just a single item we're running ... "

"Who's to say we wouldn't file a countersuit, huh? This claim of us adding drugs is malicious. Here he gets to make some wild accusation and we're supposed to stand by helplessly while he does it?"

"Well, that's why I'm calling," Deacon explained gently. "I wanted to give you an opportunity to explore this situation with your attorneys. Also, I want to get an official response to the accusation so we can add it to the piece for balance. It's newspaper protocol. Plus, if the *Sun* can remain the primary contact, we can lessen the effect on Pinwheel. But we need to act before this story reaches the other papers."

"Yeah, I get that, and I really do appreciate what you're doing here, Deac. I really do."

"Then maybe you'll hear me out on another little idea," Deacon offered.

"Another idea? Okay."

"Naturally you'll also want to run this by your legal folks, but I'm wondering if we couldn't get a highly respected third party to sort of deflect any damage. Maybe you could let them inspect your plant, and they could report no sign of any drugs. It might even serve as free advertising if they report the cleanliness and care of the production."

"That might work," Ostwald admitted. "It would make us look like we have nothing to hide, that we welcome scrutiny."

"Exactly."

"The question is, who?" Ostwald wondered. "Who would do the inspecting? It has to be the perfect person if this is to work like we intend. We don't want someone who's too zealous, if you know what I mean, yet we want someone who the public buys as having integrity."

"Yes, I've thought of that, too," Deacon said. "Remember that story from a couple months ago about the gal who found Armstrong Perzie, the big shot artist who'd gone missing under our noses for a couple decades?"

"Yeah, maybe."

"In other words, no." Deacon chuckled. "Honestly, I wonder if that coffee has forever ruined your ability to sit still long enough to read a newspaper. You do know Lindbergh flew across the Atlantic a few years ago?"

"I thought he was the fella that invented radio."

The two men laughed.

"Anyhow," Deacon continued, "it was Addie Sumner who reunited the old artist with his family and convinced him to start painting again. Our readers went nuts for the story, made her quite popular."

"Wasn't Sumner the college gal who was elected mayor a couple years back? Kind of a publicity stunt that accidently went legit?"

"Hey, you really do pay attention to the news. Yeah, that's her, and it's one more reason I had her in mind. Those are two big accomplishments—the mayor deal and the painter story—and women really identify with her because of it. She's adventurous, she's clever, and most importantly she's trusted. My daughter asks me every other week if I've heard any more about her. That's exactly who you want inspecting your plant."

"You're right, and more than you know," Ostwald agreed. "Tingle is still trying to gain favor with women, and it would be a huge boost getting the seal of approval from a gal they really respect. Damned if we couldn't almost turn this mess into a positive."

"That's what I'm thinking," Deacon concurred. "And the best way to go about it would be for the *Sun* to offer Addie a reward for proving the story true or false. It should be a reasonable amount, and it should come from us, a third party. It wouldn't sound right if Pinwheel paid to get its own clean bill of health."

"Right again," Ostwald marveled. "I assume you mean that we'd send you the money and you'd offer it as your own."

"It's only reasonable."

"Great idea, Deacon. Let me talk to Farrell about it first. He always sees things from a practical point of view. If he agrees—and the lawyers do too—then we'll proceed with your idea. I'll contact you in a couple hours and let you know if it's a go. Then you can contact her and arrange the whole thing."

"Sounds good."

"Thanks again, Deacon. I promise you that this only strengthens our desire to continue a long relationship with the *Sun*. Don't forget, we spend more of our newspaper advertising money with the *Sun* than any other paper, and it's mostly because of you."

"Well, I have a duty to offer everyone a chance at defending their reputation," Deacon explained, wanting to end the conversation on a higher plane.

"I agree completely. Well done, and thank you for the call."

"Not a problem, Jude. Talk to you soon."

Immediately after hanging up, Jude Ostwald visited Farrell O'Bryant using the side door that connected their offices. He described to his partner the phone call he'd just finished.

"Well," O'Bryant began after some consideration, "I have to admit that Deacon's idea of an inspection is rather clever. And like you say, this Sumner gal might actually enhance our reputation. The chance of her uncovering something scares me a little, though. You know anything about her?"

"Not a great deal, no. I know she was the mayor of Elberton for a couple years—elected while she was still in college—and I know she found some painter and made him famous again. According to Deacon, women love her. She is in her early 20s, though, if I'm figuring correctly. Young enough that her ambition might run ahead of her common sense."

"That's something to consider," O'Bryant agreed. "If she were to dig a little too deep, the whole inspection idea could blow up in our faces. How do you propose that we steer her while still giving the impression of a full inspection?"

"I'm wondering if maybe we couldn't pair her with a guide—one of our people. Someone we can trust who would steer Sumner away from anything we'd rather she didn't know."

"Someone like Richards?"

"No, it would look funny to have our chief operating officer acting as a tour guide. I was thinking more along the lines of someone like Miss Kellison."

"My secretary? I trust her, all right, but there are a couple things she doesn't know about, and I'd like to keep it that way."

"I'm not suggesting we make her a confidant or anything, but she's been with us a long time and worked in a few different departments. She has a decent understanding of the place, and she's proven herself reliable. We'd have her report Sumner's comings and goings. And if Sumner gets too close to something we deem sensitive, then we have Miss Kellison intervene and nudge her off course a little."

"And who knows, maybe this Sumner gal does a cursory inspection and we're worrying for nothing. Either way, she issues a glowing report to the *Sun* and women will associate Tingle with someone they trust," O'Bryant summarized.

Satisfied with the plan, Ostwald was starting to leave when he noticed O'Bryant's shoes.

"By the way, those shoes are pretty sharp. I like 'em a lot."

"Yeah, they are pretty nice, aren't they?"

"Where'd you get them?"

"I'm not really sure. Maggie picked 'em up from somewhere. I could find out, if you'd like a pair."

"I don't know, it sounds kind of strange, us being shoe twins."

"Yeah, you're probably right."

"So, when do we meet with Miss Kellison?"

"Some time after lunch, maybe. I still need to make a couple calls."

"Okay, let me know."

5

After his meeting with Deacon, Exlee returned to Aronoff's and spent his last forty-five cents on ham, eggs and iced coffee (Gold Monocle, half ice, shaken). As he ate, Exlee mentally reviewed his conversation with the editor and decided it hadn't come off half bad, although he regretted having to surrender the couple's names and address. It left him a little vulnerable in all directions, but there was nothing he could do now. The main thing was to get this big scheme launched, and he'd done that by securing a front page article in the *Sun*.

Now he could focus on the more immediate goal of drumming up a little money.

He caught the number 394 streetcar, which passed Aronoff's, and after settling into an empty seat near the back, he yawned and let his mind loose for a bit.

Exlee wasn't one for introspection, but every now and then when the weather was nice and his belly was full and he felt a little accomplished, his mind would drift inwardly. Sometimes he'd explore his deepest wishes by daydreaming, and other times he'd force himself to reexamine the past—studying the chain of events that led him to his current condition. The latter was an exercise in curiosity, and he would review his life like a scientist looking for meaning behind choices but never really finding any.

As the streetcar rolled toward downtown, Exlee thought back to his senior year at Adah Menken High School. He recalled the plans his more organized classmates had made, some aiming for college and others lining up jobs. The majority of the students, however, were like Exlee: wholly without plan. At some point not long after graduation day, they just figured adult society would slow down, throw open a door and invite them into the job market. The details were fuzzy beyond a fat, steady paycheck, but none of them was anxious for clarity, anyhow.

For Exlee, that clarity came in the form of his mother wangling him a job with her brother, John, who owned a luggage store. Uncle John didn't exactly need an assistant, but he found enough work to keep Exlee busy, and four months later John's good deed was rewarded when Exlee announced he was leaving. He had been hired as a personal assistant by two customers—a wealthy, widowed woman and her wealthy, widowed sister-in-law. They sought to travel the world by ship and desired a steady escort. It turned out to be an exciting adventure full of unforgettable sights, but when the sister's demands began veering toward the offbeat, Exlee thought it time to return stateside and begin his grown-up life in earnest. On the trip home aboard the ocean liner *Mauretania*, Exlee met an attorney who was impressed with his quick mind. The lawyer suggested that studying law might be the proper avenue for such a clever young man, even giving Exlee the name of a friend who worked in admissions at a decent college near Chicago. Unenthused, but content to let fate choose his path (or in this case a rather tipsy lawyer who thought every handsome boy should study law), Exlee enrolled at Treemont College upon completing the voyage.

Using the money he'd earned serving as a globe-trotting consort, Exlee proceeded to drift through four years of undergraduate law, studying only when killing time between coeds and suds. With each passing semester his funds and his grades sank lower, and it was only by luck that Exlee survived long enough to snag a diploma by the fingertips. He finished 137th out of 139 in his graduating class, with number 138 skipping finals to elope and number 139 in a doctor-induced coma after awkwardly falling from a sorority house window during a bloomer raid.

Exlee made a half-hearted attempt at applying to law school, but given his academic record, it was no surprise when law schools of all shapes and sizes rejected Exlee as though he were a leper trying to have an elevator held.

It didn't matter, anyhow; he was done studying. As a matter of fact, he had no ambition toward anything traditional. That's not to say Exlee lacked vigor or thirst for life—he'd always had those—but nothing practical enraptured him. So, while living in the guest room of his Great-Aunt Bess and Uncle William's house, he began to spend his time wandering the streets of Stout City, considering his place in life by observing what others were doing with theirs.

A couple of months of casual study left him intrigued with one small group in particular. The press agent corps was roughly divided into two groups: those on the payroll of legitimate concerns like banks and railroads and those who acted independently. It was the latter—the true lone wolves—who impressed Exlee. They were the kind who found you when they needed something but were impossible to locate otherwise. Exlee admired these men who leveraged their solitary hustle into a living using nothing but wits and blarney. And as far as he could tell, there was no official method of entry into their version of the game. You simply found an underpublicized person or group and convinced them that their anonymity was a tragedy which you alone could fix. And once that problem was fixed, you explained, acclaim and riches would surely rain down upon them. Simple enough, he figured. Who wouldn't pay a little to have a dream come true?

The hard part of the press agent bargain was fulfilling the promise. As the job title suggests, a press agent must establish relationships with the press. They are the de facto voice of a city, reaching more people with a single article or radio program than a gossipy hairdresser could in a lifetime. Exlee figured he could handle that easily enough since he had no problem making friends; plus he planned to present the press with material so shamelessly entertaining they couldn't refuse it.

Having decided to take the plunge into press agentry, there was only one question remaining: What would Exlee promote? Seeing as how he'd invested four years learning basic law, it only made sense that he promote something related to the legal field, so he chose attorneys for his gambit.

And because he was drawn toward challenges neglected by clear-thinking people, Exlee took the additional step of choosing to represent the lowest stratum of lawyers—the shysters who represented drunks, unruly tenants, shoplifters with holes in their pockets, and slow-footed thieves.

Of course there remained the small detail of convincing Stout City's legal black sheep that they needed representing. Initially, they were underwhelmed by his pitch and saw no reason to pay good money to this man, interesting as he may be. After all, newspapers didn't care about the menial legal chores they performed for the ugly and the damned of the city. People wanted to read about high profile divorces and sensational murder trials. Their domain was a legal junkyard, rarely yielding items worth mentioning in the press.

It was no easy task, but eventually he proved to them that the banal could be noteworthy. He created a formula for packaging contemptible acts with sad stories based on curious people. Instead of simply embellishing the basic tales of woe the lawyers provided, he tracked down their clients and carefully listened as the miscreants explained their plight. In nearly every case they were willing—no, glad—to give their side of the story, and the funny, flawed reasoning behind their deeds was the best part. In this way, Exlee gave their sordid behavior a face, which allowed newspapers to run these little stories as cautionary tales. Their indignant readership ate it up because in truth, people are just plain fascinated when free will is fumbled. The papers knew it, the readers knew it, and Exlee exploited it with just a hint of compassion.

Exlee's constant interaction with transgressors would have been a soul-crushing recipe for some, but he was blessed with the ability to separate their hardship from his buoyant outlook. In some cases, his charming indifference to their woe left the reprobates feeling strangely vindicated and accepted. As for Exlee, he found so much satisfaction in repackaging calamity and selling it to the papers that he didn't even consider it real work, which was good, because it didn't pay like real work, either.

The lawyers enjoyed seeing their names and cases in print, but it didn't change the fact that their practices only turned occasional profits. They gave Exlee what they could, when they could, and by combining these random paydays, Exlee made enough money to call his game a career.

The newspapers, which appreciated his oddly captivating filler, augmented his earnings, but just barely. Exlee might collect cash on his better pieces, but some of the smaller items fetched no more than wrestling tickets bartered from the sports desk. Certain city editors would claim a logjam of news and offer to buy two pieces for the already cheap price of one. One time, Exlee's entire pay was a surefire tip on a horse race via some mobster who had rigged things and let it slip while drinking with a reporter. Exlee had a zest for selling scenes from the legal underbelly, but it most assuredly was not a path to wealth.

Fortunately, he had a few other paying dodges, and he was looking for one of them to shake loose as his streetcar came to a stop at the corner of Broadway and Orchard Avenue.

Exlee disembarked and surveyed the surroundings while adjusting his coat and tie. This was the heart of Exlee's daytime action—a section of Broadway commonly known as Arraignment Alley because it housed the main courthouse and associated government buildings. The remainder of the area was scattered with law offices, bail bond shops, and cheap cafes.

Two blocks away—on the other side of Orchard—Exlee kept a tiny office above Madame Mildred's Wig Shop. He spent little time at his office, using it mainly to receive mail, make phone calls, and take naps when needed. Its furnishings consisted of a couch, a desk, a wastebasket, and two chairs—one for him and one for a visitor, which was rarely used. On the desk sat a phone, an empty stapler, and some scattered papers. The place was barely more substantial than the ad hoc offices he arranged around the city.

Exlee decided to skip an initial office visit out of deference to his need for money. His first stop was at the law office of Anthony DeScomo, one of Exlee's original clients. Exlee liked to check in every other day and see if DeScomo had picked up any cases worthy of an item in the papers. Most of DeScomo's clients were of Italian heritage, and when they went off the rails the wreckage could be impressive. On the downside, messy divorces were a rarity thanks to their Catholic leanings. Today, DeScomo had nothing, and he was in a bad mood. So was his secretary, Joyce. Exlee decided not to waste any banter on them and moved on instead to the office of attorney Sarah Stone.

Although she probably didn't have it, she owed him some money for a couple of quality pieces he'd recently placed with the press. One involved a prostitute newly arrived from Oklahoma who'd offered a judge services in lieu of paying a fine during her inaugural Stout City arraignment. The other concerned a woman determined to sue her neighbor for "putrid cooking smells." Exlee had actually gone to the trouble of procuring and then printing one of the neighbor's recipes for a thick custard featuring fermented shrimp. In the piece he submitted to the *Star,* he'd ended by joking that a judge should sentence the neighbor for crimes against food but shouldn't bother sentencing her to the gas chamber, since it was less toxic than her home. He'd hoped the editors would leave that in, but most of them at the *Star* were humorless, except Swede Trauper, and that was only when he was sober—usually the three days before payday.

Attorney Sarah Stone was on the phone when he arrived, so Exlee took a seat and perused an old copy of *Vanity Fair.* He was reading an article about a movie starlet and her disenchantment with Hollywood when Sarah hung up. She greeted Exlee then apologized for needing to make another call, which she did. Unsure whether to stay, Exlee glanced out the window but was distracted by a dead fly lying on the sill, its little legs sticking straight up. At least it would never have to suffer disenchantment with Hollywood. Then Sarah's call took an abrupt turn for the worse. Her voice became tense, then stern. Apparently her client was too drunk to appear at a court appearance taking place in twenty minutes—an appearance stemming from a charge of public intoxication. This at least answered the question of whether Exlee should remain. He didn't, deciding to move on to the courthouse buildings.

This was an area where Exlee spent a lot of his hours laying the groundwork for other sources of income. He spoke to judges, lawyers, clerks, and anyone else who might need his services at some time or another. The judges, for example, had to run for reelection every so often, and Exlee was a man who got around. Get him on your side, and he would say good things about you to a wide swath of society. And the way you got him on your side was to hire him for the occasional bit of public relations work. The judges were aware that Exlee was performing the same services for most everyone on a typical ballot—including opponents—so in reality, it gained them very little. The truth be told, they gladly paid for the prestige of having their names included in the hip routine that was Exlee's nightly cavorting.

Today, however, he was not having much luck hooking up with people. He'd arrived at the courthouse too close to the end of the noon hour, and everyone was in flux. Having no desire to hamper the wheels of justice or waste his own time, Exlee decided to head back to the office and check his mail.

He'd just crossed to the south side of Broadway when Joe Fields stopped him, grabbing his elbow.

"Hiya, Ex," Joe greeted him.

"Hey Joe, what's new?"

"Not a thing. Been meaning to give you this," Joe said as he handed a little cash to Exlee. "I hadn't seen you for a couple days. Sorry about the delay, it's just been ... whoops, I'll have to catch up with you later."

The light had turned green, and Joe rushed to cross the street, leaving Exlee to try to remember why Joe owed him money. He counted twenty-five dollars.

PINWHEEL

Well, whatever the reason, Exlee could now skip his afternoon visits in Arraignment Alley and head uptown, where he had some important business at the *Daily Mercury*.

He'd do that right after checking his mail. And a quick nap.

6

Every morning at 7:15, Deacon held a meeting with his right-hand "man," Emma Beltran. Her official title was assistant managing editor, but it was known by everyone who held a newspaper job in Stout City that Emma spoke for Deacon and ran a good portion of his show.

In appearance, Emma did not stand out in any way except for her eyes, which she'd inherited from her mother. They were the darkest of brown, almost black. Otherwise, she looked like a harmless 54-year-old mother, always dressed nicely and generally in pleasant spirits. No one would have guessed that she'd grown up in the worst part of Stout City, that her stepfather had been a brutal alcoholic, or that she had run away from home at 17. Her first marriage was at 18 to a boy who'd just been expelled from college for cheating during his first semester. He was shot and killed nine months later while trying to steal a keg off a beer truck for a World Series party. Her second husband ran off with a five and dime clerk, and her third husband died of a heart attack while raging about politics.

And yet, despite such an unsettled personal life, there had always remained one constant: her career in the newspaper business. She'd started as a paper girl in order to save her family from eviction, and because of her choice in husbands, Emma had always been counted on for financial reliability. She worked her way up the ladder by proving herself equally steady within the newspaper office, succeeding in a variety of roles over the years. Her ascent to assistant managing editor was accompanied by almost no fanfare. If anything, she had been begrudgingly rewarded by management, who were unsure what to do with a woman so capable. The press was historically a heartless, manly pursuit that had thrived with the top editors wearing neckties, not an asterisk. It didn't matter to Emma. Years of tumultuous relationships had made her tenacious, and she knew the quality of her work could not be denied. It didn't hurt that she loved the news business, as evidenced by her reading all five Stout City dailies over breakfast each morning. She may have looked and spoken like a garden club hostess, but she was a force who knew the paper business inside and out and rarely flinched.

Emma's steadfast advancement was aided by a strategy of hopscotching between papers, filling a vacant, higher rung whenever a paper was caught in need. She probably would have moved on from the *Sun* were it not for Deacon Lowe. He had instantly grasped her intrinsic value and wisely pledged his professional loyalty to her, promising her equal voice within their partnership in exchange for dedication and sincerity. It was not unlike a happy marriage in which each person's fundamental essence complemented the other's. She was a master at efficiently taming minutia, and he was a connector of dots trying to think a step ahead of each crooked alderman. For eleven years now, they had worked in unison, and though the staff had grown comfortable with the rare gender combination running the city desk, there remained a curiosity about the fullness of their relationship.

When Deacon's wife, Abigail, died of leukemia in 1930, it would have been natural for rumors to begin linking the editor and his assistant editor romantically, but to date, nothing resembling this had occurred. They had never been out socially, and when the work day was done, he went home to the suburbs and she went home to the apartment she shared with her only son, Jerry (an enthusiastic, unpublished poet who made ends meet by walking dogs and giving marcel waves to women who were willing to save money by having their hair done in the back of a florist shop).

The closest thing to a romantic gesture between the two editors occurred each morning when Deacon moved Emma's chair from the corner of his office and placed it near his desk for their briefing.

Today was no different, and like clockwork Emma motored into Deacon's office at precisely 7:15, both hands wrapped around a mug of coffee (Pinwheel original, two creams, one sugar). She was anxious to catch up, having been out of the office most of the previous day helping to cover a ballyhooed trial involving a woman who'd killed her husband for not paying attention to her story about a rude cashier at the grocery.

"So what's new?" she asked. "I feel so out of touch after being gone yesterday and then accidently sleeping in this morning. That's the first time it's happened in ages. I didn't even get a chance to look at this morning's edition."

"Remember me saying I was meeting your favorite guy yesterday?" Deacon asked.

They both knew he was talking about Exlee, and they both knew he'd said it to get a reaction from Emma because she did indeed have a small weakness for Exlee. She gave Deacon a smile of acknowledgement but refused to take the bait.

"And what story was Mr. Ellis pushing?" she inquired.

"Oh, you'll like this one. He's promoting the threat of a lawsuit, claiming a married couple has split up because she is addicted to Pinwheel coffee. The husband claims that a drug is being added to Tingle, and it's so strong that his wife even prefers it to relations with him."

"That's supposed to be a big deal? I preferred washing dishes to bonus time with my second husband. It was a stroke of luck for me when he took off with the Woolworth's girl. I almost felt sorry for her."

"And that brings up a good point. How much chance does this supposed lawsuit really have? Who's to say what constitutes addiction or what constitutes preferable lovemaking?"

"Can you imagine the expert testimony on *that* one if it went to court? As a matter of fact, I'm claiming dibs on covering it."

"Forget about it. After a bunch of doctors and engineers broke it down, you'd be so self-conscious you'd be celibate the rest of your life."

"And how would that be different from my current path?"

"Can we get back to the lawsuit?" Deacon laughed. "And let's focus on the addiction part. Exlee claims that the husband's lawyer has a lab test that proves Pinwheel coffee has an addictive element—or elements. He didn't explain, really."

"If that were true, wouldn't everyone be addicted? I don't see any other lawsuits or marriages breaking up over Pinwheel coffee."

"That's what I'm wondering, but then again, look at you. How many cups of Pinwheel coffee do you drink each day?"

"Including the one I have during our morning meetings, I'd say about ... um, two thousand, maybe more."

"Exactly. You drink it all day. And what other brands do you drink?"

"None," she admitted sheepishly, knowing where this was headed.

"Because they don't make you quite as giddy, do they?"

"No, that's not it. Pinwheel just makes better coffee. It tastes better."

"*Or* you've convinced yourself that it tastes better. You should try a different brand every day this week and see if you still think Pinwheel tastes better."

"Oh, what does it matter? I'm not so addicted that I'd divorce my husband or stop preferring sex."

"Yes, well, you are the opposite of expert testimony there."

"That's really mean. But even aside from that—which was terrible—I do have experience with all the elements in question, even if the marital thing is a bit dated."

"A bit? Let me think, who was the president in nineteen ... ?"

"I cannot believe you this morning. If you're trying to make me feel bad, you're doing a good job. I bet Exlee wouldn't talk to me this way."

"One more reason he's your favorite."

"And yours," she reminded him. "Let's just move on."

"Okay, back to him and Pinwheel. So, just to clarify, there is no actual lawsuit that's been filed, and not only that, he claims the husband is being represented by a lawyer named Wickenstaff. Know him?"

"Doesn't ring a bell."

"It shouldn't. It's a long story, but I happen to know a little about him from a news story some years back. He's one of those types who makes a living off of threatening letters. I doubt that boob has ever tried a case or if he could even find the right courtroom."

"Okay, but suppose this husband chose Wickenstaff randomly from the phone book?" Emma countered. "Maybe he doesn't know any lawyers, sees the name, it sticks out because it's unusual, and so he calls.

Wickenstaff isn't going to turn him down. Even a dumb lawyer knows good money when it falls in his lap."

"And he'd probably be too greedy to split the case with a competent lawyer, who'd demand the larger share if he even took the case," Deacon added, playing along with her scenario. "So, instead of doin' it the right way, Wickenstaff would go the easy route: a public shakedown in the papers using Exlee as his hired front man. Exlee does all the work for a fixed fee, which barely dents the extortion money collected from Pinwheel on behalf of the client. Wickenstaff gives a little to the husband after overcharging him for negligible representation and pockets the majority of it without ever leaving his hole."

"Which brings us back to the real question: Do we think this lawsuit is real or not? It seems strange that Exlee would get tangled up in something this big if it was phony."

"Or even if it was real, for that matter. And yet here he is, running the show on this thing publicity-wise. Here, take a look at this. It's the piece he talked me into running on the front page today."

Deacon picked up a paper from his desk, handed it to her, and watched as she read it. He liked the way she bit her bottom lip when she was concentrating on something.

"Wow. That really is quite a claim, and of course it would have to be against Pinwheel, who we can't afford to lose. Even more shocking is that you ran this on the front page."

"Yeah, Cantrell was not pleased," Deacon admitted in reference to the *Sun's* editor in chief. "It took a lot of convincing, and of course the funny part is I had no desire to go along with this thing."

"So why did you?"

"Because it's Exlee, and he's never steered me wrong before. I'm gonna trust this story has merit and take actions accordingly."

"What sort of actions?"

"Well, I've already done a few things. I called Wickenstaff to confirm this supposed lawsuit and naturally he had no comment. No surprise there. Then I called Jude Ostwald and tried to show our loyalty. I convinced him he should make a public showing of his factory being inspected by an outside party. That way they get a clean bill of health and the publicity swings in their favor. Unless they really are adding opium or something."

"Either way, we scoop the story, good or bad," Emma agreed. "*And* you're keeping Pinwheel happy at the same time you're letting someone throw a stone at 'em. It's beautiful. Who's the inspector?"

"Addie Sumner. Got the okay from them late yesterday afternoon, called her, and she agreed."

"Perfect. Love that gal."

"Also, I've contacted a lab that's going to run samples of Tingle so we can have our own results, but that will take a few days. In the meantime, I've arranged to have two people followed. The first is supposedly this Paul Wagster fella ... "

"Who's that?"

"Ah, sorry, I forgot to mention that part. When Exlee was trying to convince me to run his piece I insisted that I needed the names and address of the couple involved in the alleged lawsuit—sort of as collateral, since we're risking our largest advertiser against his unproven claim."

"That makes sense."

"It must have, because he agreed. Wrote it down in front of me. The only question is if the names he wrote really match the actual couple ... "

"Or if there is an actual couple. Or a lawsuit. Or drugs in the coffee."

"Geez, don't I know it. This one has us crawling way out on a limb. Which is why I'm covering every angle. I'm having Koenig tail whatever man leaves Wagster's address this morning. If we connect this husband to a workplace, we can at least confirm his identity and match it to the name Exlee gave me. And speaking of Exlee, I'm also having him followed today."

"You're having *him* followed, too? That feels strange for some reason."

"That's because the rascal usually has us fawning over him. But if he's going to raise the stakes, then so are we. The problem is he knows everyone on our staff, so I came up with the idea of using Jack Swanson to tail him. He was a heck of a reporter in his prime, and he retired before Exlee came onto the scene. He's been retired fourteen years now, learned that when I had his file pulled so I could call him. Exlee wouldn't think twice about Swanson if he happened to note him."

"Yeah, but Swanson retired a long time *after* his prime, and add fourteen years to that. You sure we shouldn't have someone trailing *him*?"

"Too late, I called him last night. Gotta admit that his hearing wasn't the greatest, but on a positive note, he agreed to do it for nothing. Said he longs for the days of action and was glad to get a taste of it for one more day. I didn't tell him why we were tailing Exlee, and he didn't ask, but he should be following Exlee right now."

"I'll be darned," Emma muttered in disbelief.

"Like I said, we have to assume everything so we can be ready if this goes big, no matter what direction."

"Can you imagine if Addie Sumner actually finds a barrel of opium in some janitor's closet at Pinwheel?"

The door to Deacon's office swung open with an office boy entering and gratuitously knocking at the same

56

time. Nobody ever waited for Deacon's response to the knock, and he often wondered why they bothered or what they'd do if he ever told them to halt.

"Mr. Herrick wants to know if he should take a photographer with him to the grand opening of the Fernpath Country Club," the office boy said on behalf of the paper's society reporter.

"Any picture takers available?" Deacon asked Emma.

"Just Filson. I doubt Slim finishes that streetcar accident before nine, and I thought I overheard you sending Dumaine somewhere."

"Yeah, a woman poisoned her lover with horse medicine or some such thing," Deacon explained. "Word is that she's a real looker."

"In that case, she'll have a legion of fans declaring her innocence. Nobody wants to fry a beauty."

"Lucky for you if you ever decide to knock me off. As for photographing this country club bash, I'm not so sure," Deacon mused. "People like a peek at how the other half lives, but you have to be careful not to rub it in these days."

"Plus you'd hate to tie up our last photographer in case something big shakes loose," Emma reminded.

"That's true. Tell Herrick no on the photographer," Deacon said to the office boy. "And remind him that he gets six hundred words including names ... and no Mrs. Hollins."

"Who is Hollins?" Emma queried after the boy had departed.

"An old, rich widow that Herrick is tryin' to butter up. What his intentions are depends on your imagination, but he's gotta stop shoehorning her into every society piece or the rest of the bluebloods are gonna revolt."

Emma chuckled, and then there was silence as they both tried to remember where they left off.

"So you were asking something about the Exlee-Pinwheel situation?" Deacon said.

"I don't remember now, but I do have a question. What about the wife who's supposedly addicted?"

"Good question," he said. "If we can spare a body, we should send someone to the couple's address and watch to see if she's there or if they're really separated."

"How about Koenig when he's done confirming the husband?"

"I'd really prefer to have him stay with the husband in case he meets with Wickenstaff or someone who might connect any of the puzzle pieces. Who else we got?"

"Gaston if he's halfway sober. Haven't seen him yet today. Just saw Torres, but I planned on having him do a rewrite on the trolley piece," Emma explained.

"What about Hoyt?"

"The sports editor?"

"Don't sound so surprised. He's a reporter, isn't he? He's just gotten a little full of himself since taking that spot, like these specialty editors do. Get a new title and suddenly they think they're exempt from regular newspaper work. After all, weren't you helping on that trial yesterday?"

"Yes. And I plan to go back this afternoon."

"Well, if you can do the occasional heavy lifting, then so can he. Matter of fact, Alexander could also use a dose of regular reporting," Deacon insisted, referring to the theater editor. "Give those two yahoos a phone call and wake 'em up. Tell them I wanna see them immediately. This Pinwheel story has a better chance of making or breaking the *Sun* than some critique of an opera."

"It's not the opera you should worry about," Emma warned as she stood up. "It's the ballgame. God help us if Hoyt misses it and our readers are left to wonder about the exact sequence of hits that's already summarized in the box score."

"I'm not worried because I'll send you," Deacon called to her as she walked away.

She turned and gave him a mock glare without breaking stride.

He smiled back at her until his view was abruptly blocked. A secretary had stepped into his doorway.

"Koenig is on the line again," she announced. "I didn't want to interrupt ... "

"Thanks. Put him through." He leaned toward the phone and picked up on the first ring.

"Hey, Koenig. Whaddya got?"

"Well, I tracked the husband to his job at the Van Every Tire Shop. I'm at the drug store around the corner, and I just called and asked for Paul Wagster. They said he was busy, and I hung up. Sounds like the fella matches the name and address you gave me."

"Good work. Stop by the tire joint and ask him what he knows about this lawsuit business. I'm sure Wickenstaff has instructed him to keep a lid on it, but if nothing else, maybe it'll shake him up a bit, prime him to talk sooner rather than later. After that—I know its dull business—but I need you to keep an eye on him for the rest of the day. Don't engage him, just watch and take notes."

"Will do."

"And one other thing. If he happens to meet a lawyer—at an office or if the guy just smells like a lawyer—drop Wagster and confirm the other fella's identity. Thanks."

7

Addie Sumner had never met Deacon Lowe, so she was surprised when he'd called the previous evening with a job offer. She'd been even more surprised by the impressive pay that came with it. The job would only last a week or so, including the writing of a final report, but the money would cover living expenses for three months. It had been tough pretending to weigh her decision when her brain was screaming, "I'll take it!" And she had taken it. She was there first thing Tuesday morning.

After a few minutes' wait, Addie met the Pinwheel owners inside of their executive suite on the fifth floor. She guessed they were both in their early forties, and she was instantly impressed with their vitality. Jude Ostwald was a little taller, with a longer neck and black hair parted down the middle. His mannerisms were very alert, and he gave off a sense of restrained physical prowess, like a cheetah making small talk with an antelope right before eating him in five bites and then going for a swim.

Farrell O'Bryant's verve was found in his eyes, which were quite literally Irish and smiling. They looked at you with voracity *and* benevolence, as though he knew implicitly that he was a step ahead of you, but hoped you'd be kind enough to understand. He was just beginning to bald, and his mouth seemed too small for the rest of his features. He also walked with a slight limp, even though he looked wiry and strong.

Together, the two men were a force before even uttering a word, and when they did speak it was with alacrity and passion. Addie was impressed but not intimidated, and she chose to listen attentively rather than trying to influence their opinion of her. They explained that their campus was open to her and she was free to report anything she saw. "We trust you will use enough discretion not to reveal any proprietary elements which might enable our competition," Ostwald warned, but he placed no other stipulations on her inspection. Additionally, in an effort to aid Addie, they were providing her with a guide, Miss Hazel Kellison.

Hands were shaken and polite smiles were shared before Addie was ushered into an anteroom and turned over to her new companion.

"What did you think of them?" Hazel asked after the owners had left.

"They seemed nice. You definitely know who is in charge around here."

"Aren't all bosses like that?"

"Oh, I've known plenty who don't have a clue. You've always worked here, I take it?"

"Uh huh. Since I graduated from high school. Started on the first floor, and in a way I've worked my way up."

"In a way?"

"Well, to be honest, I've had help. Lots of girls have dropped out of the pool to get married or have babies. Me, I just keep plugging away. I've had fellas ask me to marry them, but I'm not in a hurry and none of 'em were that great, know what I mean?"

"I think so. I haven't had any proposals yet, but I'm really enjoying work right now."

"I heard you were a mayor once. That must have been like a dream."

"It had its nightmare moments, but I've never learned so much so fast."

"If I was mayor I would make speeding tickets illegal. I got another one just the other day. The cop tells me I'm ten over the speed limit, but he was facing the other way. How does he know? Not to mention I don't recall seeing a sign. He swears there is one, and I keep meaning to look, but I forget. Sometimes I wonder if these cops aren't just looking for a young gal to harass a little, maybe they get some thrill out of it because their wives don't listen to 'em at home. Have to admit, though, that this last one wasn't difficult to look at. I might fight the ticket just to meet him at court. Anyhow, you're probably more interested in getting started than listening to me talk about my speeding tickets."

"I guess we can do both. Why don't we start with where they roast the beans?"

"Okay, right after a stop at the cafeteria. I haven't had my coffee yet, and around here that's a sin." She laughed.

They took the elevator down to the first floor and then turned left into the Pinwheel cafeteria, where they sat and enjoyed a cup of coffee (Tingle, straight, for Addie, and Tingle with a pinch of cinnamon for Hazel).

"How tall are you?" Hazel asked.

"A little over five foot ten, I believe."

"Wow. Do you have a tall boyfriend?"

"I don't even have a pretend boyfriend. How about you, do you have a boyfriend?"

"Sorta. I've been seeing a fella named Ronnie. He actually works here, over in the loading docks where they load the trucks. We've been out three times but I don't know. He forgot to call me a couple times last week. We went out Saturday night to the movies and everything seemed fine, but then he didn't call Sunday. So I called last night to see what's up, and he says he's just trying to take it slow because of a bad breakup he had once. He wasn't taking it too slow in the movie theater. I finally had to tell him, 'Your car keys aren't in my blouse, if that's what you're lookin' for.' My mom tells me stories about the polite boys she dated in the horse and buggy days—tipping their caps, for goodness sake. We get these modern wolves who think they're polite if the date doesn't start in their apartment."

"I guess each generation has its challenges."

"And it keeps getting worse. I'm afraid to have children, the way the world is going."

When they'd finished their Tingle, they took the elevator to the second floor and walked down a long corridor to the end.

"We're about to leave what we call the headquarters," Hazel explained when they reached the door. "Once we go through here, we'll be in the main processing building. It's much louder, so be ready. I'll take you to the office of the main supervisor. His name is Tom, and his office is on this level so he can look down on the floor."

Hazel opened the thick, airtight door, and a wave of noise blasted them. They stepped onto a wide, iron catwalk and looked down on the activity. Addie was dazzled by the magnitude of what she saw.

It was like an entire city at work, with movement everywhere. Men in uniforms snaked among the equipment, pushing things, carrying things, and occasionally stopping to study things. The most prominent feature of this vision was the giant roasters. There were eight of them along the far side with a series of hoppers and conveyor belts waiting nearby to feed and empty them like servants waiting on hot, angry masters. Fascinated, Addie studied the progress of the beans, which arrived by magical belts from some other building and were transported so far away she could only guess that she was seeing cans being stacked.

She asked Hazel a question about the cans, but as soon as the words left her mouth, Addie was aware that merely speaking loudly was useless. Shouting was required, and the effort required to repeat herself made the question seem trivial. She waved it away when Hazel looked at her askance.

Instead, Hazel led her down the catwalk to the supervisor's office. As soon as they stepped inside and closed the door, silence was restored in such a way that it felt like her ears were plugged. She almost jumped when Hazel spoke.

"What were you asking out there?"

"Oh, nothing, really. I thought I saw the coffee cans at the other end. It made me curious as to where you get them—the cans, that is."

"We make them," a nearby man interrupted. "There is a building across the way dedicated solely to cans. They take raw material, press it, mold it, stamp it, and send it over here using a roller conveyance similar to the belts you see servicing the roasters."

"This is Tom Brinkman," Hazel explained. "He's the supervisor I was telling you about. Tom, this is Addie Sumner, you probably heard about her doing an inspection."

"Nice to meet you Addie. Yeah, I heard something about an inspection but no details, really. Is this what you do for a living, Addie, inspecting factories?"

"Not always," she admitted. "I provide a range of services for different interests. Each assignment has a unique purpose based on a narrow scope provided by management."

It was a professional-sounding lie, but he had no way of disproving it, and she had only told it because she knew her competence was being tested. Someone in a dress having authority—albeit temporarily—was unknown in the supervisor's office. Her strong answer had the proper effect, leaving him a little concerned.

"So, uh, what is your purpose on this assignment?" he asked, trying to sound nonchalant.

"It's really not my place to divulge. I'll be submitting a report directly to Mr. Ostwald and Mr. O'Bryant when my inspection is complete. Right now I'm just getting a lay of the land, and it looks like you have a lot on your hands. I can't imagine how you run such a large operation."

Her answer hadn't provided him much security, but just as she intended, the last bit of flattery perked him up. Men were easy that way.

"Just to give you a better understanding of what goes on down there," he said in a slow voice, "let me run some numbers past you. The entire plant covers nearly 500,000 square feet and sits on eighteen acres. On any given day, one million pounds of coffee beans are roasted, processed, and packaged in this plant. That's over ten pounds per second, and it goes on around the clock except on Christmas, Thanksgiving, and Independence Day. It takes thirty-five railroad cars of beans per week to meet demand. Dozens more rail cars and trucks depart here each day, full of packaged coffee headed all across the country. The whole plant operation requires 647 employees, not including local truck drivers, security guards, and lunch ladies."

"It sounds like you have great responsibility," Addie said.

"I guess I sleep all right," he drawled cavalierly, "but some of us are made for this sort of thing. Every day there's some problem—usually several—and I enjoy the challenge of working through it. Tuesday, it was roaster number six. She blew a bearing, and the resulting screech was probably heard in the next county. Last week, ol' Tim

Doskins wasn't paying proper attention and lost the second finger on his left hand during a clean-out."

"That's awful," Addie said.

"Yeah, we had to shut things down and waste a good fifteen minutes lookin' for that finger. They're harder to find then you'd think. Anyhow, what I was sayin' is that unplanned things happen every day, and someone has to make sure we still meet our production numbers."

"Well, I admire your skill, Tom. I'll probably have more questions later, but would it be possible for me to take a little tour of the floor, just to get a feel for the process?"

"Normally it would be against the rules unless it were a government agency, but seeing as how the owners have given you free rein, I'll make it happen."

Tom picked up a phone and gave instructions to someone on the other end.

"There you have it," he declared after hanging up the phone. "Eddie Helmer, the floor supervisor, will meet you down there at the east door. He'll have a coat and some ear plugs for you. Just be sure not to touch anything, or you may end up like Tim Doskins."

He chuckled in an attempt to display the devil-may-care attitude it took to run a ship this big.

Hazel led Addie back inside the headquarters hallway. "We'll take the long route down. We could have used the catwalk stairs inside, but they aren't made for nice shoes, plus those fellas working in there might get distracted watching our progress. They didn't pretend to be subtle the times I've tried it. What did you think of Tom?"

"He seems to be on top of his job."

"Yeah, he's been here since the start. He's married and has three kids; I see 'em every year at the company picnic in Goodman Park. His wife is one of those sickly types, usually sits and tries to look brave and fragile at the same time. His son, who must be about 10 or 11, is getting to be a little terror. At this last picnic, he went around giving a bunch of us women hugs like he'd missed us, but his hands were busy gettin' a sample of our backsides, if you get my drift. The little urchin. He's just at that age where no one knows what's in his mind, and if you said something to his parents they'd defend their little baby and accuse *you* of having the weird thoughts."

Addie and Hazel spent the rest of the morning following the beans' progress as they were cleaned, roasted, ground, packaged, and prepared for delivery. Addie was sure she had walked several miles by the time they were done visiting the various departments related to the processing. The scale of the operation left her in awe, and there were still several buildings they hadn't visited.

"I'm not used to that much walking," she explained after they had returned to the quiet of headquarters. "Maybe we can look at the rest of the campus tomorrow."

"I was hoping you'd say that. Let's eat lunch now, and afterward I'll arrange a visit to the can manufacturing plant for tomorrow."

"What about the offload warehouse facility? I think that's where Eddie said the beans started."

"Yeah, there isn't much to see there, really. They just pull bags off the rail cars and stack 'em in a warehouse. Then they dump 'em in hoppers. Pretty dull stuff, really, and it's difficult to get to."

"I'd still like to see it, even if it's for a few minutes."

"Sure, I'll just run that by management and make sure it's okay. I know there are some safety concerns in some of these separate areas—it's why they keep them separate in some cases. Exotic germs and falling bags—that kind of thing. I'd have to clear it with the legal department."

"Seems like a lot of red tape for just a warehouse."

"I know, but I'm just the messenger, and like I said, I'll speak with management and do my best. Say, what did you think of Jackson Prescott?"

"Which one was he, again?"

"The one in charge of the cooling vats, where the beans go directly after roasting. He had the really curly hair."

"Oh yes, him. Well, it's kinda hard getting to know someone when you have to shout to talk, but he seemed all right. Maybe I'm wrong, but he didn't seem overly pleased to see you."

"You noticed that, huh? Basically, he hates me, I guess. We actually dated for a little while a year or so ago. I should have known better. On our first date he picked me up in a jalopy, and I was so embarrassed at the thought of being seen in it, but I didn't want him thinking I only date a fella for his money. Well, then we got to the restaurant, and he said he wasn't real hungry and maybe we should share something. Said it would be romantic. Ha! Romantic, my foot. Then afterward, when he was dropping me off, he had the nerve to ask if he could come in. I knew where that was going and shut him right down."

"That was quite a date."

"Yeah, well, it got worse. His stupid ex-girlfriend called me and told me she was still trying to work things out with him and I needed to give him the air. I had no idea who this mama was, but she wasn't in charge of my life and I told her so. The next time I went out with Jackson ... "

"You went out with him again?"

"Better me than this dingbat ex-girlfriend. She actually had the nerve to show up on our last date, acting as though she happened to run into us. Can you imagine? I have no idea who picked out her clothes, but I was completely embarrassed for her, and that idiot Jackson was talking to her like it was no big deal—like she didn't just interrupt our date on purpose. After that, I was done with him. That's what you were picking up on when you said he hated me."

"I didn't exactly say ... "

"A friend of mine heard they got back together after we broke up, and supposedly they fight all the time. Honestly, I think some men just like to be miserable. That's all I can figure. There is no other reason for going out with a troll like her."

They entered the cafeteria, picked up trays, and got in line to be served.

"Oh, my lord," Hazel exclaimed.

"What?"

"Over there against the wall. See that guy with the bushy beard?"

"Yeah."

"I went out with him one time over a year ago. He's a truck driver for Pinwheel, and he never eats lunch here in the cafeteria. I wonder if his truck is broken."

Addie wasn't listening. The coffee station was next, and it felt like the man in front of them was taking forever.

8

Hoyt and Alexander stared silently at the green house on Moccasin Street. They had been in Hoyt's car for almost two hours, waiting for a glimpse of the wife at the center of the Pinwheel lawsuit. So far they'd seen nothing. And adding to the frustration was that all of the blinds were drawn—even if she were home, they couldn't tell.

"I hate to beat a dead horse, but I still don't understand what the hell we're doing looking for a wife that may or may not be at this house or even exist, for that matter."

This from Hoyt, the sports editor, who was still miffed at being demoted to this assignment. His temporary partner, Alexander, the drama editor, was not exactly giddy about the whole thing, but he was more open-minded.

"It is not ours to know," Alexander philosophized. "We just have to trust Deacon and go with what he told us."

"All he told us is that this couple is supposed to be separated, meaning we are straining our eyeballs to prove she's gone. Think about it—at what point do you prove that something isn't?"

They lapsed into silence, turning their attention to a stray dog trotting down the near sidewalk. It paused briefly to drop and lick itself, then bounced upright and watered a nearby tree before merrily disappearing around a corner.

"Dogs."

"Yeah."

Their eyes returned to the green house. Still nothing.

Alexander took a sip from his paper coffee cup (Gold Monocle, a little sugar and a lot of cream) while Hoyt frowned at the sound of the sipping. Cabin fever was beginning to amplify little things, and Hoyt was particularly susceptible to such annoyance. For his sanity—and because Alexander couldn't talk and sip at the same time—Hoyt took the extreme measure of initializing chitchat.

"Assuming we're ever released from this bondage, you got anything good planned for tonight?" Hoyt asked.

"Actually, I get to review a special performance of *Hamlet* at the Hollingsworth Theatre."

"What's there to review? Don't they always use the same script and the same ending?"

"Generally yes, but ... "

"And don't they always stick with the same outdated language?"

"Yes, because the beauty of Shakespeare is in the words," Alexander explained. "Attempts at so-called modernizing invariably fail because his work is really a poetic rhythm grounded in the language of that time. The magic simply does not translate."

"Well, they could at least change the ending every now and then—reward a guy for two hours of deciphering gibberish. Maybe they could even jazz it up while they're at it," Hoyt offered. "So instead of Juliet killing herself, she mourns for Romeo by becoming a hooker—it's a stretch, but people grieve in funny ways. Then, let's say one of her johns gets a little obsessed, and she kills him with poison, and the cops connect the fella's murder with the poisoning death of Romeo, and she does ten years at the big house wearing some skimpy prison outfit. I'm tellin' you, real people might watch this stuff."

"Real people already have motion pictures to satisfy all their decadent, sophomoric needs," Alexander chided. "Shakespeare endures in its natural form because it is a cup of cool water for each new generation of thinkers who thirst for beauty. The rest of you can keep petting your sweethearts in the darkened theater while some god-awful gangster flick sets the mood."

"See, that's the difference between us. I cover sports because the ending is never known. That's where the real drama is—wondering who will win or which player is going to be the hero. That's why thirty thousand will be at the baseball game this afternoon."

"Ah, yes, the drama of whether team A will win its twenty-third game or team B its twenty-sixth. Based on your earlier logic, wouldn't it be more fun if the batter suddenly decided to split the umpire's head open with a bat then shimmied up the foul pole and bellowed dirty pub songs while the crowd threw peanuts at him?"

"Would you believe I've seen most of that? A second baseman named Jerggans played piñata with an ump's noggin at a game I was coverin' in Spokane. It made quite a sound. Sportswriter next to me looked up thinking Jerggans had just cracked a triple. As for the other, I was in Montana—either in Billings or Butte or Bozeman—and a fan got loaded and climbed the left foul pole. No pub songs for him, though. Kept yelling that he was Jack and that was his beanstalk."

"And I once reviewed a junior college production of *Jack and the Beanstalk*. And now we've come full circle."

Silence settled over the car once more as fresh entertainment arrived. A garbage truck was slowly working its way down the opposite side of the street with a pair of workers taking turns hoisting loads of rubbish into its hopper. Neither Hoyt nor Alexander could decide if the workers had the worst job in the city or the greatest.

"I hate to complain, but I'm getting awfully hungry," Alexander announced after the truck had moved on.

"Yeah, well, I'm flat out starving," Hoyt growled. "I'm also gettin' sick and tired of staring at an empty house."

"Maybe we should find a phone and call Deacon, see if his plans have changed."

"Or we could act like real reporters. Isn't that the line he was feeding us, claiming we're getting too complacent in our editorial roles? So let's finish this off like actual reporters so we can get some damn lunch."

Upon uttering this declaration, Hoyt jerked his door open and got out of the car.

"What are you doing?" Alexander asked in a loud whisper, still playing the role of sleuth.

"I'm gonna go poke around that house like a reporter would. You wait here and keep watching in case the nonexistent wife appears on the roof."

Before Alexander could voice his admonishment, Hoyt shut the door and walked in the direction of the house.

Left behind, Alexander could only mutter warnings as he watched his foolhardy partner cross the street and walk up the driveway to the green house. First, he tried to peer through a side window. Not finding anything there, Hoyt moved to the front porch, where he crouched and tried to spy around the edge of the drawn curtain in the front window.

"You idiot," Alexander murmured as he scanned the neighborhood, hoping there were no witnesses.

Hoyt's next move was to a side gate, where he stood on his toes to look over the top.

"Don't do it," Alexander whispered.

He didn't. After surveying the backyard, Hoyt turned around and looked back at the car, pantomiming a shrug and raised palms to indicate he had seen nothing useful. Alexander shrugged back involuntarily and relaxed, anticipating Hoyt's defeated return. The sports editor had other ideas, however. He returned to the front porch, where he knocked on the door.

"No, you fool," Alexander hissed.

Just then there was a sudden knock at the car window next to Alexander's head, causing him to squeal and spill some coffee on his pants. He turned to behold a grinning, elderly woman.

"What do you want?" he asked angrily through the window.

"Roll down your window, pervert."

Alexander gasped in shock and furiously rolled down the window.

"Did you just call me a pervert?" he demanded.

"I've been watching you two stalk Mrs. Wagster all morning. Don't you think I know what you're up to?"

"You most certainly do not," he replied tersely.

"Well, if you're a Fuller Brush salesman, you're awfully determined to sell to the one house, and slow about it, too."

"No, you don't understand ... "

"Oh, I understand. My Ollie, when he was alive, would mow the lawn twice in the same day to get a look at Mrs. Wagster. I never said anything because I couldn't blame him. She's a pretty thing, and oh, those legs—I'm surprised Oliver never mowed his toes off while trying to get a good look."

"But ... "

"But nothing, I've got news for you; your friend can snoop all day and he won't find her."

"How do you know?" Alexander asked.

"I watched her leave about a month ago with three suitcases. The big type. Maybe she went on a long trip, I don't know, but I haven't seen her since."

"Was she alone when she left?"

"Nope, her husband helped her load 'em in the car. He's still there, though. Comes and goes like usual, except he gets home later. Probably eats his dinner out with her being gone. Oliver would've eaten cat food or starved to death if I ever left him for a month. He could barely toast bread."

They both paused and looked up at the sound of Hoyt's shoes crossing the street. He was returning to the car.

"I could've warned him," she explained, noting his discouraged expression.

"Well, why didn't you?" Alexander challenged. "We've been here half the morning."

"Wait until you're eighty-seven years old someday with no reason to get up each morning. You take entertainment where you can get it."

"You mean like watching Mr. Wagster load suitcases?" Alexander scolded.

"Or watching two perverts huddled in a car."

"I told you we're not perverts; we work for the *Sun* newspaper. And we were *not* huddling."

"If you say so." She winked. "But if you do work for the paper, be sure and report that dog licking himself."

With another wink, she turned and walked up the pathway to her house, Alexander glaring at her the entire way.

"Who was that?" Hoyt huffed while climbing into the car, red-faced and out of breath.

"Nosy neighbor. She says the wife left a month ago with suitcases. Also called her Mrs. Wagster."

"Great!" Hoyt said with a clap of his hands. "We have our answers. Now let's get something to eat."

"Well, if you're game, there is a place near here that serves some divine Peruvian food. Ever tried it?"

"Nope, and I'm not about to start on an empty stomach," Hoyt proclaimed. "Something like that could kill a man who's as out of shape as me. I'm thinking maybe Lou's instead."

"Oh my lord, have you ever studied that kitchen? Talk about something killing you. Let's split the difference and have some barbeque at Snitch Brown's."

"We have a winner."

Hoyt started the car and pulled away from the curb while Alexander gave a final look toward the old woman's house. He hoped she caught the full fury of his scorn.

9

Tuesday's dinner rush was underway at Troscanza's, home of the finest Italian cuisine in Stout City. The restaurant's kitchen, which had been a quiet, gleaming showpiece earlier in the day, was now a steaming cacophony of hisses, shouts, and clangs. Chef Marco LaRocca and his bedraggled crew battled to keep up with demand, their sauce-stained uniforms causing them to look less like trained culinary artists and more like Valley Forge survivors. Still, it appeared they might be gaining ground until a new setback occurred.

It was a plate of tagliatelle bolognese that had been rejected by a disgruntled customer who claimed the pasta was overcooked. Upon hearing the news, Chef Marco shook his head in dismay and called over his sous-chef, Martinus, for a conference. Martinus was informed of the charges that had been leveled against the tagliatelle, and then, with grave solemnness, they each plucked a noodle from the dish, and after some contemplative chewing, swallowed and debated their findings. A nearby grill chef who was eavesdropping offered the opinion that perhaps the customer's palate was inferior. Uninvited, the fish chef offered an opinion to this opinion, using a combination of English, Italian, and swearing to suggest that the diner be evicted. Marco rolled his eyes.

"Anyone else have an opinion on the tagliatelle?" he loudly asked the crew. "Anyone? I desperately need the opinion of one more cook who was not involved in its preparation. Please, just one more."

The crew, knowing Marco was venting his frustration, remained silent. Except one.

Tony, the ancient dishwasher in the back, unleashed some Old World cursing over his shoulder as he continued scrubbing plates. It was vitriol for vitriol's sake, and the crew burst into laughter. Order was restored.

Exlee Ellis watched with amusement as he sat quietly in a far corner of the kitchen eating a bowl of risotto alla milanese. The meal was a gift from Chef Marco, as was each dish that Exlee enjoyed here, usually three or four times a week.

The two had met several years ago at the horse track, where Marco was distracting himself after a career setback. He'd just lost his junior sous-chef position at an Italian eatery on the east side after being falsely accused of striking a coworker. The double sting not only left him despondent, it left him without a good reference. The story appealed to Exlee as a wrong that should be righted and one that would residually profit him. (If he had ever bothered with a business plan, this would have been Exlee's in a nutshell.)

After leaving the track that day, Exlee had stopped by Troscanza's and asked to speak with the owners. He was told they were unavailable, so he left a message saying he'd been contacted by another press agent in San Francisco who'd asked him to deliver a message for his client. The client was one of the preeminent Italian restaurants in the city, and their signature chef, Marco, had fallen in love with a woman visiting from Stout City and quit his job to follow her back home. His employer was supposedly despondent over losing such a remarkable chef and was pleading with the top Italian restaurants in Stout City not to hire Marco. Talk him into returning to his former job—with the woman, if he liked—and they would double his pay.

Exlee delivered this message to Troscanza's for three straight days, then on the following Monday he had Marco show up in search of a job. Needless to say, Marco was employed as soon as he mentioned his name.

Not only was Chef Marco hired, he was given a salary and position exceeding what his limited credentials normally would have earned him. His genuine talent and hard work did the rest, and he secured the respect of the owners and his kitchen mates. Ultimately, Chef Marco rose to the heights of his fictional reputation.

And Exlee, as always, enjoyed his cut of the winnings. In exchange for free food and drink, Exlee promised the owners he would keep Marco's hiring a secret from the interested parties in Frisco. Marco took it a step further by promising food for life and even reserving a makeshift table in the kitchen corner for Exlee.

The arrangement came with strings attached, however. As a third party, separate from the kitchen staff, Exlee had been unofficially designated the final arbiter in crew debates. Usually, these controversies involved something trivial like movie starlets or baseball players, but occasionally it was a question of whether some personal action or theory was acceptable in normal society. Exlee was as flawed a judge as one could find on many matters, and they knew it, but they accepted the majority of his decisions anyway. If nothing else, his rulings provided closure.

Tonight, closure on the disputed tagliatelle was needed, and Marco set the forlorn dish on Exlee's table in the corner.

"What do you think?" Marco asked sullenly.

Knowing his friend needed a laugh, Exlee performed accordingly. He stabbed a forkful of the pasta and held it up to the light where he could inspect it, slowly turning the fork to and fro in the interest of full discovery. Then he stuck the specimen in his mouth and chewed thoughtfully, occasionally pausing to process a newly discovered variation within the bite. Finally, after swallowing and chasing it with a gulp of wine, he issued his verdict: "The customer has the palate of a donkey with a head cold."

Chef Marco was unsure whether Exlee was being honest or not—nobody ever knew, really—but he was pleased by the performance and the verdict. He returned to battle satisfied.

Exlee waited until Marco had departed before scraping the remaining tagliatelle into a nearby trash can. The pasta was definitely overcooked.

After enjoying the remainder of his wine, Exlee got up and started to exit through the back door whence he'd arrived when a temptation gained the upper hand in his mind. Troscanza's was a particularly fruitful venue for meeting his type of woman, and he wondered if he shouldn't have a little peek into the dining area.

As with all things Exlee, his taste in women was confusing and seemingly contradictory. Logic dictated that Exlee would enjoy the company of carefree, overt women with questionable morals (and to be fair, he more than enjoyed such women when no one more suitable was available). However, given his druthers, he would always choose the type of woman who generally had no use for an amiable but insolvent rogue like himself. Such a woman might be found at a university, or a museum, or volunteering with some society aid group—sometimes all three, plus a church visit. Traitwise, she tended to be smart, responsible, and cautious. She also had a tendency to wear glasses, which, unbeknownst to her, only acted as a tonic to Exlee's desires. By some quirk of nature, Exlee was helpless for the likes of a four-eyed librarian with virginal ambitions—a cruel counter to his rakish goals.

Now, whether he was simply attracted to refined women or he was a sucker for challenges, it's hard to say. This much was certain, though: Exlee's kind of gal was hard to snare and even harder to release. She expected ample rapport before accepting the first invitation for a date, and she assumed committed romance thereafter. Only then would breathtaking intimacy be presented as dessert, and once dessert was served, their "love" was a fait accompli.

Perhaps it was true love that Exlee craved. Or maybe what he sought was even more dangerous—maybe his was an oversized desire to temporarily own a woman, body and soul, to experience new variations of total victory. How else to explain the effort and feeling he injected into his seductions, knowing that the cruelty of a one-sided parting was inevitable? Easier trysts with easier women would have been ... well, easier. Only Exlee could know what drove him to chase transitory love with grounded women, and in all likelihood, he had never asked himself.

So instead of enjoying his gratis pasta and heading out the back door, Exlee decided to take a gander at the customers, just in case his next love should be taking a dinner break from her volunteer work at the home for unwed mothers.

He entered the dining area through the waiter's service door and moved cautiously along the periphery, seeking to remain unnoticed in the shadows. But while he was waiting for his eyes to adjust to the dimmed lights and cigarette smoke, he heard his name called. Squinting, he surveyed the tables and caught sight of a raised arm waving at him. Exlee waved back, but it wasn't enough.

"Get over here, Exlee," a male voice demanded playfully.

Exlee surrendered and moved toward the table. As his view improved, he noted that the table contained six guests staring back at him, four of them unknown and two quite familiar: a city councilman and his wife—the wife an ex-girlfriend of Exlee's. One glance and he knew she was still his type, minus the wedding ring.

"Hello, Theo." He greeted Councilman Roth.

"Pull up a chair and join us," Roth said. "We're celebrating a visit from old friends."

Exlee needed no convincing that a celebration was under way based on the six flushed faces around the table and the three empty wine bottles in the center of it. He joined them after borrowing a chair from the neighboring table.

"Exlee Ellis, I'd like you to meet Bill and Mildred Hoskins and Duncan and Bessie Sanderson," Roth announced. "We're all chums from our days at Loyola, which is why we are celebrating. Tonight sort of marks the anniversary of the first time we were all together as freshmen ... on a hayride, of all things."

"Except for me, remember? That's when I had my tonsils out," Mildred corrected.

"That's why he said 'sorta,' " her husband, Bill, explained.

"Anyhow, I'd like you all to meet Exlee Ellis," Roth continued. "He is undeniably Stout City's favorite son. As to how and why, though, don't ask me, I have no idea. He just is and always will be."

Everyone laughed heartily at this, even though the joke meant little to those on the outside. The wine made their effort easier. Exlee smiled graciously and glanced at Kate Roth, but she did not return the eye contact, nor did she laugh as hard as the others.

"In the interest of full disclosure," Roth continued, "I should also make it known that Exlee here was Kate's boyfriend for a period of time—before we were married, I should add."

Again laughter, but slightly more restrained this time due to the unwieldy nature of the confession. Bessie Sanderson's curiosity was piqued, however, and she proved to be a woman unburdened by tact.

"Now I remember where I heard that name," she cooed naughtily. "As I recall from conversations with Kate, it was a very hot and heavy relationship, which might explain why Mr. Ellis is a favorite."

"Maybe you should give him a try." Her husband, Duncan, laughed. "All I get from you is the heavy and none of the hot."

Bessie turned and slapped Duncan on the shoulder. "You should talk; you've put on more weight than me. When we got married you were a beanpole, they could hardly find a tux that fit you."

"And it's too bad they found one."

Bessie gave him another whack on the shoulder. It was one thing to disparage her in public, but it was quite another to steal her shtick. Issuing bold, outrageous comments was her act, and now with a little wine in him, Duncan thought he was going to make this a two-man routine. Not so fast, honey.

"So now that we have Exlee in the hot seat," Bessie continued daringly, "maybe he can tell us what ended the romance between him and Kate."

"Bessie, that's terrible," Mildred interjected.

"I'm actually sort of curious, myself," Roth added.

"I'm afraid we all are, for better or worse." Bill laughed.

Exlee glanced at Kate, knowing how much she disliked this sort of thing, but she was not looking back. "Well, I don't really have a very good answer as to what ended it," he began. "I guess it wasn't one thing in particular. Kate, of course, was wonderful, just as she is now, and I, uh, probably didn't deserve such a gal. We all know Theo is a better catch anyhow, right?"

"That's debatable, and I barely know you," Bill quipped to moderate laughter.

"That really was a rather empty explanation for a favorite son," Bessie admonished flirtatiously. "Was it another woman that ended it?"

"No woman could top Kate," Exlee offered with a grin.

"Another sidestep. Well, our curiosity has only increased, so I suppose it will be up to Kate to settle this," Bessie said sweetly, turning her gaze toward the councilman's wife. The eyes of the rest of the group joined her.

"And to think you were a bridesmaid in my wedding," Kate teased.

"I was, and I'm still dying to hear your answer," Bessie teased back.

Kate smiled politely and fixed her eyes on Exlee for the first time. He was about to hear the truth he'd escaped; the truth that she had reflected on for years.

"The answer isn't simple. There's virtually nothing absolute that can be said about Exlee," she began. "I very seriously doubt whether he has any real concept of himself, actually. He only knows he is appealing and that it allows him to get away with anything. As a matter of fact, he counts on it—both his appeal and getting away with anything. He doesn't exactly mean to cause harm with his desires, but he has a good idea that harm is in the cards. He will say and do curious, sweet things, and most of them will be genuine. He will even take your breath away when he is fully engaged. In general, though, I have never met anyone so capable of greatness and yet so comfortable with mediocrity—if that. And that's the strangest part about the fascinating Exlee; he really is content with nothing. All he needs is the occasional thrill to satisfy his appetite, but other than that I wonder if he needs things like normal people do—a shoulder to cry on, praise, even close friends. It makes him extra special or extra sad, I'm not sure which. All I can tell you is that I loved him truly, but he didn't seem to need it, and that's as close to an answer as I can provide. A little long, but somebody had to fill in the blanks for him."

There was a moment of awkward silence before Exlee intervened.

"What she really means is that I scratched her favorite Fats Waller record and debated politics too loudly with her cat."

Everyone laughed. Too much seriousness had been averted at the last moment.

"The cat is still alive, although heavier since you saw her," Roth informed Exlee. "And we both plan to vote for Roosevelt—the cat and I."

Kate smiled gracefully at her loves, past and present. How amusing that they should share the same artistry for changing a subject—and so enjoy doing it.

"See, it all worked out for the best," Exlee summarized. "As far as I can tell, most everything Kate said about me was true. So now, you all be the judge: Did she choose the right man, or what?"

"Theo said he was picking up the tab, so I vote for him," Duncan wisecracked.

The quip captured the essence of Kate's condemnation. Theo picked up tabs and votes while Exlee placed bets and poked fun. Kate locked eyes with Exlee to see if he'd caught it, but as usual, no part of him was saying, including the eyes.

"Listen, I've enjoyed being raked over the coals, but I better move on before Mrs. Sanderson digs any deeper into my past," Exlee said as he rose to leave. "It's been a pleasure meeting you hayriders, and I hope you all have a nice visit."

"Wait a sec, I haven't even gotten to the reason I called you over," Roth insisted. "I thought maybe you could enlighten me on this Pinwheel business. Someone called my attention to a little item in the *Sun* and mentioned you were the front man on this deal."

"Not much I can add, really," Exlee said. "I guess we'll know more when this thing gets to trial."

"Another nonanswer from Exlee," Roth proclaimed, turning to his wife. "I don't suppose you can fill in the blanks on this one, honey."

"I speak *some* Exlee, but I'm far from fluent. There's no shortage of women who have training, though." She smirked.

"Yowza, that's one way to tell him good night." Duncan laughed.

"So you really are peddling the Pinwheel story?" Theo pressed Exlee. "I told the fella he was probably wrong, that you don't like the stakes getting too high, but, um, well, this is interesting. You should stop by my office sometime this week, Ex."

"I will," Exlee promised out of habit. "In the meantime, you all have a great evening."

Exlee gave a quick wave to the group along with a final glance at Kate. There was a message in her eyes, but he dared not linger trying to interpret it.

He departed, leaving the table silent until Bill remembered something was missing.

"Where on earth is my replacement tagliatelle?" he wondered aloud.

10

"The *Daily Mercury* ran a neat little piece on us this morning," Emma announced as she took her seat for the morning briefing. "At the bottom of their editorial page. They mocked us for running a front page story with no sources or names other than Wickenstaff, who they said was 'an attorney unfamiliar with morality.' It ended by saying we were unduly provoking harm toward the biggest employer in Stout City."

"I'd be angrier if it weren't true," Deacon groused.

Emma started to comment but decided to switch subjects. "How did our editors fare with their sleuthing?" she wondered, having left at lunchtime the previous day to continue helping with the Mayes trial.

"They survived, even performed like real reporters," Deacon replied. "Alexander interviewed a neighbor woman who said the wife left a month ago with big suitcases and hasn't been seen since. So, the separation between husband and wife seems to check out. And they confirmed that she was Mrs. Wagster, so the names and address that Exlee gave me check out."

"We just don't know if this identified couple has anything to do with the Pinwheel lawsuit ... or if there is a lawsuit," Emma summarized.

"Exactly. But I'm still having Theising look into their past in case this thing is real. That way we'll be ready to spring a feature while the other papers are still getting started. Hopefully it'll stop them in their tracks."

"We could use a home run."

"The question is if we have one. Isn't it funny how we never doubted Exlee until he offered us the inside track on something large and promising?"

"Speaking of Exlee, what did the older ex-reporter think? I, um, can't think of his name."

"Swanson. The one who followed Exlee yesterday?"

"Yes, him."

"He should be here any minute to give us his report," Deacon informed her. "In the meantime, I should mention that Addie Sumner called me late yesterday afternoon after her first day inspecting Pinwheel."

"How did that go?"

"Fine, I guess. Sounds like she met with the owners and then got a basic tour of the factory—which is quite a journey, apparently. Said she would try to dig a little deeper into key areas today."

"No barrels of opium yet, huh?"

"Not yet." Deacon chuckled. "And, no, you can't go over there and plant one just to guarantee us a big story."

"You flatter my muscles. How much do you think a barrel of opium weighs, anyhow?"

They were interrupted as Deacon's office door swung open, followed by a knock.

"Mr. Swanson is here to see you," a secretary announced, departing before anyone could reply.

In walked a fine looking elderly gentleman dressed completely in tweed, including a flat cap where his hair used to be. Accenting his beautiful three piece suit was a walking stick, which he hung on Deacon's coat rack upon entering.

"Hello, Jack, glad to see you." Deacon greeted the visitor. "Here, have a seat. Jack, this is Emma Beltran, my right hand man. Emma, this is Jack Swanson, one of the *Sun's* all-time greats."

Jack bent and shook Emma's hand before turning, sizing up his seat, and plopping into it with a groan.

"I tell you what, I feel anything but great today," he admitted. "I'd forgotten how much physical effort goes into tailing someone—gotten too darned old since retiring."

"Nonsense," Deacon declared. "You look better than ever. Matter of fact, I don't recall you dressing this dapper when you were working your beat here."

"That's because I didn't. Never put much thought into my dress until a couple years ago, and then only because I got remarried to a swanky old gal who likes to dress me up like a doll."

"Congratulations." Emma beamed.

"That's one way of lookin' at it," the old man quipped. "But enough of this baloney. I'm sure you're waiting to hear about Exlee Ellis, not me."

"Well, we sure appreciate you pinch hitting like you did," Deacon said. "I know it was short notice and quite the arduous task, but we couldn't think of a better man to save us."

"I'm not sure I saved anyone," Jack groused in an effort to hide his obvious pride, "but I took some notes ... that are here ... somewhere."

Jack patted his breast pocket, then began an exhaustive search of all the pockets in his jacket and trousers, finally discovering the little notepad in the breast pocket he'd started with. After a deep breath he flipped open the pad and began squinting, which led to a second search, this time for his reading glasses. Those procured, he prepared to read his notes, when an opening thought occurred, causing him to lay the notebook in his lap.

"First of all," he explained, "you told me he generally got a late start to his morning due to, um, an active nightlife ... "

"Uh huh."

"Well, let me tell you, he uses every bit of his mornings to sleep, and then some. I almost gave up waiting to see him leave his place, thought my senility was complete and the fella had slipped past me, but nope—he finally came amblin' out about 11:30, freshly scrubbed and yawning."

"Sorry about that. I rarely hear from him before noon and wasn't sure exactly how he spent his mornings," Deacon said.

"My guess is in bed. And then he goes home."

Greatly amused by himself, Jack laughed hard enough that it required a handkerchief, which required another search of his trouser pockets. After finding the handkerchief and drying his eyes and wiping his nose, he picked up the notepad from his lap and proceeded without further delay.

"As I was sayin', with him sleeping so late, he starts his day by having breakfast for lunch, and he did this at an establishment called Sully's. He had an egg—scrambled—and a hot dog—if you can imagine starting your day with such a thing—and coffee over ice. The fella that runs the place already had the coffee cooling in a back refrigerator, which tells me Exlee must be an expected guest there."

"If he didn't pay, then yes, he was expected," Emma remarked before taking a sip of her coffee (Tingle, two creams and one sugar).

"Funny you should mention that. He rarely paid for anything all day, including this odd breakfast-slash-lunch. So anyhow, after leaving Sully's, he stops at a newsstand for a copy of each Stout City paper. These he pays for—go figure. After that, I follow him as he walks about six blocks to an office above a wig shop in Arraignment Alley. No sign on the door, but when I inquire in the wig shop below, the battle ax who runs the joint confirms that it's his office. I couldn't blow my cover trying to get any closer, so I waited across the street. He exited the building half an hour later—probably after reading his papers in peace—then he visits the Red Cross office."

"The Red Cross?" Deacon asked with astonishment.

"Yes, sir. Although, I'm pretty sure he was seeking charity rather than offering it. I was afraid to follow him inside such a small office, so I watched through the main window. I'm no lip reader or expert on body language, but I know when a woman is being chatted up, and ol' Exlee was doing his best to impress the gal at the front desk."

"You'll notice neither one of us is surprised," Emma said.

"Just out of curiosity, what'd she look like?" Deacon asked.

"Couldn't say how old she was, but short brown hair and glasses."

"Him and the glasses," Deacon mused.

"He was doin' his best to steam hers, that's for sure. But fear not, he gets down to business next."

"It had to happen sometime," Emma figured.

"His next stop is the courthouse, where he makes a series of visits to ... here, let me read them so I get the order right: Judge Collins in his chambers, Judge Westphal in her chambers, the fella who runs the newspaper and cigar stand near the elevators, the three women who were *supposed* to be serving customers in the cafeteria but were gathered around him gossiping instead, and then various tables within said cafeteria. One of these tables contained a lawyer I recognized—

Gladwin—and another table contained a security guard who I once wrote a piece on long ago after he was caught stealing a woman's shoes from her porch. Cops found dozens more from other women when they searched his house. I remember distinctly that he liked the ones with little buckles on 'em. Claimed his time in the military did something to his mind. And now here he is sitting in a courthouse with a pistol hanging from his hip. I don't know, I guess we're all safe as long as we don't have on heels with the little buckles."

"This Gladwin lawyer, what do you know about him?" Deacon asked.

"Well, of course I've been out of action for a few years, but when I was working he was a big shot in training. His father and uncle had been successful attorneys. Anyhow, last I knew of him he was over at the firm of Watkins, Wells, and Harrington, where he was more of an inside man—developing legal strategy, wooing clients, that sort of thing."

"Was it just Exlee and Gladwin at the table?"

"No, there were two other fellas I didn't recognize. I couldn't exactly listen to their conversation, as I had to sit far enough away not to attract Exlee's notice, but they were laughing, and I'm almost positive I heard something about a football game. The whole visit lasted about three minutes."

Deacon and Emma looked at each other and shrugged lightly.

"After the cafeteria, I must confess that I lost him for a few minutes. The older you get the more nature calls, which isn't a problem when I'm home because it actually gives me something to do for a few minutes."

Emma laughed.

"No, I'm not kidding you. The foundation of my day is built around three meals and checking the mail. And to make it worse, I can't eat half my favorite food anymore, and I haven't received a love letter in decades. In other words, my life is bland food and past-due bills, and *that's* the part I look forward to."

"What about your new bride, the one who has you looking so snazzy?" Emma countered. "I'm sure she adds happiness to your life."

"That depends on what you mean by happiness. She talks a lot, so I never want for company. As for the kind of happiness that needs no talk—only when the stars align. I'm telling you, nothing works right anymore."

Emma buried her face in her hands while Deacon just smiled and shook his head.

"You asked." Jack smirked. "But enough of my complaining, let's get back to Mr. Exlee Ellis. So I picked him up again as he was leaving the building permit office, and then he hit the streets of Arraignment Alley again. He stopped at a dry cleaner's but dropped nothing off nor picked anything up. He bought a pack of gum from a drug store but put it in his pocket without chewing any, and then he stopped by his office for a few minutes. I took a chance and lingered outside the door. Sounded like he was talking—a one-sided affair, so I figure he was making a phone call or two. After that, I waited across the street again until he left. Then he visited a couple lawyer's offices ... "

"Which ones?" Deacon asked.

"Uh, let's see here." Jack paused as he looked back over his notes. "The first one was Griszinki and Tomar, and the second was, um ... Vennett. James Vennett. Looks like he spent six minutes at one and eleven minutes at the next."

"Neither of those rank too far above Wickenstaff, do they?" Deacon asked Emma.

"Not familiar with Vennett, but I know Griszinski has actually tried cases in court. Mostly bankruptcy."

"Sorry to interrupt." Deacon apologized to Jack.

"Not at all. I'm here to do a job. Should I continue?"

"Please."

"So, after leaving Vennett, he stopped here at the *Sun* ... "

"Darn, sorry to interrupt again. He stopped by here to deliver that second piece from the husband and his lawyer," Deacon explained to Emma. "I'm sure you've already seen it in this morning's edition."

"I meant to ask you about that. They were a little harder on the wife in this one," Emma said. "You can tell me more when we're done. Jack is going to kill us if we keep stopping him, aren't you, Jack?"

"No, ma'am. I couldn't handle prison food. So anyhow, after leaving the *Sun*, Exlee proceeds to depart from downtown altogether, taking a bus uptown to the, um, Press Section."

All three frowned internally at the mention of the Press Section. This was where Stout City's other newspapers were headquartered. Their common occupancy in the newer, more vibrant part of town added to their prestige. By contrast, the *Sun's* location in old downtown underscored her fading reputation—left behind, both physically and in terms of relevance.

"So, after getting off the streetcar," Jack continued, "he, um, visited the *Daily Mercury* for about forty minutes, and then he ran a couple errands."

"Just the *Daily Mercury*?" Emma asked. "None of the others?"

"Just the *Merc*."

Deacon and Emma exchanged another look, this one with more depth to it. They knew that Exlee visited other papers; it was a vital part of the press agent's hustle. If he was any good, he also frequented radio stations and magazine publishers and anyone else whose product reached the masses. But Exlee had only visited the one paper—their nemesis—and he'd stayed for forty minutes. The combination of these facts triggered a mutual curiosity, but they said nothing for now.

"Anyway," Jack continued, hurrying to fill the awkward silence, "after that little visit, he stopped by the telegraph office and sent one telegram. Once again, I didn't dare get close enough to become conspicuous, so I can't give you any details as to what he wrote. What I was able to observe was that he didn't have to pay for it. Did he get elected mayor of Stout City while I was taking a nap one day?"

"No." Deacon smiled. "He just has a knack for working things in his favor. I'd explain it better if I fully grasped the science behind it."

"Well, I must say I got a kick out of following him. I'd do it again if needed.... Oh, wait, I almost forgot my last entry here. After the telegram, he stopped in a bar called Printer's Ink—one of those dashing places the young ones go to—and he had a draft beer. Then he went further uptown where all the night spots are and slipped in the back entrance of Troscanza's. I figured he was grabbing a bite, and my old bones were beat anyhow, so I called it a night. Hope I covered it all like you were expecting."

"Better than we were expecting," Deacon crowed.

"Yes, thank you so much," Emma added. "I see how you earned your ace reputation."

"That's enough of that," he grumbled while rising from his chair. "You two are full of it, but you can still be sure I'll pass those quotes on to Louisa when I get home ... if I can remember."

"I can write both quotes down for you."

"I meant if I can remember how to get home," Jack said with an impish smile while collecting his walking stick. "Call me if you need any more help. I can always postpone checking the mail until evening."

And with that he was gone, leaving Deacon and Emma alone.

"He was something else," Emma declared. "I'm so glad I got to meet him."

"Yeah, this worked out really well, although I'm not exactly sure what we learned. Can't really say that the lawyers he mentioned mean anything, but that *Mercury* visit ... that felt funny. Maybe I have this unreasonable belief that his loyalty is to the *Sun* first, I don't know. It's a ridiculous notion."

"It's no worse than what I'm thinking," Emma said. "What if the Pinwheel story is complete fabrication? What if he is conspiring with the *Daily Mercury* to deceive us into running a fake story designed to embarrass our biggest advertiser?"

"And leave us publically exposed for blatant libel—libel against the hand that feeds us. It would be provoked suicide for the *Sun,* and then the *Daily Mercury* could collect the corpse for pennies on the dollar."

"When you look at it that way, it is odd that he chose to give us an exclusive on this wild sounding tale, leaving the *Mercury* free to sit back and take pot shots at us. One might even conclude it was part of a plot ... but Exlee isn't like that, is he?" Emma asked with a mixture of hope and concern.

"I don't know. Either we're being played or we're playing ourselves, I have no idea which. It's like trying to find our way in a thick fog at midnight."

There was a heavy silence as they each considered the ugly possibilities. Emma stared at the floor and sipped her Tingle while Deacon tried to distract himself by going through the small pile of letters, notes and missives that had collected on his desk since he'd departed the previous day.

"Hey," he suddenly exclaimed. "See if you can catch Jack real quick. Ask him what time Exlee sent the telegram yesterday. The one after the *Daily Merc.*"

Emma dashed out of the office as Deacon reread the paper in his hand. A minute later she returned. She'd caught Jack, who was reminiscing with one of the older editors on his way out.

"According to his notes, it was 5:50 in the evening," she informed Deacon.

The editor picked up the telegram lying in front of him.

"Then this is the one he sent. It's marked 5:52 p.m.," Deacon crowed.

"What does it say?"

"It says he wants to meet us for lunch today. Both of us. At Jupiter's. His treat."

They looked at each other with furrowed brows, trying to comprehend.

"Both of us. For lunch. With him paying," Emma finally repeated. "None of these things has ever happened before."

"And remember he sent this immediately after visiting the *Daily Mercury*, although he doesn't know that we know."

Emma slowly dropped into her chair. "That sure adds fuel to the paranoia."

Deacon picked up the telegram and read it once more.

11

Pinwheel's owners had carefully instructed Hazel Kellison on how to shepherd Addie Sumner during her inspection. This made sense, as any business would want some parameters when throwing its doors opens for scrutiny from a third party. On the other hand, Addie had been mandated to provide a true picture of Pinwheel. Thus, the two parties—Addie and Pinwheel—were working together in an uneasy alliance, each wanting the other to succeed but not at the cost of their own reputation. The corporation would try to hide its warts, and Addie would try to discover them. It was a game of sorts, and Addie was taking it more seriously than Pinwheel's owners would have preferred ... had they fully known.

Unfortunately for Addie, discovering warts in an operation covering several acres is nearly impossible without a hint, and Hazel the tour guide had worked hard to deny her any. Too hard, actually. Hazel's vigilance was so strong that when Addie happened to inquire about anything the Pinwheel owners deemed off limits, Hazel would redden and hesitate while she considered a polite way of dampening the subject. Her anxious pauses might just as well have said, "You're getting warmer," and her answers, "You're red hot."

Hazel had reacted in such a way twice while leading Addie on a tour of Pinwheel the previous day.

The first happened in the main offices while they were passing through the bookkeeping section. When

Addie asked if she could sample the files, Hazel had blushed and started to explain that "certain Security Exchange and Department of Commerce regulatory statutes might be interpreted in a manner making it unlawful for an uncredentialed visitor to have specific forms of unaccredited access to certain areas." Not only had Hazel's unusual discomfort struck Addie as interesting, so had her sudden command of legalese. A suspicious mind might have thought Hazel was quoting a line fed to her by superiors, and Addie had a suspicious mind. She'd had some experience in governmental affairs—having served as a small-town mayor—and recognized authoritative double-talk when she heard it.

Hazel's second case of uneasiness occurred when they were discussing the offload warehouse. She explained that it was a separate structure where the sacks of coffee beans were unloaded from railroad cars, stored, and ultimately opened and dumped into hoppers. This was the genesis of the conveyance system that delivered the beans to the roasting floor. Furthermore, Hazel had reluctantly explained, due to the nature of the station's atmosphere—dust, heavy objects, dangerous steps—the place was basically closed to non-warehousemen for legal and insurance reasons.

Addie was particularly suspicious about this banned area. After all, wouldn't a separate building be the perfect place to add some sort of addictive drug to the coffee, maybe in the form of a coating undetectable to the casual observer?

Having arrived for her second day of inspecting, Addie remained in her car and considered her options. She desperately wanted a peek at the offload station, but she knew there was no subtle way to make it happen. Hazel had already explained that it was restricted as well as somewhat isolated on the Pinwheel property, erasing any chance of an accidental, meandering visit. If Addie were going to see the station's innards, she was going to have to badger Hazel into submission or sneak in there and risk being removed from her job for trespassing. She wondered if she could claim a mental breakdown or amnesia if caught. "Maybe I could claim I was high on Tingle," she joked with herself.

As Addie sat, debating the finer points of ethics, she happened to spy a security guard meandering, doing whatever security guards do. To a law abiding citizen, this would have been an obvious sign from above, a deterrent sent by the angel Gabriel—don't even think about doing something borderline criminal. But to a stubborn woman in the throes of curiosity, it represented something different. What she saw was an ally, albeit an unwitting one.

Addie scrambled out of her car and shut the door without looking. "Excuse me, I'm wondering if you could help me," she called to the guard.

"Yes, ma'am, I'd be glad to try," he offered alertly, moving toward her.

The guard was short—several inches shorter than she—and thin, which everybody seemed to be these days, three years into the depression. He was probably in his early 40s, with a mustache too big for his face and a tattoo of an eagle too big for his forearm. Addie figured he was an ex-sailor, probably having served in the World War.

"Thank you," Addie responded to his offer of help. "I remember seeing you yesterday during my tour of the plant."

This was a lie, and she paused to see if the bluff would take hold.

"Yesterday?" he asked. "I spent most of the day near the loading docks on account of some reported thefts I ain't authorized to discuss. Maybe you saw me there."

"Exactly where I saw you!" Addie exclaimed. "I was getting an inside look at the plant as part of my inspection work for Mr. Ostwald and Mr. O'Bryant. I'm sure you know all about it."

"Oh, sure," he agreed. "We get, uh, bulletins and such."

"Isn't that a lifesaver? You see, I'm a little lost among so many different buildings, and I'm supposed to report to the offload station. I have a feeling that you are the perfect man to help me get there."

"I guess I know this place better than anyone here," he admitted. "As far as offload goes, though, it would be much easier if you went through the east wing of offices and took the second floor service bridge to the rail dock. It's a little longer that way, but with you bein' in a skirt and heels ... "

"You wouldn't believe what I manage to do in a skirt and heels," she joked, much to his discomfort. "The truth is, I'm already late, so if you wouldn't mind guiding me by the outside route, I would be so grateful, and I'm sure Mr. Ostwald and Mr. O'Bryant would be, too."

"All right," he agreed, excited at this rare opportunity to show off his trekking skills. "Follow me, and we'll get you there in one piece, pronto."

And with that he turned and strode confidently toward an alley behind the administration building. Addie jogged to catch up while glancing at her surroundings, hoping nobody was watching.

Valor having gone to his head, the security guard continued setting a rather frisky pace. Addie was forced to abandon her furtive gandering so she could focus on keeping up. At the end of the alley, the guard dashed up some wooden steps to his left and motored down the backside of an auxiliary dock before turning right down another alley and left to the front side of yet another dock. By now, Addie had broken into a half-run, carrying her handbag like a football. She was sure the entire world could hear her heels beating the wood planks.

They stopped at the bottom of another set of stairs and stood on the gravel edge of two railroad tracks that ran between the docks. Addie waited for him to continue, but he was busy surveying the scene with a discouraged look.

"This is the railroad spur," he informed her. "See those six rail cars over there? They came in yesterday late and are being unloaded this morning. That's the offload warehouse next to 'em. You need to be on that dock across the way, but the problem is this other railcar—the two bay hopper car the railroad musta left behind for some reason—probably too lazy to move it to a siding. It's blocking the only set of stairs to that dock from here, and it's up against it tight."

"So what do we do?" Addie asked.

"Not much we *can* do ... unless I was to sorta help lift you up across the way. That might get dicey, though, considering all the different, um, considerations."

"I'm willing to give it a try after coming all this way."

The security guard frowned and emitted a low moan before stepping over the tracks and into the shadow of the other dock. Addie carefully followed, then stopped and watched as he sized up the task. The dock was a little taller on this end due to a slight decline in the ground's elevation. Lifting her up by the waist was out of the question. It was a good thing, too, as the difference in their heights would have made each feel silly.

"Tell you what I'm gonna do," he finally explained. "I'm gonna kneel on the ground and you'll use me like a step. That should get you close enough, although I hate gettin' your nice clothes dirty, rolling around on the dock."

"I should be fine, I think."

The guard shrugged and dropped to his hands and knees hard against the dock. He was about to suggest that Addie remove her heels, but it was too late. She stepped on his back and wavered unsteadily while he tried to muffle his whimpering as the heels dug in deeper. Finally, she attempted her ascent, and with great effort managed to get her upper body over the edge of the dock. She didn't have the arm strength to pull herself completely over, though, and she teetered on the dock's edge between success and failure. Looking up and noting her precarious circumstances, the security guard scrambled to his knees and began shoving upward on her shoes. Their combined effort was just enough to push her to the summit, where she landed face first on the dock.

The guard staggered away from the dock and turned to admire his handiwork.

"I said I'd get you there in one piece." He beamed.

Addie, rising to her feet, slapped her hands free of dirt and adjusted her skirt. Everything seemed to be in order, though slightly less comfortable.

"You're a man of your word, thank you. Would you be so kind as to toss me my handbag, please?"

He did so, bidding her farewell as she caught the purse. "I'm gonna head on back, but, um, good luck with your inspection, and just ask for me if you need anything else."

He turned and sauntered away before she could get his name. "Thank you again!" She waved.

After checking her outfit once more, Addie moved down the dock toward the offload station. She heard male voices as she neared. Just then a man exited a rail car, startling both of them.

"Hi there, can I help you?" he asked doubtfully, having never encountered an attractive female visitor on the docks before.

"Actually, I believe you could be of great help." Addie smiled. "I'm currently undertaking an inspection of the plant at the request of Mr. Ostwald and Mr. O'Bryant, and this is my next stop. This *is* offload, correct?"

"Yep, sure is."

"Excellent," she answered crisply. "Let's go inside here and have a look."

Still confused by Addie's unforeseen appearance, and further flustered by her aplomb, he obeyed as though he were 8 years old again.

They entered a large warehouse. It was dark except for a few overhead bulbs and whatever sunlight could penetrate the half-dozen grimy windows far in the back. What could be seen, though, was awe-inspiring. Burlap bags laden with coffee beans were stacked in giant rows as far as the eye could see. They extended in every direction, hundreds if not thousands of them silently awaiting their turn in the roaster. Addie couldn't have been more impressed had she been standing among the Egyptian pyramids.

The rest of the scene felt pedestrian, at best. There was a tiny shack-like office to the immediate left of the gaping entrance. It was made of plywood and glass, big enough to hold no more than two men at a time. Dusty clipboards holding curled paper hung on the walls. Next to the office was a large industrial scale, and next to that were various carts, hand trucks, and other wheeled implements used to move the sacks around.

In the center of the warehouse was a large clearing that represented the heart of the operation. Everything, even the great walls of bean sacks, stood back from this open space, where three large, iron grates were set in the cement floor. Below the grates were the hoppers that fed the conveyor belts, which in turn transported the beans through the cleaning screens and onto the roasting floor.

What Addie didn't see in her initial glimpse was anything that might contain an additive.

So focused was she on discovering something nefarious that she didn't immediately notice the nine other men inside the warehouse. They sat to the far right of the last hopper grate, resting on a low row of bean sacks like it was a park bench.

"Oh! Hello, fellas," she greeted them upon cognizance. "You move all these sacks in here by yourselves?"

"In one trip," one of them wisecracked to the goofy chuckling of the rest.

Addie smiled and proceeded to explain yet again what her purpose was and that it was mandated by Mr. Ostwald and Mr. O'Bryant. Once again the mention of the names had a sobering effect on the countenance of each listener. Addie was finding this convenient, though somewhat amusing, as anyone could flaunt the names just as easily and with no authority.

"They told me the name of the supervisor here," she lied, "but I've met so many employees since yesterday that I've gotten confused and forgotten."

One of the men on the sack bench stood up and walked over to her.

"That would be me, ma'am. I'm Curly Sieber. We were just restin' after unloading the last of that car and before we began dumping."

"Curly, that's the name," she said with feigned recall. "The owners said you would give me a quick tour of the offload warehouse, and I really do appreciate you taking the time."

"Uh, sure, I'm glad to show you around. There's still a few minutes left in our morning break anyhow, and …"

"Oh, I don't want to interrupt your break," she interjected.

"Not at all," he assured her. "You can pretty well tell everything about this place from where you're standing, but we can start on the left, over here, if you'd like."

He was right, there wasn't much more to see, just an endless maze of burlap sacks. She did notice, however, a handful of pinups adorning the back walls, mostly magazine covers from *Tattle Tales* and *Spicy* depicting women with coquettish expressions and striking figures but not much in the way of clothes.

Curly had forgotten about the warehouse "art," and the first one they encountered struck him like a thunderbolt. Neither party acknowledged it, and Curly was quick to point out some innocuous fact about something in the opposite direction. This was repeated several times, much to the discomfort of both of them.

By the time they returned to the front of the warehouse, the crew's break had ended, and they were piling bags of coffee beans next to the grates.

"Right now we're going to add beans to the hoppers," Curly explained. "From there they'll go through a series of washing stations to remove any foreign particles. There's even a magnetized portion that pulls any metallic particles. We don't always know when the belts will be started for a new roasting batch, so it's our job to make sure the hoppers are supplied. When that's done, we'll start unloading the next boxcar. Those are our two main jobs, unloading and dumping. Another batch of men will be clocking in soon. We have overlapping shifts to make sure the cars are emptied before the next ones arrive."

"The dumping is actually kind of mesmerizing." Addie smiled. "Mind if I watch for a bit?"

"Not at all. Just stand over here; you'll have a good view while stayin' safe."

She complied and watched as the men continued moving bags into position using large carts. Meanwhile, Curly took his place alongside two other men atop the grates, and with a simple, well-practiced flick of their knives, they sliced open bag after bag, allowing the beans to cascade into the grating with a small roar. It was hypnotic but otherwise innocent-looking. Addie saw nothing that would even hint at an addictive drug being added from this location.

She meant to ask Curly how they decided which bags to select for dumping, but she hated to interrupt his work. Plus, she needed to get going.

When Addie finally met up with Hazel, it was past ten o'clock.

"You look like you've been busy." Hazel laughed, noting the somewhat disheveled look that Addie had acquired during her dock gymnastics.

"Just one of those days," was Addie's noncommittal answer.

"Okay. Well, now that you're here, where would you like to start today?"

"I'd like to visit the roasting floor again, if you don't mind. And then maybe I could spend some time in the financial area?"

"The roasting part is easy enough; I'll just call Eddie and have him meet you. As for the financial part, I'll have to get back to you after I've checked on schedules and things."

"Great. Maybe you'll know something by lunch?"

"I'll work on it, I promise."

"Thanks. And now I'm wondering if I shouldn't actually start in the cafeteria. I've been craving a fresh cup of Tingle all morning."

"Mind if I join you?" Hazel asked.

"Of course not."

"Good, because you are going to die when I tell you about Lyman calling me last night."

"Lyman ... I don't remember ... "

"The truck driver with the bushy beard? We saw him in the cafeteria yesterday at lunchtime?"

"Oh yes, I remember now. I don't think you mentioned his name."

"And probably for good reason. Hey, Addie, did you know there is a piece of wood in your hair?" Hazel asked as she removed it. "It's like a splinter."

"How odd," Addie said, wrinkling her nose. She took the sliver from Hazel and after studying it for a moment, placed it in her handbag without further comment.

"Maybe we should talk about your night, instead," Hazel said.

12

Deacon and Emma arrived at Jupiter, the restaurant, one minute before noon. They didn't see Exlee immediately, but that was to be expected. Exlee was the rare person who could be quite early or quite late in equal proportion.

"May I help you?" the young hostess asked with bored courtesy.

"Well, we're meeting someone who we don't see," Emma answered while looking around. "His name is Exlee Ellis, and he ... "

"Oh, Exlee is already here," the hostess exclaimed with a smile. "If you'll just follow me."

Emma trailed closely as the hostess wound her way past faux marble columns and vases resting on pedestals, décor that was supposed to hark back to ancient Rome. To most patrons, it was a stunning vision of classical opulence, but to Deacon it represented a distracting mishmash of dynasties, continents, and cultures.

Deacon was so distracted by the incongruous decoration that he fell behind as the hostess led them to their table. When he finally returned to the business at hand, he was hopelessly lost, forced to wander about the cavernous room craning his head around faux marble columns until he spotted Emma waving at him.

Everyone has a hobby that makes them an amateur expert in some field. It may involve quilting or field hockey or bird watching or even the finer points of cooking an egg. In Deacon's case, it was ancient civilizations. He'd caught the bug in elementary school, creating a diorama that captured the majesty of the Parthenon in an upturned shoebox. This lifelong passion was mostly a private affair, but occasionally his trove of knowledge reared its indignant head in polite company.

"Sorry about that," he said upon arriving at the table. He shook Exlee's hand before sitting next to Emma. "I got busy trying to figure this place out. Apparently nobody involved in decorating knew the difference between ancient Rome and classical Greece or even Egypt; they might just as well have named this place Zeus or The Nile, for goodness sakes. Frankly, if it can't be done right, then they should surrender and base the ambience on Jupiter's namesake, the planet. Moons and constellations are timeless, and there's less chance of creating such a confusing aura."

Deacon then pointed out some of the grosser errors in the decor, oblivious to the looks exchanged between Exlee and Emma. When Deacon had finished his litany of sins, there was a moment of silence as his two companions waited to confirm that his mild outrage was exhausted. Exlee finally spoke.

"First time I've ever heard him seize the floor for more than three sentences," Exlee declared. "And he uses it to denounce a restaurant decorator for his history skills. Does he do this sort of thing often when I'm not around?"

"Naturally, it doesn't come up often, but I always learn something interesting when it does," she explained while giving Deacon a supportive smile. "Then again, we don't visit restaurants or discuss much outside of local news."

"That is such a shame," Exlee lamented, shaking his head sadly. "I understand keeping a professional relationship and all, but look at Emma's eyes, those incredible dark brown beauties. Honestly, Deacon, you are a stronger man than me."

"That's not saying much. You've set the bar pretty low," Deacon answered dryly, refusing to take the bait.

"Okay, I can't argue there." Exlee laughed. "But seriously, Deacon, what would you do without her? We both know she really runs things at the *Sun*. Suppose she got snatched up by the *Daily Mercury*, what would you do then?"

The mention of their goliath rival and potential saboteur caused Emma and Deacon to wonder. Coming from Exlee, who was causing them real suspicion, it felt like a taunt, and it provoked a strong reaction.

"I'd tell the *Daily Mercury* where they could go," Emma boasted. "Loyalty means something to me; it's not just a passing condition. And always remember there are more important things than money and prestige."

"Is that advice aimed toward me?" Exlee asked with surprise. "I thought it was generally agreed that I was a failure in both those departments."

"I'm just saying certain opportunities aren't always what they seem, and aligning yourself with trustworthy friends is preferable in the long run."

Exlee didn't answer, but instead smiled and held his gaze on her, trying to decide what was really behind her words. Under the weight of his look, Emma switched her gaze to Deacon, who was poring over a menu.

"Have you decided what you're having?" she asked him.

"Not yet," Deacon lied. He hated telling others what he was ordering. Their response was always pleasant enough, but there was an undeniable hint of disappointment if he didn't choose something sufficiently gourmet.

"Well, I've narrowed my choice down to two," Emma said. "Should I have the Hades Salad or the grilled Uranus filet?" she wondered aloud.

"I'm afraid to ask what grilled Uranus is." Exlee frowned.

"In this case, it's duck," she explained. "I believe Uranus was the god of sky, as in birds, as in duck."

"As was Jupiter of *Roman* mythology, whose name is emblazoned on this restaurant," Deacon informed them with heavy sarcasm.

Emma peeked nervously at Exlee, who pretended to scrutinize his menu. The waitress arrived and took their drink orders. An iced tea, a Neptune Nectar, and a cup of Tingle. ("Black, please.")

When the drinks had been served and the food orders taken, Deacon could no longer stall his curiosity about their meeting.

"I must say we were a little surprised by your telegram. Meeting for lunch is rather formal relative to our usual newsroom conversations."

"I was just thinking about that," Exlee agreed. "The last time we were all three together was last week, near Hoyt's desk. Which reminds me, I owe Emma something."

Exlee reached into his shirt pocket and produced a five dollar bill, which he extended to Emma. She smiled but held up her hand, stopping the transaction.

"I have to keep you coming around," she said, flirting. "Let's make it double or nothing on the Illinois game. You get Army and three points."

Exlee pretended to consider the prudence of this wager, making a show of it by squinting and rubbing his chin. Not that it mattered, since he'd already placed bets on both sides of this one.

"It's a deal, but only if I get four points."

PINWHEEL

"You know, the thing with you, Exlee, is that I never know if you really care about the points or even the outcome," Emma admitted with narrowed eyes. "And the way you smile when you make a bet makes me wonder if you aren't part of a fix or something."

"I'll take that as a yes," he answered.

They reached across the table and shook hands.

"So you brought us to lunch for a bet?" Deacon asked.

"Not exactly." Exlee smiled. "I have a follow-up to the Pinwheel items I gave you Monday and Tuesday. This time it's a response from the woman and *her* lawyer. I told you this story would be a hot one. Here, read this."

Exlee removed a folded sheet of paper from inside his coat pocket and handed it over, watching with anticipation as Deacon unfolded it and began reading. Emma's eyes shifted back and forth to each man. She knew the game was getting bigger, along with the risk.

"I know you hate this," Exlee said humbly, "but if you could run this one on the front page like the last two ... no big headline or anything, just, you know, front page."

Deacon handed the paper to Emma without taking his eyes off of Exlee. He heard the supplication in Exlee's request, but the increasing danger of this game was testing the editor's renowned unflappability.

"That's kind of you—not demanding a sixty-point, up style, banner headline—otherwise, I might think you were surpassing any favor you *may* have accrued with me over the years," Deacon said with calm sarcasm.

"Don't be angry. You know what I'm trying to do here. We discussed this last time and agreed it's a big fish and we're going to reel it in like one, to the benefit of both of us. You just have to trust me, which shouldn't be hard seeing as how I've never led the *Sun* astray one time ... well, very rarely, and not on anything this important."

"And that's my concern, Exlee. This is important. I kid you not when I say this story could finish the *Sun* if it blows up in our face. A paper has to be sturdy to survive for nearly a hundred years, but the way it stands now, two people—you and I—could topple it with this thing. I want to trust you, I really do, but your appeals are becoming increasingly difficult ... "

"Who is this Spencer attorney who's representing the wife?" Emma interrupted, looking up from the paper.

"Just a lawyer." Exlee shrugged. "Been around since I started."

"He operate alone?"

"Yeah, out of an office in Arraignment Alley. Remember that piece I sold you a few months ago, the one about the grandmother who kidnapped her grandson because she didn't think the daughter-in-law was feeding him right? She was Spencer's client. He also does a lot of bankruptcy these days."

"So if we left here and stopped by Spencer's office, he would confirm this story you handed me?" Deacon asked impatiently.

"Sure. I just don't understand this ... this treatment. It's a large story, yes, and you have a lot at stake, I get it, but I trust my people, and I'm stickin' my neck out the same as you."

Deacon and Emma both looked at him gravely, fearing that he was bluffing but wanting desperately to believe him. Sadly, once something is viewed through the prism of suspicion, it can be difficult to see it any other way, especially if the potential for ruin exists. Doubt was causing Deacon and Emma to connect dots differently than they would have before. Hearing that Exlee had visited the *Daily Mercury* would have meant nothing previously, but now it meant everything, especially since he'd arranged this lunch immediately after stopping there the day before—a lunch where he escalated the fear by introducing this new item.

"This story has legs," Exlee continued. "You two need to embrace the fact that you're scooping it—and what a beauty it is. Tell me what you just read isn't something."

Emma cracked a small smile. She had to admit it was a very funny piece. The wife, through her lawyer, was claiming that the husband was jealous because she found more happiness in a cup of coffee than he found in his bowling leagues, racy detective magazines, and cheap beer. If she were to use the same logic he was using, then maybe she should sue the publishing company, since he so thoroughly enjoyed the gals in the detective stories with the "bosoms everywhere." She also noted that the rumors of his amorous failings were not entirely true and that she had been with worse. Not only that, she was willing to forgive him and reunite under one roof if he would just accept her brewed happiness. If he loved her like he'd promised when proposing six years ago—on the boat ride at the carnival—then he would want her happy as long as it wasn't stopping his happiness. She overlooked so much regarding him, why couldn't he just share her with Tingle?

"It is something, all right," Emma agreed. "But surely—if nothing else—you can tell us when the husband's lawsuit will be filed. That's what's really leaving us exposed. Once that's filed, it's real news. Until then, we're courting libel with the biggest firm in Stout City."

"Honestly, I don't know a date. Last I heard, they were just working on some affidavits."

"Well, honestly, I don't know if the editor in chief is going to keep giving us the green light," Deacon countered. "He was beyond reluctant when this started and basically told me I'd be the one paying the price if this were a hoax of some sort."

"And I totally understand that," Exlee insisted, "but I'm being paid to make this story splash, and there are other papers that can do it bigger and faster if you're not up to it."

Deacon leaned back in his chair and frowned as an awkward silence hung over the table. This was the second time in three days that Exlee had made a threatening statement, and Deacon sensed a transition of power that he did not like.

"Well, the friendly battle lines seem clear enough," Emma joked in an attempt to ease the tension.

"It's not a battle, it's just business," Exlee explained. "Oh, by the way, I read about Addie Sumner doing an inspection at Pinwheel and that the *Sun* is sponsoring it. Your idea, Deacon?"

"It just sort of came up in conversation when I was getting their rebuttal to your initial piece," Deacon lied. "Since the *Sun* is caught in the middle, it makes sense to cover both angles."

"Couldn't agree more, it's a nice play. You just better hope Addie doesn't find anything too bad, or Pinwheel might think you were working with me to set them up."

He started to say more, but the food arrived, and after pleasantly commenting on each other's dishes, they dug in. Silence settled over the table.

"This is actually kind of nice, having a good lunch at a good restaurant," Exlee decided near the end of the meal. "I was just thinking you two should get out of the office every now and then and eat like this—talk about something other than newspaper shenanigans. That's what teammates do, they share things."

Deacon refused to engage in this trap, chewing his food and looking past Exlee as though he hadn't heard a word. Emma, meantime, feigned interest in her plate of food, probing it with her fork like she was searching for gold.

Stonewalled, Exlee sampled some more of his Mashed Vesuvius Potatoes and chewed silently before commenting again.

"It could even be dinner. No sense in rushing home every night when you could enjoy each other's company in a relaxed atmosphere."

Emma smiled politely and Deacon nodded as he chewed.

"And it wouldn't have to be here," Exlee continued. "Nobody wants to waste their hard earned money on a place that thinks the Byzantine Empire and the Roman Empire are related."

Deacon tried as hard as he could to continue ignoring Exlee's line of conversation, but the need for correction was physically painful.

"The Byzantine Empire was actually a part of the Roman Empire," Deacon explained.

Emma caught the grin on Exlee's face and realized that he'd just won a bet with himself.

On the taxi ride back to the *Sun's* office, Deacon and Emma strategized.

"Cantrell is not going to appreciate me trying to run this third piece on the front, even if it is below the fold," Deacon said, referring to the editor in chief. "I'm really wondering whether we should stall this until we know more about the lawsuit—or nonlawsuit. Or until we get our laboratory results back, which would at least prove or disprove that the coffee is somehow drugged."

"That could be days, and when Exlee doesn't see it tomorrow, he may just take it to one of the other papers, including the *Daily Merc*—if he's not already planting this on their behalf. This is getting so complicated, and I got no sense of anything from him at lunch."

"Me either," Deacon concurred with a sigh. "And what really makes me nervous is his confidence in this story. Last week he was pleased to get twelve bucks from us for that item about the husband and wife shoplifters who'd just emigrated from Czechoslovakia. Now he's calling the shots on front page material and threatening to switch allegiances. Maybe he never really did put us first—we've just been getting first dibs because we're the paper nearest Arraignment Alley—*if* we really were getting first dibs. I swear I'm starting to reexamine everything back to when I met him and gave him his initial break."

They were silent for a block before the managing editor continued.

"It comes down to this: Who could prove the potential lawsuit quickest? Exlee and his lawyers are probably in cahoots, whether this is real or not. The *Daily Mercury* wouldn't admit anything if they were involved. That leaves the husband and wife. We don't know where she is, so then we're down to the husband, right?"

"Right," Emma answered. "Although we aren't even sure if he is connected or just a red herring."

"Well, he's all we have at the moment. I say we try and get him to talk—not by traditional means, mind you—he's probably still maintaining silence. But remember how Koenig tailed him and mentioned his eating out for supper after work and then a bar visit? That's the kind of activity you'd expect of a separated man. So maybe we have a reporter follow him to the bar and then go inside and act like a talkative stranger and see where it goes. We got nothing to lose, and after a couple drinks, maybe the husband says more than he should."

"Especially if the reporter is a woman. And I don't mean me," she added quickly.

"Not a bad idea. Who we got available for reporters—femalewise?"

"DeMoss ... "

"Too matronly."

" ... and Currouthers."

"Too rough. She's worse than a Teamster. Who else?

"That's it for reporters. We have office gals," Emma suggested.

"Hey, yeah. How about the one who sits near the hall entrance? Underneath the fan."

"Wow, no hesitation there."

"Well, you have to admit she's rather attractive," Deacon opined.

"She's downright beautiful. If I had half her looks, I'd have married some millionaire instead of hanging around newspaper offices my whole life."

"And what would you do as a millionaire's wife?"

"I don't know. I'd read books all day ... while sitting in a bathtub full of champagne."

"I could go for that myself," Deacon conceded. "Know any millionaires?"

"No, and they're reserved anyhow. Reserved for women from important families or women who look like Miss Redding."

"Who's Redding?"

"The one you just suggested, you dope. Your crush underneath the fan," Emma answered.

"Oh."

"Truthfully, though, she seems to be smart enough if you want to try her out on the husband. I can't believe I'm trying to talk you into this. It's all Exlee's fault."

"Speaking of crushes."

Emma didn't deny it. Instead, she started looking through her handbag. "He actually gave me a note for you. He made me promise not to read it and that I was to give it to you later. This seems later enough, and ... Aha, here it is."

"This must be the same note I watched him write while you visited the ladies' room before we left the restaurant," Deacon decided. "He said it was for you."

"All I know is he handed it to me on the way out and told me it was for you."

Deacon shook his head as he opened it.

My dearest Deacon, the note began, to Deacon's annoyance, *I know I bother you with the Emma talk, but it's been two years now since your wife died. It's time to remove the mourning blinders and start enjoying more of Emma. She's always been a special friend, and you can't tell me you wouldn't love those brown eyes up close. Please think about it. XOXO, Exlee.*

Deacon finished reading the note and folded it, showing no expression.

"What did he say?" Emma wondered, fearing it was more trouble concerning the Pinwheel situation.

"Nothing. He just had a thought."

Emma turned toward her side window and watched the city pass by until she thought she heard a chuckle. She turned back to see Deacon smiling.

"What's so funny?" she asked.

"It's difficult to stay mad at an idiot who ends his note with hugs and kisses."

13

Farrell O'Bryant and two other men were waiting to tee off at the fourth hole of the new Fernpath Country Club. There was a foursome ahead of them just moving onto the green.

"I know this is a new course, but damn, where'd everyone come from?" Jim Jefferson complained.

"That's what I'm wondering. I thought there was a depression going on," Farrell agreed.

"There must be, the way you were huntin' for that lost ball a while ago. You want me to loan you a few bucks so you can buy some extras?" Zeke Fish asked.

"What was the hurry? I knew we'd cnd up waiting here anyhow, so I might as well look for my ball, depression or no depression."

"Yeah, and I noticed after all that looking you found it just inside the fairway."

"That was a drop. I added a stroke."

"Uh huh. What did you get on that last hole?"

"A five after adding that stroke."

"A five? After you three-putted? Either you can't add or you're a brazen cheat."

"Says the man who calls every other drive a mulligan. We haven't even teed off on the fourth, and you've already claimed more mulligans than the Boston Police Department."

"That would be funnier if you didn't use it every time we played."

"To be fair, he used a pub instead of the police department last time," Jim said.

Zeke looked over at some nearby trees, and the other two men followed his gaze. They watched as a man emerged.

"Would you look at that?"

"He finally made it. Where you been, Jude?"

"Sorry, boys, I had to finish up some work, but you can put me down for three birdies so far. Matter of fact, I'm pretty sure I'd have eagled that last hole."

"That's just about the same way your partner has been scoring himself. Makes me wonder how accurate those Pinwheel quarterly reports are and whether I should sell before you get audited."

"Then you could buy stock in a real company like Blue Checkered Coffee."

"Or buy some regular socks. Are those your wife's?"

"Actually, I'm pretty sure they're *your* wife's. You should check with her when you get home and see if she accidently put mine on."

"No thanks. If I proved you two were seeing each other, I'd have to do something about it."

"Hey, the group ahead of us are all on the green. We should go ahead and hit. That's gotta be 350 yards away, right?"

"It says 327 yards on the card."

"Just to be safe, we can have Farrell go first. Anything over two hundred is guaranteed to land in another fairway."

"Jim would make more sense. They'll be at the next hole by the time he gets done with his mulligans."

"I'll show you a mulligan," Jim said as he teed up his ball. He took one practice stroke and then gave the ball a ride. It was long and straight, and they watched silently as it bounced a few times and came to rest in the middle of the fairway.

"Damn, Jim, I guess you'll be playing this hole alone."

"Let's take a vote on whether that's a mulligan."

Jim just smiled.

Jude teed up next.

"Are you serious? You're gonna waltz in here late and tee up second?"

"Actually, I should have gone first, based on my imaginary eagle on the last hole."

Jude teed his ball and then, in order to get limber, he went through a whole series of lunges and twists, followed by several practice swings.

"I bet your wife falls asleep waiting."

"I bet his wife falls asleep during."

Jude ignored them and carefully lined up his drive before unleashing a violent swing that sent his ball rocketing to the left. "Stay in play, baby," he coaxed. But it didn't, and instead landed directly in a grove of trees.

"Just use Farrell's method. Take a drop and lose three strokes."

Zeke carefully placed his tee in the ground and then gently set his ball on top. Then he stood very erect, studying the fourth hole with his hand shielding his eyes from the sun.

"All right, Columbus, let us know when you've discovered the New World."

"Quiet," Zeke instructed. "Quit trying to distract me."

He stood over the ball and looked back and forth from the ball to the green, trying to create a positive mental image of his shot. Finally, with a slow, controlled swing, he lofted his drive. It drifted lazily to the right, landing in the fairway twenty yards from Jim's drive.

"Not bad ... for your aunt."

"My aunt actually plays golf. Aunt Jo. She took fourth place in the ladies' tournament at her club in McKeesport."

"What a coincidence. You'll be taking fourth place in our group today."

It was Farrell's turn to tee off. He swung left-handed, which annoyed everyone for unknown reasons. After a couple practice swings, he stepped up to his ball and gave it a violent thump. As was the case most of the time, his drive sliced left. The ball hit the edge of the fairway and bounded into the thick rough not far from Jude's ball. Farrell cursed and slammed his club on the turf, which made everyone laugh. They counted on his temper for entertainment.

"Look out for rhinos when you're in that jungle."

"Wanna borrow my nine iron machete?"

"You two shut up and go play your easy little fairway shots," Jude scowled.

They all picked up their bags and prepared to leave.

"When's this place going to have caddies, anyway?"

"From what I heard in the clubhouse, they didn't hire enough of them. They weren't sure how much traffic the course would get when it first opened. So, apparently they ran out before we arrived."

The two groups separated—Jim and Zeke toward the middle-right of the fairway and the Pinwheel partners toward the jungle on the left.

"Any troubles at the office?" Farrell asked as they left the tee box.

"No, not really," Jude answered. "I was already running late when Miss Kellison stopped in to give me an update on the inspection. Remember us wondering how meticulous Addie would be? Well, her latest plan is to work through the end of the week, which ought to tell you something. Four full days. That is no casual inspection."

"No, it is not, but that could still work in our favor. The more things she's impressed with the better we'll look."

"So far, from what I can gather, she hasn't found anything troublesome. She did mention to Miss Kellison yesterday that she was interested in seeing the offload warehouse, which you and I agreed wasn't the best idea. Miss Kellison played up the dullness of a warehouse and described its minimal function—she even added some mumbo jumbo about safety issues because of dust and falling bags."

"Good for her," Farrell declared. "That's just what I'd have suggested she say."

"And it may have worked. Apparently Addie didn't mention wanting to see the offload warehouse today."

"If it does come up again, I do have one idea involving some of the blending beans. We could use them as a diversion or, uh, replacement or something, if you see what I'm driving at."

"Yep, and it makes sense. Keep in mind, though, that we don't want to overreact if we don't need to, or do something that could be exposed as a blatant lie."

"I understand, but there are some things I'd rather have exposed than others. And to be honest, if Drutoa were going to be exposed, it would happen among the pencil pushers. Offload could only tell her so much."

"Well, I'd prefer she not even discover a starting point."

They had arrived at the approximate area where their golf balls had departed civilization. It was a spot where the row of trees lining the rough expanded into a grove. The ground at their base was thick, wild grass covered by layers of leaves. If ever there were a place devised to swallow golf balls, this was it.

Jude and Farrell stood silently on the edge of the fairway, estimating the odds of finding their golf balls.

"I don't know."

"Yeah."

Gingerly, Farrell took two steps into the chaos, where he stopped and scanned the vicinity. Then he used his seven iron to carefully probe the mesh of deep grass, half expecting to find his ball, but more concerned he would discover an angry rattlesnake.

Well aware of his friend's fear, Jude waited until Farrell bent down for a closer look in the grass before hissing loudly. Farrell jumped back in panic, waving his outstretched club at the ground like it was a sword. It was all Jude had hoped for, and he did a little jig while he laughed.

"I knew you were going to do that," Farrell exclaimed. "You're such an idiot."

"I'm not the one poking around in that mess."

"Well, neither am I," Farrell decided as he quickly hopped back onto the safety of the fairway. "And since I did the looking, you can provide the new golf balls."

"You call that looking?"

"It was more than you were willing to do. Now give me a ball."

Jude surrendered and handed one to Farrell, then dropped one for himself on a spot where the fairway crested just a touch. Farrell tossed his ball a little farther out.

"For the record, we found the original balls, right?"

"Darn right we did."

Farrell stood over his new ball, and just as he drew his club back, Jude hissed.

PINWHEEL

Farrell interrupted his swing to laugh, and then he began to chase Jude, threatening him with the club, which he now held over his head like a weapon. With silly laughter, Jude pretended to escape by running in a circle around their bags.

Zeke and Jim, who had just finished playing their shots onto the green, paused to watch them from afar.

"There's something that ain't right about those boys," Jim droned.

It was a thought shared by the foursome waiting behind them.

14

Just before Everidge Boulevard begins ascending out of Stout City, there is a big, round curve. If the driver times it just right, he can accelerate on the curve's exit and gain some extra momentum for the incline. This was part of Deacon's drive home every evening, and he knew exactly when to accelerate. He'd done it thousands of times, having lived in the same home for more than twenty-five years. The sights along the route had changed, but that big curve before the hill was exactly the same as the first time he'd navigated it.

Deacon hadn't been the managing editor very long when he and Abigail decided to buy a house in the suburb of Arden Heights. His paycheck had gotten a little bigger, and so had the children, Evelyn and Chuck. It seemed like the right time to advance their living condition. Arden Heights was newish and clean, filled with ambitious young families ready to settle into suburban bliss. The downside was that it added nearly twenty minutes each way to Deacon's commute, but he didn't mind, knowing the joy it brought his family to live in a better neighborhood.

Their house at 2476 Honey Nettle Drive was brand-new, part of a subdivision that had just been completed. The house was light green with white trim. A fancy brick pathway led from the sidewalk to their front porch, and a pristine cement driveway on the far side led to a detached garage behind the house. Hullet Elementary School was only a couple blocks away, and the neighborhood youth enjoyed its large play area during school and after.

Abigail, a former library assistant, looked after the home and children, but found time to collect used clothing for the needy, chair an art guild, make quilts, handle the family finances, and occasionally umpire pickup baseball games at Hullet. She liked helping with homework, hated vacuuming, and was a fearless attempter of new recipes.

She thrilled to hear their garage door swing closed each evening, partly because she loved Deacon and partly because she missed having a teammate to talk with like she'd had at the library. Ironically, Deacon returned home seeking quiet, but because he loved Abigail, he accepted the pent-up avalanche of conversation awaiting him. When she finished describing the minutia of her day, Abigail would ask about his, only to receive summaries such as, "Just the usual," and "It went pretty well."

But after a shower and dinner, Deacon would regain some zest, and they would talk while guiding the children through the steps leading toward bedtime. His pride in family often swelled during these hours, watching the children squirm and giggle during a bath or observing the tender relationship between mother and offspring.

When the children were finally asleep, Deacon and Abigail liked to sit in the living room and read magazines, sharing the funny and interesting things they came across. This was also the time when they would share their choicest news, hers involving neighborhood gossip and his involving funny things overheard in the office. Sometimes serious topics like politics or in-laws were broached, but only if the outrage were excessively large.

PINWHEEL

Two decades slipped by quickly, and as the children evolved, so did Arden Heights. The trees, newly planted everywhere when they arrived, grew large and full, adding charm to the area. They also hid some of the neighborhood's aging. Sidewalks had cracks, curbs were scuffed with tire marks, and nearly every house needed a few shingles replaced. Even the noise increased, thanks to the ubiquity of automobiles—many houses now sported two cars, three if you included teenagers' jalopies.

The subdivision's first wave of grown children began to disperse. Evelyn, the eldest Lowe child, married a mail carrier named Dennis, and they now lived in Kansas City with their three children and one dog. Chuck was an unmarried professor at Nebraska State, where he taught the joys of Homer to unwilling students.

Alone once again, Deacon and Abigail made plans to travel. Destinations were being vetted and dates arranged when Abigail suddenly became sick with cancer. Before either of them could really come to grips with this surprise, she was dead and buried, and the house on Honey Nettle experienced no more laughter.

Rounding the curve this evening, Deacon accelerated at the precise moment needed, and his '29 DeSoto Six leapt toward the hill, passing a car in the next lane that had floored it too late. Everidge Boulevard straightened into a long, steady climb, and Deacon was careful to keep momentum without pushing the upper end of third gear. He passed another driver who had peaked too early and then another who was fading. Subconsciously, he was engaging in a battle, but the other drivers weren't the opponents, they were just the proof of his efficiency. Nothing else entered his mind during the climb, and when he crested the hill, a wave of satisfaction washed over him. He couldn't describe a perfect ascent, but he knew it by feeling.

For many years, this stretch of road had helped to cleanse his mind of the day's worries, but now it served an additional purpose: to help him temporarily forget what the evening held—loneliness.

He arrived home and closed the garage door behind him. At one time, the perfectly balanced door had glided shut with precision, but now it flew down and slammed with a whomp. The springs needed replacing, he reminded himself before quickly forgetting until the next night, when he would remind himself again.

Deacon entered the empty house and turned on the kitchen light. A note from Anna, his housekeeper, lay on the kitchen counter reminding him of some minor household repairs that were needed. It also gave cooking instructions for the casserole she'd constructed and left in the fridge.

He set the note down and hesitated. All that stood between him and a nice meal was turning an oven knob and inserting a dish, yet it seemed like so much. Once you started down that path it was oven mitts and serving spoons and plates and finally the washing of those items. He contemplated whether to skip the process and snack on some cheese or an apple but knew Anna would note her untouched creation and feel hurt the next morning— or worse, chastise him for not taking care of himself. He dutifully turned the knob, and while the oven preheated, he went upstairs and changed from his suit into a pullover shirt and light cotton slacks.

After dinner he treated himself to a glass of scotch, intending to relax and daydream about nothing in particular while sitting in his favorite easy chair. It wasn't long, however, until thoughts of work slithered in, chasing daydreams out of the picture.

PINWHEEL

At first it was the same old worry of the *Sun's* demise and his subsequent casting about for a position elsewhere. He imagined the patronizing grins he'd receive when walking into the offices of his former competitors, the feelings of bitterness as he was interviewed by men not as accomplished as he.

But Deacon was not one for moping—even imaginary moping—and soon his thoughts turned to solving the Exlee dilemma. He looked at it from every slant, trying to find one thread of reason that would preclude Exlee from being a possible turncoat. For example, wouldn't the two lawyers Exlee was "working with" be afraid of ruining their reputations if this Pinwheel thing was pure fancy? Nope, Deacon argued back at himself, the lawyers were already third rate, they had no reputation to lose. Maybe they even had something to gain. Something from the deep pockets of the *Daily Mercury*.

Then Deacon's thoughts turned to Exlee's new agenda of selling Emma as a romantic possibility. During the several years the three of them had interacted, Exlee had never maneuvered the conversation in that direction. And today Exlee had even gone to the trouble of sending a heartfelt, persuasive note. Would a turncoat do that? Yes, if he wanted to assuage his guilt.

Deacon refilled his glass with scotch and took another swig. He leaned back in his chair and closed his eyes, trying to picture being alone with Emma. He chose a park bench for his imaginings and tried to create a romantic feeling between them. She was desirable, he had to admit, and they really did think with one mind most of the time. But even in his experimental dream, an amorous connection felt out of place. When he pictured leaning toward her for a kiss, the imaginary Emma looked at him uneasily and leaned back slightly. Deacon quickly opened his eyes before she slapped him or hollered for a cop.

He took a long sip of scotch and studied the shadows on the wall. A car drove by, its headlights briefly scattering the shadows, and then it was dark and quiet again. It was hard to believe, but right in that same spot there had been a time when two children in pajamas had run over to him and exchanged hugs and kisses before bedtime, their hair still damp from bathing. Abigail would patiently stand at the edge of the room admiring the tender scene, waiting to put the children to bed so she could finally relax for the evening. Funny how it all seemed like nightly routine then; nice but insignificant. What he wouldn't give now to kiss one of those damp heads that smelled of sweet shampoo. Or to watch them settle into bed while he stood in the doorway with his arm around Abigail's waist, ready to turn out the lights.

Suddenly, Deacon got up and walked to the bedroom that he and Abigail had shared. He turned on the light and opened the closet. After sifting through the clothes, he withdrew a dress—brown with a pattern of little pink and green flowers and a neckline of lace. He'd never found the courage to discard her things in the closet, and this one was his favorite. He laid it on the bed and stepped back to admire it but found the angle dissatisfying. He hung it from the coat rack in the corner instead. That was better, and he sat on the edge of the bed and tried to picture Abigail standing there wearing it. It was pleasing for a moment, but Deacon began to feel foolish, and then he began to feel a little angry. What a waste that Abigail—his Abigail—should be rotting in the ground while this dress looked so fresh and colorful.

Emotion began to fill him, and he hated it, blaming the extra glass of scotch. It was too early for bed and Deacon wasn't in the mood for reading, so he returned to the living room, flipped on the light, and turned on the radio, moving the dial back and forth until he found some upbeat jazz. From a nearby corner he retrieved a coffee can full of golf balls and his putter. He dumped the balls on one edge of the large Afghan rug and then, against the other edge, he laid the can on its side. Then, using his putter, he gently struck the balls one by one toward the can. The fourth shot was right on target, causing a hollow, metallic clang as it rattled into the coffee can (Pinwheel original).

Deacon halted play for another sip of scotch and to turn up the volume on the radio. He stood over the next ball and imagined himself at Oakmont on the fourteenth green, with Emma standing in the gallery, anxious for him to succeed.

His putt came up just short, and the clock on the wall said he still had one long hour until bedtime.

15

Deacon wasn't entirely himself the next morning. The extra scotch hadn't done him any favors, and his imaginary romancing of Emma, which had seemed safe at night, felt uncomfortable now that he was sitting across from her in the light of day.

He felt compelled to act a touch more aloof than usual this morning, irrationally convinced that Emma could sense having been the object of his tentative dreams. Emma, of course, was instantly aware of the aloofness, but she traced its cause back to Exlee's blatant matchmaking at yesterday's lunch. Woman's intuition, as it's falsely labeled, is in reality an innate ability to catalog any unusual wrinkles in daily life and match them to other cataloged wrinkles.

Deacon had moved Emma's chair into place, but the friendly banter which always inaugurated their morning briefings was stiff and ponderous this morning. Only when they launched into the business portion of the meeting did the natural rhythm of their relationship reign once more. The rhythm was so natural, in fact, that neither of them recognized the transition.

"So, I got a note from Koenig saying he and Miss Redding followed the husband after work last night but that he went straight home," Deacon said. "Obviously, Miss Redding couldn't knock on his door and casually meet him at home, so hopefully when they follow him tonight he returns to his routine of eating and drinking on the town."

"Just our luck," Emma mourned, "he plays good boy on the one evening we want to ply him with secretarial beauty."

"You know, when you put it that way, it sounds rather shameless, encouraging some staff ingénue to flirt with a married man."

"Are you serious?" Emma asked with a look of incredulity. "After all of the stunts we've pulled over the years in the name of increasing circulation, you think *this* is the line in the sand? Have you forgotten the time that you talked that greenhorn reporter into actually marrying an ambassador's loony niece? And to top it off, we never even got any inside dope from him afterward. For all we know, those two have bred three loony kids because of us."

"Funny you should bring that up," Deacon said. "I keep meaning to tell you that I met that fella in front of a hotel not too long ago. He was in town for an agriculture convention. He's dropped out of the newspaper game— no surprise there; you think I'd talk a kid with real reporter potential into marrying for a story? Plus, she wasn't bad looking. Crazy as a loon, but really, when you got past that she had a certain attractiveness ... "

"If by 'attractiveness' you mean she was curvaceous, then yes, she was abundantly attractive."

"Really? I don't recall that," Deacon deadpanned while Emma rolled her eyes. "Anyway, what I was saying was that he ended up in Elberton, and now he's the assistant branch manager of a farm implement dealership. What's the green one?"

"John Deere."

"That's it, works at a John Deere dealer. He seemed very happy, and when I inquired about his wife, he told me they were still married. He even thanked me for bringing 'em together. Said they had two children and a bunch of fruit trees on the acreage surrounding their house. Sounded idyllic to me."

"Yeah, well, I bet she's still loony."

"Probably, but men figure most women are crazy to some degree or they wouldn't marry a man. In his case, he must have weighed the loony part versus the attractive part, and somehow it worked out using his math."

"Yes, I'm familiar with man math. Anyhow, let's get back to what started this—you claiming to feel immoral about using Miss Redding to chat up the husband. Maybe the truth is that you'd prefer saving her for yourself."

"Cut it out, wouldya?" Deacon protested. "I only said I sort of feel bad, and only then because we're using a seemingly innocent young girl. I was only thinking it would make more sense to use an actual prostitute. We're not destroying any virtue that way, and if they ended up, um, doing what she does for a living, I'm sure the truth about a lawsuit would be easier to extract, men being what they are."

"I can't decide if I'm appalled or impressed."

"Well, it's only a thought. And now that I think about it, it would be too risky since working girls aren't exactly pillars of confidentiality. Even more importantly, management would never authorize trick money when we already have a gal under salary."

"Now I'm officially appalled. I hope this thinking at least applies to both genders. That way when we need a male to seduce information from a wife, we look in-house first."

"Please, Emma. Every fella at the *Sun* would volunteer. We'd have to institute a policy for choosing one, and I have a very bad feeling that management would support seniority as the mechanism. Do you know how long some of those guys down at the printing press have been here?"

"Yes, and I've seen them," she confirmed in a tone lacking compliment.

There was a lull in the conversation as Deacon sifted through the small, scattered pile of papers on his desk. A manila envelope caught his attention, and he removed its contents and perused the data, making small noises as different items resonated. As she waited, Emma sipped on her coffee (Tingle, two creams and one sugar).

"This is a report from Sanderson," he finally informed her. "Can't remember if I told you, but I had him reassigned from the Whitney scandal so he could spend a couple days checking into the background of the Wagsters."

She smiled politely, having been the one to reassign Sanderson.

"Pretty impressive what he came up with in a couple days," Deacon added before becoming absorbed in his reading and drifting off.

"Care to share?" Emma asked after waiting long enough.

"Oh yeah, sure." He flipped the report back to the first page. "Paul James Wagster and Vivian Ann Wagster, maiden name Garrison. Looks like they both grew up in Stout City. He went to Chester Arthur High and she went to, uh, Tompkins High. Both graduated in 1921, meaning they'd be about, um, 30 years old. Doesn't appear that either went to college. Paul currently works at Van Every Tire Shop, and as far as we can tell she stays home. Um, let's see ... nothing about kids here, although I'm not sure ... wait, it says Paul was married previously to a woman who lives out of state now."

"No name?"

"Nope, just says 'a woman.' Okay, here we go. Looks like Sanderson tracked down somebody who went to school with Paul and knew him for a while afterward. I guess they were friends but drifted apart. Anyhow, the friend says Paul's parents were average—whatever that means—that his dad worked at a tailor shop. They were Protestant ... 'one of the funny-named ones,' the friend says."

"That narrows it down. I always thought Presbyterian was a funny name, though."

"In that case, we'll declare him Presbyterian. Why not? The friend goes on to say Paul wasn't the best student and may have flunked a couple classes. He also spent a little time in trouble for fighting with ... it says a trombonist. Is that right? Who fights with the marching band?"

"I don't know, but it takes a lot of brass."

Deacon looked up from his report and stared at Emma, who shrugged and then hung her head in mock shame.

"It goes on to say that he—the husband—worked at an auto parts store after graduating but got fired. The friend thinks Paul and another employee were running some sort of timecard scam where they covered for each other. The friend lost track of Paul not long after that."

"Sounds like the type who might get mixed up in a questionable lawsuit," Emma surmised. "I guess that puts us a shade closer to something, whatever it is. What does it say about the wife?"

"Not as much. Mostly what Sanderson found in the Tompkins High yearbooks from her time there. Says she was in a couple organizations, the Cotillion Club ... "

"Probably forced to join by her mother."

" ... and the Literary Society."

"Which means she's more reader than writer, or she'd be on the school newspaper as well."

"Maybe she likes poetry," Deacon suggested. "If things didn't work out with her husband she could be a match for your son."

"She'd be barking up the wrong tree."

"It also says she played on the field hockey team her sophomore and junior years but not her senior year. What do you make of that?" Deacon asked.

"Maybe she had a boyfriend, or maybe she wanted an obligation-free senior year, a chance to play and be silly. I had a friend—more of a close acquaintance—who got ahead in school so she could have more freedom her senior year. She ended up breaking her leg in two places riding in a car with some kids after a party. They'd all been drinking, and the driver slid into a telephone pole. She had a cast and crutches during the winter of her senior year. Had to be helped around whenever she was outside in the bad weather."

"Is it just me," Deacon wondered, "or does that strike you as a cautionary tale for life in general? Spend your working adult years saving and planning for retirement—your junior year, so to speak—and then something happens and it was all for naught."

"Are you talking about your life?" Emma asked cautiously.

"Yes and no," Deacon said after a pause. "Not that we scrimped too much or anything like that, but we did worry about savings and put off certain activities and trips and so forth. The funny thing is I still remember Abigail joking about me taking care of myself healthwise. Said she didn't want to be all alone when she was old."

"I'm sorry, Deacon. I didn't mean to make you ... "

"It's fine," he soothed. "Matter of fact, last night I was just thinking about her. Not that I really forget her, just that every now and then it's a little stronger. I, um ...
"

He paused to consider sharing his thought. Emma wanted badly to tell him he needn't say any more, but she was too curious. He rarely mentioned Abigail.

"So what I did was I pulled one of her dresses out of the closet and kind of studied it," he admitted. "I'm not sure if that's strange or even if keeping her clothes in the closet is strange. I don't know. It's not like I dwell on the stuff or anything, but ... I just don't know."

"Nothing about any of it is strange," Emma said encouragingly. "It's not like there are rules or calendars governing the situation. Time will help you reconcile things and figure out your future. I guess you could say that you still have your senior year."

"You might be right," Deacon agreed, smiling softly. He felt better about the dress episode, and for a moment he saw Emma the same way he had last night while he was golfing. It made him nervous, and he returned to the report.

"Sanderson included an article he traced down in the dead files. It lists Vivian as a bridesmaid in a Trimple-Schofield wedding. That was four years ago, and it shows her as Wagster, so we know she's been married that long. Sanderson also wrote a note saying he's going to try and find another member of the wedding party and see if he can learn more about Vivian."

"She is definitely the unknown piece to this unknown puzzle," Emma declared. "I would really love to find her and have a little chat."

"Or we could send Victor the press operator to charm her socks off."

Emma was about to comment unkindly when the phone rang. Deacon spoke a few sentences and hung up.

"That was Dixon from advertising. Says the Penny Wise Grocery is threating to pull their advertising after we ran that story about their owner."

"You mean the fella who tried to run over his wife but missed and smashed the doorman at the Excelsior?"

"That's the one. Same story the other papers ran. The only difference is the other papers had already stopped selling ad space to Penny Wise because they weren't getting paid. We're the only rag desperate enough to keep running their ads without pay, and now they're hinting that our reporting of this incident makes us even."

"Speaking of the *Sun* being desperate ... "

"What about it?"

"I was going to tell you when we started, but you seemed to be in a strange mood. The *Daily Mercury* ran an article this morning making fun of us."

"Do I want to see this?"

"No, but you should know," she said. "Here, I cut it out for you."

She pulled the clipped piece from her tote bag and handed it to him. He read it silently at first, but his vexation caused him to read the cruelest portion aloud. "The setting *Sun* is so desperate for publicity these days that they have chosen to question the integrity of our city's most successful institution based on mere rumors. That they bite the hand which feeds them and still receive more is a testament to the enviable patience of Pinwheel's ownership. We applaud this fine corporation for their loyalty, and we will continue to applaud them when they rightfully discard the services of a desperate paper like the setting *Sun*."

When he'd finished, he calmly placed the clipped article into his wastebasket. "That was fun," he said. "Now I'll return the favor with something closely related."

"What's that?"

"When I walked in this morning I was greeted by the news that our Pinwheel story has been picked up by the wire services, and it's starting to show up in papers across the country."

"How lovely."

"How lovely, indeed. If I find out Exlee and the *Daily Mercury* ... "

"I really don't think ... " she began before another phone call interrupted her.

Deacon answered and listened for a moment before covering the mouthpiece.

"It's Councilman Roth," he whispered with furrowed brow. "He wants to talk about the Pinwheel lawsuit."

"I'll be back," Emma mouthed while plucking Sanderson's report from Deacon's desk. She wanted to read it for herself, especially the part about the obscure wife.

16

The mother, aged sixty-four, sat alone in robe and slippers at her breakfast nook reading the *Daily Mercury* and drinking coffee (Tingle, one healthy dose of bourbon). She looked up when her daughter came shuffling in wearing gold silk pajamas and pink slippers. Her hair was unkempt, and her face clearly stated that she found waking up painful.

"Good morning," the mother pleasantly greeted her.

"Morning," replied the daughter as she entered the kitchen and fixed a cup of coffee (Tingle, lots of half and half and a generous helping of sugar). She took a couple of sips then broke off a piece from a biscuit sitting nearby and ate it. Apparently deciding the biscuit was tolerable, she took the entire thing and moved to the breakfast nook, where she sat at the other end from her mother.

"Is that all you're having?" her mother asked. "I left some bacon for you, and there's still another grapefruit."

"We go through this every morning, Mom. It takes me awhile to wake up and decide what I want. I'll probably eat some bacon, but I just need to wake up."

"Well, you don't need to be rude about it, Vivian. I don't think I'm a bad person for getting up early and making breakfast for us."

"Oh, please don't do that." Vivian groaned. "I appreciate that you make breakfast, I'm just not a morning person like you, Okay? I don't just wake up all polite and chipper. I need some coffee first."

"It seems like you need it all day. I've never seen someone drink so much coffee, and I sure don't remember you drinking this much of it when you still lived here."

"I've noticed you keep a cup handy most of the day."

Mom smiled. "Well, I have to admit this is some extraordinary coffee. It makes my head float a little bit, and there's no harm in that, although I should ask Dr. Hyntner when I see him next."

"If anything, he'll tell you to cut back on the ninety proof 'creamer.' "

"Don't start that again, dear. It's only a nip here and there, and I've heard some very reliable sources say a little is good for your system."

"Yeah, a little a day, not a little every hour. And speaking of me living here before, I don't remember you drinking at all when I was growing up. Maybe you started after the divorce. I probably wasn't paying attention then."

"Your father didn't like to keep alcohol in the house. His father—your granddad Garrison—was a big drinker, and I think he was afraid he'd end up like him, although I don't believe that one becomes a violent drunk because they keep a supply on hand. You either become one or you don't, and if you do, then you'll find it when you need to."

"I didn't know Granddad was a drunk. I knew he drank, but ... "

"He had mellowed quite a bit by the time you were born. And after he saw you and Jim, he tried to do even better, although it was too late in a way. He had done so much damage to his body. It's why he died young. Your father always resented that a bit—that he made an effort to cut back for you and Jim but not for his own kids when they were little."

"I guess that makes sense."

There was a lull as they each drank their Tingle. Vivian started to ask again if her mom's "nipping" started after the divorce but knew she would just get defensive. She thought of a better question anyhow, one she couldn't remember if she had ever asked directly.

"So why did you and Dad get divorced, anyway?"

"I've asked myself that for years, but I still don't have a simple explanation. Actually, I do. We just didn't care enough about each other anymore. The difficult part is trying to decide how it happened and if something could have been done. It wasn't like one day we woke up and looked at each other and said, 'I don't like you anymore.' We just quit doing things for each other. I quit ironing his shirts and he quit asking me to. Then we each got stubborn and refused to even talk about it. He would iron his own or take them to the dry cleaners, and I wouldn't comment. We didn't fight about it, we just didn't talk about it."

"So you divorced over ironing?"

Mom laughed. "No, that was just an example to show you how we started living separate lives in the same house."

"What about the sex?"

"Vivian Wagster! I knew you'd ask that—and in just that way, too. There are some things that aren't your business, but I will say it was complicated. I didn't just quit buying groceries because we weren't talking much. And he still worked and paid the utilities. We kept living for a while; we just didn't like each other for some reason, and that's the part I've never fully understood. Your father was—and is, as far as I know—a good man."

"That's so strange. I don't remember any of that. You two must have been good actors because I recall him laughing sometimes at things you said, and he bought you Christmas presents and things for your birthday."

"Well, you were not quite a teenager. If we'd still been together when you were, you'd have begun noticing. We were friendly and we shared a lot of things, so it wasn't really acting. I don't know how to explain it other than it was a big weight that hung over us—this failure to keep liking each other after we'd been so in love at one time. It kind of made us feel foolish, and I guess we just decided if we were ever going to be happy again it would be individually—by starting our lives over alone. You must be having some thoughts like that about Paul if you're here."

"Isn't it funny how I never put the two together—your divorce and now me living here, separated from Paul? I'm sitting here listening to you, and I'm not even thinking about my marriage."

"Well, they're quite different when you think about it," Mom offered. "You see my problems from the view of a daughter, which is very different than being the wife. I think there's a difference in the men, too. Your father was a straight arrow, he was never going to be like his dad. But Paul was always a little on the bad side. Even you admitted it before you married him."

"He's not evil or anything. He just thinks there's a shortcut to everything, and he'd rather try something risky than do it the long, slow way."

"You mean he's lazy."

"He's not lazy," Vivian argued. "I mean, he's not overly ambitious or anything, but he doesn't sit around and expect me to take care of him."

"Like Raymond?"

"Oh my God, why do you always have to mention him? I was young and stupid, okay? And he was so gorgeous."

"And on the bad side. You were always attracted to would-be ruffians. I always wondered if it had something to do with rebelling against your father. You seemed determined to be with the opposite type of man."

"Why does everyone think there's some social reason behind everything? Do you hate peanuts because your mom wouldn't take you to the circus? I get so tired of it. Maybe I was just born a certain way, and when I grew up I liked a certain kind of guy. Dad could have been a raving drunk like his father, and it wouldn't make me suddenly want some wimpy, nice guy. Parents are always feeling guilty and then trying to pass their guilt on, which just makes it worse."

"I really don't think I was trying to pass any guilt on, Vivian. I just said I wondered if it had anything to do with you marrying somebody like Paul, who you're obviously having problems with—although I don't know what they are, because you barely say anything about it. You've been here almost a month, and I all I hear is that you needed to be apart to think things over."

"That's because it's true," Vivian said. She finished her cup of coffee and went into the kitchen to fix another. She returned to the nook.

"Okay, here's the deal," she began. "We've been fighting about money a lot lately. Obviously, the depression is killing everyone, but, well, Paul had his salary reduced at the tire shop. And he still doesn't want me to work, so here we are, getting poor when I could at least try to help. We've fallen behind on the house and the car ... "

"He should have kept that one job at the warehouse. You told me he was making good money there."

"They let him go from that job, so there wasn't much he could do about that."

"I'm pretty sure they wouldn't have let him go if he were working hard and one of the better employees."

"It doesn't matter, Mom. All I'm saying is that things have gotten bad enough that we even looked into bankruptcy. We've just gotten too far behind on things. So anyway, that's the main problem. Well, sorta. We start arguing about money, but then we start arguing about each other. He doesn't want me to work because he thinks it's a man's job to make the money ... "

"Your father was the same way, not that I really wanted to work outside the home."

"So anyhow, what I'm saying is that I gave in to him. I loved working when I did. I got to be with people and earn my own money. But I stopped when we got married, and I was already a little unhappy about that because I had to feel guilty about how every nickel was spent. But now it *really* makes no sense if he's having trouble at work. His pride is getting in the way, and so we fight because it's crazy to look into bankruptcy when we could solve it if he wasn't so stubborn. So I get mad at him for being stupid, and he gets mad at me for acting like he isn't capable of supporting us, and it just turns into the same old argument night after night."

"Oh, I'm so sorry to hear this."

"Don't feel sorry for me. It just makes me feel worse, like I'm some sort of pathetic child."

"Okay, I'm sorry."

Vivian rolled her eyes. "So finally we just decided that we should stop fighting, and the only way to do that was to be apart for a few weeks. Oh, and he was working on this idea that someone gave him that sort of involved me, but I wasn't so sure I wanted to be part of it."

"Another shortcut?"

"Yes. If it works out, I guess there's a decent amount of money involved—enough to start over somehow. It's not a bad idea, really, and there is some truth to it, it's just that I hate the way it has to be. Already the whole thing has gotten weird, and it just started, really. So, either it'll work out or I may be here for the rest of my life."

"What do you mean that there's 'some truth to it'? That doesn't sound very good, like it might be illegal or some such thing, and you really don't need to get mixed up in some crazy scheme and end up in jail because of Paul."

"No, it's not like that ... I don't think. I just mean that it involves something with me that's hard to prove."

"That's the other part that bothers me. You keep saying it involves you, like you're some sort of hostage or something. Is it a blackmail thing? I've read about those in the paper and they just break your heart."

"No, Mom, it's not blackmail. I'd have to have something of value to be blackmailed."

"If what I read is true, there are women who are cornered into using their bodies as payment for whatever trouble they've met."

"Well, for one thing, my body may have had value at one time, but I'm thirty now."

Mother and daughter took a drink of coffee and waited.

"What's the second thing?" Mom finally asked.

"Oh, I don't think I had one."

"Well, I have two points. First of all, wait until you're my age before you start talking about bodies falling apart. And second of all, you still have really nice legs, you said so yourself. You should be proud of that."

"I guess I should. Our neighbor across the street, Oliver, used to mow his lawn all the time so he could look at me when I had the front drapes open. He was actually a sweet man. I didn't feel too bad about it. He died not too long ago, though."

"That's too bad," Mom said as she got up and started to clean the kitchen.

Vivian passed behind her and poured the remaining Tingle from the coffee pot into her mug.

"Do you hear anything from your father these days?" Mom asked.

"I got a birthday card from him. He signed it, but it was Joan's handwriting on the envelope."

"Men are bad about remembering things like birthdays."

"Or anything else involving other people. There's probably a better chance of Paul knowing some baseball player's home run average than knowing his own mom's birthday. He's lucky he has me—or did."

"Honey, I hate for you to think that way. You need to stay positive."

"I'm going to go take a bath," Vivian declared.

"When you're finished, don't forget to use that face cream I bought you, honey. It's supposed to do wonders for stopping little wrinkles."

Vivian walked out of the kitchen and into the hall as though she hadn't heard a thing. She stopped in her bedroom and got some underthings then entered the bathroom, locked the door, and began running the bath water.

She studied her face in the mirror. There were indeed little wrinkles. And she still hated her eyebrows. She returned to the bathtub and tested the water. She gave the hot water knob a twist. She took off her pajamas and looked in the mirror again, pivoting and stretching different ways, trying to find an angle that was flattering enough to put her mind at ease. But all that Vivian saw were flaws. She pushed her stomach in with her hand, angry over its disloyalty.

PINWHEEL

After turning off the faucet and gently working herself into the tub, Vivian noticed she'd left the towel on the other side of the room.

She closed her eyes and thought about those precious years between leaving home and marrying Paul.

At the time, she wouldn't have called them precious. It felt more like drudgery. She was working as a local operator for Iowa Bell on their main Stout City switchboard. She had to wake up at 5:30 each morning, get dressed, gulp down breakfast (God, why didn't they have Tingle then?), catch a streetcar, and fight through humanity just for the privilege of doing what she didn't really want to do. And, oh, how rude some of those callers were, complaining about things she had no control over. One elderly woman had argued bitterly that the ring of her phone was too loud, causing her kitty to be anxious. She insisted that Vivian, and only Vivian, proceed to her house immediately and fix it. She didn't want some smelly repairman to track mud in her house, scare the cat, and molest her with his eyes. Oh, but the worst calls were those involving lovers' quarrels—the passion and the lunacy and the phones left off the hook in protest.

Exhausted, she would return each evening to the tiny apartment she shared with four other tired girls who'd spent the day experiencing the same thing. But there was camaraderie born of this daily trial. They would laugh about their worst customers while dressing to go out for dinner. Some nights they didn't get home until midnight. The hours of work were a drain, but the surrounding frivolity was pure and unencumbered. And the best part was the endless, vague hope that makes youth so priceless. The five didn't know whether their hope would end in a promotion or a husband or a talent scout from Hollywood; they just knew it was all possible, and the curiosity kept them working hard and sleeping hard, never knowing which day would bring them their dream.

Vivian finally cashed in her hope in exchange for a husband. Paul was handsome enough and confident. He had a warehouse job at Sears Roebuck, and while he wasn't extravagant with his spending, he wasn't a tightwad either. Sure, he could get a little moody when he didn't get his way, but who doesn't? More concerning, maybe, was his risk-taking when it came to employment. He'd admitted being fired from an auto parts job for bribing a coworker to punch his timecard. Another job at a musical instrument warehouse had been lost when he demanded that he be promoted or he would quit. They held the door for him. But this daring style worked both ways. Another job had been secured when he bluffed with impressive references from people he'd never met. Paul's willingness to gamble on job security was even more pronounced considering he practically insisted that Vivian stay at home.

But did she really want to work again, or was she simply longing for a taste of that hope she'd felt once upon a time?

Vivian climbed out of the tub and walked across the bathroom to her towel. Splat, splat, splat. As she dried herself off, she wondered what to do about Paul. That was the question, really. Did she still love him? If she did, then she needed to find a way to fight for him. But what if loving Paul was bad for her?

She dressed and returned to the kitchen.

"I'm going to run some errands," she told her mother. "Need anything?"

"Actually, I stay pretty caught up these days with you going out every morning."

"I just want to make sure we don't kill each other."

PINWHEEL

"I wasn't complaining," Mom said with a sweet smile. "Here's five dollars for gas. You might pick up some more Tingle, too."

"You read my mind," Vivian answered while putting on a sweater.

If her mother had really been able to read Vivian's mind, she'd have known that the first errand was always a purchase of the *Sun*—to be tossed after Vivian read an update on her life.

17

Near the end of the third floor corridor in City Hall, Exlee entered Councilman Roth's office. He was greeted by Violet Genzer, a trusted, veteran secretary who was on her fifth councilman.

"Exlee Ellis," she marveled. "To what do we owe this great honor?"

"The honor is all mine, Vi. Word on the street is you got a new hairdo, and I was stopping in to admire it. And I gotta say, it really does look good."

She looked at him dubiously. "And what exactly would you say has changed about it?"

"The added curl and the lighter color."

"See, anyone else would have guessed at one thing, but you had to gamble with two. And that's what got you. There is no change in color."

"Must be the lousy lighting in here." He grinned, enjoying being exposed by a clever woman as much as she enjoyed having her looks discussed by a desirable man.

"The only thing lousy in here is your blarney." She smiled. "Now tell me what you're really here for."

"Theo asked me to come by."

She picked up the phone and let Roth know Exlee was here to see him.

"Go on inside," she said after hanging up.

Exlee entered, closed the door quietly behind him, and took a seat as Roth continued writing something.

"Just one second," the councilman said without looking up.

Exlee used the delay to look around and study things more intently than usual. He'd visited this office on several occasions but had never had the opportunity to blatantly stare at things, like the framed diplomas. Exlee had never known that Roth graduated from Dartmouth or that he'd received his law degree from the University of Chicago. On the same wall was a photo of Roth shaking hands with George Sisler, which made sense; everyone knew Roth was a big St. Louis Browns baseball fan, although no one understood why he'd opted to give his heart to a perennial loser like the Browns.

The shelves behind Roth were filled with books—mostly utilitarian and mostly of a legal or business nature. A couple books of poetry were tucked along the edge, and Exlee wondered if they were gifts or if Roth had a secret love for symbols and meter. Neither was written by Emma's son, but Jerry was probably too avant-garde to have his writings held in bondage by book covers, anyhow.

Exlee's eyes moved to the desk, and he spied two framed photos standing next to the phone. One showed two girls in velvet and bows, and the other he recognized as his former girlfriend turned councilman's wife, Kate Roth. Her smile in the photo was stunning, especially in comparison to the half-bitter smiles she'd offered him at Troscanza's two nights previous. Exlee managed to pull his eyes away just in time for Roth to look up from his work.

"Exlee, I was just thinking about you this morning. I'm glad you're here."

"I can't take much credit. You asked me to stop by when we met the other night."

"Believe me, I haven't forgotten that evening. From the time you left until we got home and into bed,

Kate mentioned three separate times how glad she was that she hadn't ended up trapped with you. She was protesting a little too much, if you get my drift."

"Nuts." Exlee laughed dismissively. "She was absolutely correct when she recited all of my faults. We'd have driven each other mad by now."

"Listen, if you two keep this up I'm really gonna start getting jealous."

"Jealous of me? No, no, no. She ended up with the right man. Seriously, Theo, she picked a winner."

"I bet you wouldn't be saying that if I were delivering Chinese food for a living."

"That's just the thing, though; we both know you'd never be anything less than a bigwig. It's who you're meant to be, and she knew it."

"Funny you should say that, because I thought I knew *you*—even if I couldn't explain what I knew. Total change of subject, sorry, but this is why I really wanted to speak with you."

"Sure," Exlee agreed. "Go ahead."

Roth paused to take a drink of coffee (Gold Monocle, whatever Vi put in it).

"Here's the deal: You're all about enjoying life in your own way, and I applaud that," Roth began. "I may or may not even be jealous half the time. It's just that ... Okay, what I'm trying to say is that for all of your whimsical ways, you've always been dependable in certain productive areas—behind-the-scenes knowledge, an endless supply of acquaintances—you get the picture. And one of the major reasons why you can pull it off—why you can work a dead man to your advantage—is that you don't overreach. You keep your game short and wide. That's why this Pinwheel thing surprised me when I heard your name attached to it. Playing with Pinwheel is like poking a bear in a cage. You better have the goods, because when that bear gets loose ... "

Roth left the warning hanging in the air so Exlee could absorb it.

"Yeah, I get it," Exlee conceded. "Pinwheel is Stout City's biggest employer, and they have the means to injure my career if I toy with them. And from your perspective as a councilman, you need them to thrive so the city can survive this economy. All makes sense. Maybe there's more to it than that, who knows?"

"Hell's bells, Ex, you gotta show a playing card every now and then. You're too used to plotting solo. This conversation goes nowhere, you have my word on it. Now show me a card or two, 'cause I got a good one for you."

Exlee looked at Roth with a twinkle in his eye, intrigued by this new tone in their relationship.

"Maybe I'm not holding any cards worth seeing," Exlee suggested. "And maybe you prefer small-time Exlee, the naughty mascot who brings fun but no danger."

Roth chuckled and leaned forward, resting his arms on his desk.

"So that's how we're gonna play it, huh? I should have guessed. You are one hell of a bluffer, Exlee, but sometimes I think you go there a little too often, like maybe it's more satisfying to beat someone and make them look like a chump at the same time—have them lose to you while they're holding the better hand."

"I didn't say I was bluffing, I just offered the possibility."

"Nobody declares they're bluffing. That would defeat the whole purpose. Tell you what, I'll show you my whole hand, and then you'll understand why I'm convinced you're bluffing about this lawsuit. You ready?"

"I'm listening," Exlee said.

"So, after I heard this rumor about someone making a case against Pinwheel and you, of all people, being the front man, I decided to dig a little deeper. This was after you played coy at Troscanza's the other night. Now, I won't say who told me or how I found out—but I tapped into a couple respected connections, and the word I got was that this Pinwheel stunt is not on the level. Didn't get much more than that, but this is from a source I trust deeply, and it was clearly stated that this thing is fixed."

Exlee just nodded slowly with that maddening trace of a smirk on his face.

"Either you already knew the game was crooked or you're still trying to bluff," Roth finally declared. "The trouble is I've shown my hand—or the hand of someone I trust implicitly—and unless you have a royal flush hiding, you can quit bluffing and just take my advice: Fold. Get out. Do what you do, be who you are, and this city will forever be your playground and the rest of us your adoring pawns."

This seemed to kill Exlee's smirk, and he folded his arms with a small sigh.

"Now it's my turn to decide whether you really showed me the cards or *you're* bluffing," Exlee countered. "When I look at this from your angle, getting me to fold solves your problems. There is nothing to be gained from me pushing this Pinwheel matter—from your perspective, anyhow."

"So, you think I'm telling you this to make my life easier?" Roth asked with an unhappy smirk. "I'm happy because the city is happy because Pinwheel is happy, is that it? And maybe I prefer you as, what was it, a naughty mascot instead of a cleanup hitter? Or maybe you think I want to knock your hand away from the brass ring because the brass ring is legally mine?"

They both knew that last part was about Kate, and they both knew this had taken a turn toward the personal. Tension hung in the air as Exlee carefully decided on a response.

"Listen, Theo, let's not do this. I know you trust your source just like I trust mine. This Pinwheel action could go many different directions, but you gotta respect me for playing it the best I can, right?"

"Of course I do. And perhaps you don't believe me, but my main concern—the reason I asked you here and the reason I shared that with you—is that I don't want to see you smashed for no reason when you have a good thing going on. I'm just afraid for you because I really do like you, and it still doesn't make any sense why you've chosen to get mixed up in something so large."

"Maybe I'm doing it just to prove to myself that I'm capable," Exlee offered, seeming sincere. "Nobody really wants to be the president of the United States, but they'd like to know they could do it."

"Actually, everybody I've ever met is sure they would make a great president. It's just *you* who doesn't really want the job. Maybe that's why you'd be perfect. Lord knows you could hypnotize Congress. Then again, it wouldn't matter, because you'd gamble away the Treasury on some wayward bet with Bulgaria."

"Now you're just trying to flatter me."

They both laughed.

"Well, I'd better get going," Exlee lied for the benefit of all. "But I really do appreciate you sharing your information."

"I hope this all works out. What did P.T. Barnum once say? 'There's no such thing as bad publicity.' "

Exlee rose and moved toward the door. "Actually, it's unknown if that's his quote, but I do know he was a master of *succès de scandale*. And one last thing," he said, stopping and turning. "I'm not after the brass ring. We both know it's where it belongs."

"Tell that to the brass ring." Roth laughed.

Exlee exited and shut the door behind him.

"Care to join me for a late lunch?" he asked Vi.

PINWHEEL

"I'd end up paying. Plus, I wanna be able to say I'm the one woman in Stout City who's never said yes to you."

"I hate to burst your bubble but that's a pretty long list. I still love your lighter hairdo, though."

She waited until the door closed and she could hear him walking away, then she pulled a mirror from her purse and looked at her hair from several angles. It really did seem lighter, she had to confess.

18

Addie had grown so fond of the Pinwheel cafeteria and its endless supply of free Tingle that she'd begun to daydream of a scenario in which they were so pleased with her report that they offered her employment. This wish was in direct conflict with the neutrality she was supposed to be exhibiting during the inspection, but that Tingle was sure heavenly.

The food wasn't bad either, and they sold it at cost. Addie had just finished stuffing herself on meatloaf, au gratin potatoes, fresh fruit, and pudding. She had no desire to move, but her chaperone, Hazel, had arranged a date for her on the third floor with the "gals in accounts receivable."

"Hello, everyone." Addie greeted them when she arrived at their group office. "I'm Addie Sumner. Maybe Hazel mentioned my visiting."

"Oh, yes, she advised us of your visit earlier," said an older woman standing near some filing cabinets. "If you'd like, you can join us at the table. After lunch we all gather around and sort the mail for our department. It's been presorted by another group, so that all the letters containing payments are routed to us. Invoices get mixed in occasionally, which we gather and send to accounts payable. We've devised a system that allows us to process the payments faster this way."

As the woman lectured about their system, Addie silently filled an empty seat at the table and shared a polite smile with the four other women, who had paused in their work to smile back. Each had a stack of mail in front of her from which she selected a piece, skewered it with a letter opener, and examined its contents. She then scribbled on the paperwork with a pencil before adding it to one of six piles in the middle of the table. The checks were laid upon a single impressive mound.

When the lecturer had finished her efficiency spiel, she officially welcomed Addie and then had each woman introduce herself. They were Erma, Hester, Margaret, and Sadie. It seemed like a happy group, no doubt heavily influenced by having just returned from the glorious cafeteria, where they had probably, combined, soaked up a gallon or two of Tingle.

"So, what do you think of Hazel Kellison?" Erma asked Addie to a mixture of smirks.

"Well, I guess she's all right," Addie conceded. "Seems awfully well known in each department."

"Yes, the boys around here consider her the, um, company ambassador, I guess you'd say."

"Because she's visited most of their countries," Hester quipped to a round of giggles with naughty undertones.

"That's why she hates 'ol Johnny boy across the hall, 'cause he won't join the club. Course, I haven't heard of him joining anybody's club yet. Probably because he acts a little full of himself."

"You always say that, Erma. I think he's just kinda serious and doesn't want to get mixed up in no workplace theater."

"Excuse me, Mrs. Dorman," one of them interrupted, directing a question toward the efficiency lecturer, who now sat at the head of the table. "There's a note in this one sayin' Paske died and now their store belongs to Stanzwick on account of Stanzwick buyin' out the Paske widow, but he's changing the name to Food Faire, and the new name doesn't match the check or the invoice."

"For now, circle the ... you know what, never mind. Put it back in the envelope and give it to me."

This exchange of legitimate business conversation momentarily shamed everyone into focusing on their work, and except for the sound of letter openers gutting envelopes, the table was silent.

Addie, with no real chore of her own, studied the women at the table. Besides the manager, Mrs. Dorman, who looked to be about sixty, there were two other women who seemed middle-aged, Hester and Erma. Of the younger pair, Margaret wore a wedding ring and Sadie did not. All of them were dressed appropriately, although Erma embellished herself with flamboyant accessories, from a polka dot headband to colorful Bakelite bracelets on both wrists. Hester was clearly the prettiest of the bunch but looked tired, with dark circles under her eyes. Sadie, who appeared to be part Asian, was also pretty but made no effort to bolster her appearance. Margaret stood out for her intensely curly hair, which barely restrained itself for the sake of workplace decorum.

Having sized up her tablemates, Addie figured the current lapse in conversation offered a good time to inject herself.

"So what do you all think of working here?" she asked, instantly regretting the generality of her query.

"It beats the soup line."

"Don't listen to her, it's real nice here. A lot of my girlfriends are jealous."

"You need better girlfriends, then," Sadie joked.

Margaret, the one slighted, stuck her tongue out in response.

Addie tried a different tack. "I met the owners yesterday, and they seemed on top of things."

"Can't argue much there," Hester admitted. "They always come up with new ideas to keep the company going strong—like the new brand Tingle. We were getting fewer checks for a while—because of the economy and all—but ever since Tingle, things have begun to improve."

None of the women disagreed, nor did they seem interested in contributing to the topic.

"What about personally? You ever talk to them?" Addie asked, hoping to provoke something.

"Me and the owners golf together at the country club," Erma clowned. "I keep tellin' them to give you girls a raise, but they don't seem to listen."

"Well, say it louder," Margaret joked to laughter around the table.

"The owners have been very generous to us," Mrs. Dorman loyally intervened. "Even when things were tighter last year."

"Oh, I wasn't really complaining," Erma growled, annoyed at her manager for showing off in front of their visitor. "They actually seem like great fellas even though I read more about 'em in the papers than I see them."

"You think that's unusual for a company this size?" Mrs. Dorman asked.

"No, not exactly. I was just answering Miss Sumner's question ... "

"Call me Addie."

"Okay, Addie's question. It would just be fun to talk to 'em more, I guess. I don't know."

"How about we all meet in the cafeteria each Monday morning and share what we did over the weekend? Can you imagine what they must do?"

"And can you imagine telling everyone what you do on a typical weekend? It would scandalize us."

There was more laughter since the butt of the joke was Margaret, straightest arrow of the bunch, as far as they knew.

"Whoops, got our first transposer!" Sadie declared, holding up a check.

PINWHEEL

"Dollars or cents?" Hester asked, in keeping with tradition.

"Dollars. A drugstore in Rochester, New York. Wrote it for twenty-eight dollars instead of eighty-two."

"Probably the wife wrote it wrong on purpose. She's saving up behind his back to run away with the milk man."

"Oh my gosh, Erma, you sound like you're overly familiar with the idea."

"Just start a new pile with it," Mrs. Dorman interrupted wearily.

Vaguely chastised, the women paused the chitchat. Erma and Hester exchanged grumpy expressions as a means of lampooning Mrs. Dorman. She saw it with eyes subtly lifted from her work but ignored it for what it was, a staff who were happy and comfortable.

"So, Addie, how about you? You have a fella?" Erma asked.

"Nope. I keep my eyes open, though."

"A tall, pretty girl like you probably just intimidates some of the numbskulls that pass for men."

"If you ever decide you really want a man—and I don't recommend it—you can have my husband," Erma offered. "He'd rather sit in the dark than change a light bulb."

"Yeah, well, my Fred told me last week that he needed a fishing trip with his friends because of bein' stressed at work. I told him to join the club."

"Tell him he should try a day of work plus cooking, cleaning and mothering when he gets home."

"Yeah, tell him he should try having a baby sometime and see what *real* stress feels like."

"Can you picture a man in labor? If it was up to them to have babies, the human race would have died out shortly after the Garden of Eden."

"Hah, my Stuart complained that his feet were killing him from pacing during the birth of our first boy. Pacing?! Try labor on for size. My first child had me in labor for almost twelve hours."

"That's nothing, my second—Mary Jean—had me in labor for seventeen hours. They had to feed me intravenously."

"I wish my first had been that easy. I was in labor for twenty-seven hours without a bite of food. Our doctor was called away, and apparently they forgot to mention this to the rest of the hospital because no one showed up forever. Finally, Fred went looking for someone, and just then the baby started crowning and I thought I'd have to deliver it on my own. To this day I think all of that labor did something to Charles. He's six and still sucks his thumb at night."

"That's not unusual," Mrs. Dorman lied supportively.

"I guess I was just lucky," Margaret chimed in. "My pregnancy was easy—no morning sickness—and when I had Elizabeth it was less than two hours after arriving at the hospital."

"That *is* lucky," Sadie, the non-mom, congratulated her.

Silence fell over the table as the women bitterly recognized Margaret's victory by means of the "easy birth" loophole. Being the biggest martyr is great, but only when simple happiness is unavailable.

"Here's one of those supply invoices from Drutoa," Margaret announced to Mrs. Dorman. "Are we still keeping those separate?"

Mrs. Dorman's first reaction was to glance at Addie, who pretended not to be paying attention. The alarm in Mrs. Dorman's look was palpable, though, and Addie made a mental note about Drutoa.

"Hand it to me, I'll take care of it," Mrs. Dorman instructed.

The rest of the women showed no reaction and continued with their banter. "Gonna watch your movie again this week?" Erma asked Hester.

"Saw it again last night at the Rialto and almost stayed for the late showing. I'm hooked."

"What movie is that?" Addie asked.

"*Bed of Roses* with Constance Bennett and Joel McCrea. Have you seen it? It's so wonderful," Hester gushed. "It's about these two bad girls—Okay, prostitutes—who get men drunk and steal their money. It's actually a comedy, and Bennett and McCrea fall in love in the end. I've seen it more times than my husband can stand. He won't go anymore, and I have to keep begging different girlfriends to go with me. I just really love it for some reason."

This caused the women to discuss leading men, which led to discussions about leading women, then mansions, California, New York, Chicago, the latest women's fashions, girdles, diets, food, relatives, mothers, and then food again.

The gabfest was sporadically interrupted with matters concerning actual work, but nothing caused a reaction from Mrs. Dorman like "Drutoa" had.

Satisfied she had a clue about something interesting and ready for some quiet, Addie eventually excused herself, thanking the sisterhood for their hospitality. She would be sure to mention to the owners what an organized, efficient effort they had put forth. Mrs. Dorman blushed.

After stopping on the fifth floor to consult with Hazel, Addie decided to call it a day right after a visit to the cafeteria for a bit of Tingle.

19

Deacon was a little late for his afternoon visit to Aronoff's. He'd been detained, managing a breaking story involving a bank robber who'd forgotten what his getaway car looked like, having stolen it on the way to the bank. The robber had then fled on foot, eventually ducking into a movie theater, where he thought he might blend with the crowd as they sat in the dark. It was dark, all right, but it was a matinee featuring a weak romance picture titled *Today We Live*. The crowd consisted of four people, all women.

There wasn't much of a crowd at Aronoff's either, and Deacon instantly spotted Exlee Ellis sitting at the counter enjoying an iced coffee (Gold Monocle over ice chips, shaken).

"I suppose you're waiting for me," Deacon surmised as he took a seat next to Exlee.

"Orange or lemon?" Aronoff interrupted.

"Um, surprise me." Deacon asked Exlee, "We used to conduct nearly all of our business at the *Sun*. What gives?"

"Nothing, really, just like to change things up occasionally."

"Yeah, well, the change in this case is coinciding with your Pinwheel project. Not sayin' it's a big deal, but it does fit with your unusual behavior concerning this story."

Aronoff sat a glass of lemonade in front of the editor, who studied the contents before drinking them half down.

"Maybe it's all in your head," Exlee proposed.

"Maybe, maybe not. I'm pretty aware of when and where we meet, and this is the third straight occurrence outside of the *Sun*, which by my calculations is unprecedented. Again, not a big deal, but you asked."

"Okay, let's say you're right. You do sound a little sore about it, though."

"That might have something to do with a phone call I got from Theo Roth this morning. He claims he has it on good authority that the Pinwheel case, which you are pimping, is fixed. You and I both know that of all the councilmen he has the best view of Stout City's underbelly. Remember a few months back? He knew the battalion chief was gonna die before the chief even knew he was sick. In other words, my fear that this story is poison to the *Sun* is lookin' real serious, Exlee. Real serious."

"Yeah, I happened by his office not long ago. He told me the same thing."

"Well, either that spooked you too or you're in on the fix, pal."

"Or you're all getting bad information. It's a real possibility, you know. You and Roth have both swung and missed before. Once again, I'm asking you to trust me, Deacon. I've always played you straight and you know it."

"But what if *you're* being played? I trust you as much as I can, Ex, but I don't trust the people you're working with. Heck, I don't even know who's on your team in this one. It's gotten so bad that last night I started wondering if maybe you'd played me straight all these years *knowing* you were gonna sucker me on this huge bluff later. And now this call from Roth. And yet, for some reason, I can't conceive of you willingly sabotaging me and the *Sun* for your own personal gain. You can see how this whole thing is making me a mental mess."

"Then you're really gonna hate this," Exlee said with a wince. He pulled out a folded sheet of paper from his inside coat pocket and handed it to the editor.

"Please don't tell me this is what I think it is," Deacon said. He finished off his lemonade—wishing it was pure grain alcohol instead—then unfolded the paper and began reading.

It was a rebuttal from the husband and his lawyer. They were discouraged to read the comments made by the wife, which insinuated that the husband preferred his vices to her and that he was an ineffectual lovesmith. Furthermore, it was with great sadness that he read her public confession concerning an abundance of former lovers. This confession was obviously a testament to her love of intimacy and further proof that Tingle must be mighty powerful to become preferable to the tender touch of her own husband. Despite this turn of events, he still loved his wife and promised that the public would understand better once the truth came out in court.

Deacon laid the paper on the counter and stared at Exlee. A weary smile creased his lips.

"You realize how absurd this is becoming, right? No matter how much doubt I build against this being a legitimate story, you keep bringing me more of this stuff like it's no big deal. Bottom line, I'm a fool for going along with a fool."

"Remember what a fool you thought I was the first time we met?" Exlee reminisced. "It was right here ... no, I think it was a couple stools over."

"You kept staring at me. It was so uncomfortable that I was the one who actually started the conversation. Now that I think about it—was that your plan?"

"Oh, no. I was prepared to ambush you with all the news from Arraignment Alley that you didn't know you'd been missing. It's just that when the opportunity arose, I panicked a little."

"A little? You looked at me like I was an ax murderer. Which is funny, in hindsight, because I've never seen you panic about anything."

"I don't know how to explain it. I was younger and unsure of my new self-created role as an agent, plus I'd heard so much about you that I had an image in my head of some noble statesman who changed lives with a thumb up or down. I almost gave up the whole idea of this press agent business right then and there."

"It would have saved me a lot of trouble."

"Aw, come on, Deacon. You're just sore about this current deal, but it'll work out. And think of all the brilliant pieces you've placed in your paper thanks to me."

"You have brought me some lulus. Do you realize there's a whole load of old ladies who look for those crime bits you bring me? I get letters from them telling me that. Somehow, reading about a part-time call girl whose hotel client turns out to be her husband starts their day off right."

"You remember that one, huh? The older women like their tawdry stories, makes 'em feel alive. But they also like the humanness of the story. That's my opinion. In the case you just mentioned, the couple had a fight for the ages, but they were both guilty and in the end it made them stronger because their love life went through the roof."

"You do have a way of spinning degradation with a hopeful outcome."

"Thanks, I appreciate that. In that case, however, there was third chapter. The husband ended up using the tricks he learned from his wife on a gal who worked at a pet store. The husband and wife divorced, and the wife got pinched for forging checks and ended up pregnant by a prison guard with the clap. I still have hope for all involved, though."

"You never told me about the follow-up."

"Yeah, I sold that part to the *Herald*. Gotta keep everyone in the game, right?"

"I sure wish you'd given this Pinwheel potato to someone else. It's slowly killing me with each piece you bring me."

"Ah, but we've made it this far. What's one more piece, more or less?" Exlee asked.

Many answers arose in Deacon's mind and none of them was nice, so he simply picked up the paper, carefully refolded it, and placed it in his coat pocket. He shook his glass of lemonade, drank its tiny remains, and placed a nickel on the counter. Then he remembered a question for Exlee.

"Oh, I meant to ask you a moment ago—how did you know it was me that first time? You said you'd only imagined me up until then."

"Aronoff's wife, Sybil. She was working the counter, and I bribed her twenty-five cents to tell me when you entered."

"A quarter? Is this true, Aronoff?" he asked the shopkeeper, who was nearby wiping the counter.

"Is what true?" Aronoff asked.

"That your wife once took a twenty-five-cent bribe from Exlee."

"Probably. How else can we afford to bribe the health inspector?"

"That's a good one." Exlee laughed.

Deacon stood up to leave. "Please don't bring me any more of these," he told Exlee.

"It's all gonna work out and we're gonna live happily ever after, which reminds me, have you asked Emma out to eat yet? I really think it would help your mood."

"I'll ask her out when I'm sure I still have a job, and you're not helping in that department. You need to stop this Pinwheel thing before it blows up in somebody's face."

"Or makes us all fabulously wealthy and desired by everyone we meet."

"Good-bye, Exlee."

The editor departed, followed a minute later by the press agent. The only customers remaining were a pair of teenage sweethearts in a corner booth enjoying a surprise coffee milkshake (one cup Tingle, four scoops vanilla ice cream, chocolate syrup, and whipped cream). It was a parting gift from Exlee.

Deacon returned to the *Sun* and was about to enter his office when he remembered a task. It wasn't a pleasant one, and he sighed before turning and visiting the office of Gilbert Cantrell, the *Sun*'s editor in chief.

"Hey, Deacon, what have you got?" Cantrell asked.

"The third act of our current headache."

"Another letter from the Pinwheel couple?"

"Yep. This one from the husband."

"And you want to know what I think?"

"You're the boss."

"For better or worse. Here's what I think about this third letter: In for a penny, in for a pound. I'm completely uncomfortable with antagonizing Pinwheel, but I value your instincts for how things fly in Stout City. Who knows? Maybe I'm going too far in trying to please you. I've always felt like an outsider since leaving Kansas City to take this job."

"You know you don't owe me anything, Gilbert. You've earned your title and have proven worthy of it since you've been here."

"That's nice of you to say, Deacon. I knew what I was getting into by taking this job. I knew the *Sun* was struggling, but the pressure has been more than I expected. Well, that's neither here nor there. I guess we're in this together, and if it all goes south, we'll just deal with the consequences. Keep doing what you're doing, but use caution where you can, please."

"Thanks, I will." Deacon started to say something more about Gilbert being valued but thought it might sound patronizing, and that wasn't good for either of them. He left with a simple nod of the head.

Gilbert tapped his fingers on the desk and glanced over at the *Daily Mercury* lying nearby. It was folded to the editorial mocking the *Sun*. He picked it up and read it for the sixth time. It felt just as brutal as the first five.

20

Miss Jenny Redding thought she knew just how hard-boiled the newspaper business really was. As a secretary in the *Sun's* editorial department, she was privy to some crass conversations. Murders were discussed with the same buoyancy employed in recounting a child's birthday party. A political scandal that threatened the well-being of the entire city engendered no more emotion than a lunch order. Jenny often wondered if anyone in the building possessed a soul.

Riding around with Koenig, the reporter, for two evenings did nothing to ease her mind.

Koenig, who'd followed the husband, Paul Wagster, all week, was acting as Jenny's guide and protector as they sought an opportunity for Jenny to entice secrets from Wagster at his favorite after-work bar. Wagster had gone straight home the first night they'd tried, and so Koenig and Jenny were now spending a second evening together, waiting and watching.

This surveillance was a dull, plodding exercise that afforded far too much time for idle conversation. And Koenig, the supervisor of this operation, who saw himself as an educator for the inexperienced secretary, did most of the talking. At first he'd confined his instruction to methods used in getting an unwitting subject to talk. Most of the tricks involved conventional wisdom ("Men love to yap to strangers about their importance at work"), but there were more straightforward devices like getting the subject drunk. Not much of a drinker, Jenny was alarmed by this part of the seminar, which exposed her to the Mickey Finn, cut whiskey, and drink swapping.

After these lessons had been exhausted, Koenig filled the remaining class time by entertaining Jenny with stories gleaned from thirty-three years as a reporter. During his career he had seen coronations, dogs rescued, babies born, and even wedding proposals. Yet Jenny would hear nothing from this catalog of blessed events, the entire lot having failed to make a dent in Koenig's memory. What she heard instead would alter her sleep for several months.

Whether Koenig was indeed soulless or he was just trying to impress an attractive girl, he held nothing back, giving the wide-eyed secretary his premium material. Take the Vincent Crandall execution, for example. As the *Sun's* sole representative at the electrocution of the murderer, Koenig was able to expound on many details the general public would not have considered. His enlightenment on the smell alone was worthy of a two-credit course.

It was an unnerving soliloquy made even more impressive by the fact that he never lost his train of thought as Wagster left work, got in his car, and drove away. Koenig just kept talking as he deftly weaved through traffic and ran stop signs in order to keep track of their prey.

Jenny was relieved when Wagster stopped at a bar called Bibb's Crib and went inside.

Koenig wished Jenny good luck and told her that, for now, he would wait outside. She smiled bravely and departed with an energetic wave, much to the dismay of her instructor, who had just finished reminding her not to call attention to him.

Leaving the still of the evening and stepping into the bright liveliness of Bibb's Crib was a sensory jolt for Jenny. Music blared from a Wurlitzer jukebox. A middle-aged couple danced next to it, their style completely out of pace with the song. Cigarette smoke drifted everywhere, and warmth emanated from the combined presence of the patrons, who laughed hard and talked loudly to be heard over the music. Jenny, who did not spend time in bars, was certain that if Dante's *Inferno* had a tenth circle, it would feature Bibb's Crib.

She scanned the scene carefully, looking for Wagster. She finally spotted him at the bar, where he was engaged in conversation with his neighbors. The sudden reality of her task frightened her, and she might have flown had the alternative not been more time with Koenig.

Slowly, Jenny made her way to the bar, and as the angle of her view changed, she was relieved to see an empty bar stool next to Wagster. She took the seat and laid her handbag on the bar, looking stiff and uncomfortable in this environment.

It took a few moments, but Wagster finally turned in her direction and was pleasantly surprised by what he encountered.

"Hi, there," he greeted her.

"How are you?" she responded stiffly.

"I'm better now." He grinned. "My name's Paul, what's yours?"

"Jenny."

"I once dated a gal named Jenny," he remarked.

"Really? What was *she* like?"

"To be honest, she was rather annoying."

"Then why'd you date her?"

"Because she would." He chuckled, his cheeks reddening a little. "I was kind of a chump back in school."

"Not anymore," she assured him, trying to be flirty. "And now that you're not a chump in school, what are you?"

"You mean, what do I do?"

"Sure."

"I'm a manager at a tire store. It's not a bad way to make a living, keeping those fellas in line who work under me. I've got bigger plans in the works, but this will do for now. For one thing, the pay is too darned good. Every time I think about doing something else, I get a paycheck that changes my mind."

"That sounds pretty swell," Jenny gushed.

"Yeah, I suppose it's swell, all right," he conceded with blasé manliness. "But like I said, I'm working on something pretty large right now. Can't really go into it, but when it's all settled I could be rollin' in the dough."

"Say, you're not a mobster, are you?"

"Nah, I'm too independent for those fellas. I've been involved in some things in my past, though; let's just say there are some cops who know me by name," he bragged, leaving the extent of his danger to her imagination.

"Now you really have me curious with all this secrecy. Can't you give me a hint about your big money plan? I'll tell *you* a secret," she offered naughtily.

"Oh, yeah? What kind of secret?" he asked, his face turning lusty.

"You have to tell me yours first."

"All right, I'll tell you this much: It involves a huge corporation, and it's totally legal, what I'm doing."

"That sounds exciting," she exclaimed. "How did you come up with this idea?"

"It wasn't completely my idea, to be honest. Someone knew about some stuff happening in my life, and they also knew I was the right kind of person. The two things sort of combined into this deal I'm working on. It's hard to explain, really, but when it's all settled I should be doing pretty good, moneywise."

"You're driving me crazy with this teasing."

"I already said more than I should have. Now what's your secret?" He dared her with wolfish anticipation.

All of this on-the-fly decision-making was beyond Jenny, who was neither a skilled actress nor a slippery reporter. The comfort of her desk seemed so far away as Paul leered at her and the sounds of the bar's debauchery pulsed in her ear. She had no secret, but she needed one.

"Promise not to tell anyone," she said, stalling for inspiration.

"I swear."

"Well, my secret is a little embarrassing."

"Those are the best kind."

"Are you sure?"

"Never been more sure of anything."

"Okay, my secret is that ... I don't wear anything when sleeping," she admitted.

"Nothing?" he whispered.

"Nothing," she whispered back.

"Holy Toledo," he marveled. "That must make sleepin' awfully difficult for your husband."

"I guess we'll find out when I have one. How 'bout you? You have a wife?"

"Sorta. We're separated. She's a great gal and all, but ... it's mixed up."

"I'm sorry to hear that," Jenny consoled. She was preparing to dig deeper when the bartender interrupted by setting drinks in front of them. Jenny hadn't heard mention of drinks since she'd sat down.

"They're on me," Paul said. "Everything's on me. Just enjoy yourself."

And did she ever. The first drink was a shock to her nearly virginal system, but it did wonders for erasing any anxiety. Bibb's Crib began to feel warm and comfortable, like sitting in front of the fireplace the day after Christmas.

The second drink actually made the songs from the jukebox sound magical, as though she were truly hearing melodies for the first time in her life. Each successive song became a personal favorite. The cigarette smoke now smelled rich, and the boisterous laughter seemed like something from a charming medieval fairy tale.

The third drink was where Jenny's joy reached its zenith and Paul's began to wane. No longer concerned with her responsibilities as subtle gatherer of secrets, she began sharing instead.

Sadly for Paul, none of what she shared was nearly as interesting as her sleeping in the nude. There were mother problems, a sister who lied about everything, an ex-boyfriend who told a friend that he thought she was too needy, and a landlady who hated her, although Jenny had no proof of this.

It was about this time that Koenig entered Bibb's Crib and took a seat near the door. He was concerned about the length of Jenny's stay and wanted to make sure Wagster was not abusing her in a dark corner. Instead he observed that Jenny was abusing Wagster. The man's discomfort was obvious even from a distance.

In the midst of her fourth drink, Jenny noticed Koenig and waved eagerly, nearly sending the reporter ducking under the table. There was no need for worry, however, as Wagster cared less about who she was waving at and more that she'd stopped talking for a moment. Prior to the wave, she had been describing her recent yearning for a baby. She wanted so badly to have one of her own, to play with its little toes. Paul was understandably nervous about the direction this was headed.

When a fifth drink was placed in front of Jenny, the watchful old reporter knew it was time to rescue his wayward pupil. He moved to the bar and introduced himself to Wagster as Jenny's Uncle Jeremiah. After some pleasantries, Koenig gently led his "niece" toward the exit.

Jenny knew she had misbehaved, and as they moved through Bibb's Crib she tried to mollify Koenig by loudly explaining what she'd learned from Paul. Through the large smile plastered on his face, Koenig shushed her until they reached his automobile, where he had her repeat what she remembered. He copied it all down in his note pad. There was little chance she would remember any details when she awoke in the morning, and he figured it was just as well.

She was sound asleep by the time they reached her boarding house, and Koenig dutifully carried his neophyte reporter to her room. He laid her on her bed, took off her shoes, and pulled the covers over her.

Just for fun, on the way out of the house he winked at the landlady.

21

Emma finished her breakfast with one final forkful of toast and fried egg. She always alternated between the egg and the toast until the final bite, when they were consumed together. Somehow it just seemed like the fair thing to do out of respect for both items.

She quickly rinsed her plate and fork and laid them in the strainer, then placed the skillet in the sink to soak. Her final kitchen act was to get another cup of coffee (Pinwheel original, one cream, one sugar). That left half a pot of coffee for her son, who still slept, having returned in the middle of the night as was his custom. They didn't see much of each other, mostly in the evenings after she returned from work and before he did whatever gregarious poets did.

Jerry was 28 years old and was living with Emma until his career as a poet flourished commercially. The other option was saving money from a steady job. Emma knew neither of these things was likely. Jerry was too artistic and self-consumed for mainstream employment, and his poetry was so fantastic as to be unintelligible even to his most loyal friends. If there was meaning in his verse, then it was hidden behind symbolic symbols of symbolism. For years Emma had actually hoped that his efforts were drug induced, but had come to the sad conclusion that he was generally sober when writing. As a confirmed bachelor, he would live with her until she moved, she died, or he found a generous roommate.

Emma sat her coffee mug on the kitchen counter and unfolded her copy of the *Daily Mercury*. The *Mercury* was the last of the five Stout City dailies she digested each morning, sort of like reverse dessert. Emma didn't want her dislike of the paper to influence her reading of the others, so she saved it for last. And yet, she had to admit that the *Daily Mercury's* vast resources allowed it to provide wider, deeper coverage of the news, even if it was provided in a sensational, classless sort of way.

And the paper was shameless in flaunting its size and style. This morning's edition contained another article poking fun at the *Sun* for running silly, baseless items concerning Pinwheel. "While we are intrigued by coffee whose reputation for delight borders on carnal, we feel that the setting *Sun* may have resorted to exaggeration where it is not needed. Suffice it to say that Pinwheel provides the finest cup of satisfaction in America, and whether one partakes before or after other pleasures is not for public consumption."

"Oh, now *they're* going to deliver a sermon on exaggeration?" Emma asked the pots and pans.

Emma was annoyed to such an extent that she skipped the *Mercury's* sports section, which she privately acknowledged as the best in the city. She picked up her mug and moved to the bedroom, where she got ready for work.

Thirty minutes later she appeared on the sidewalk in front of her apartment building on Ninth Avenue. Emma Beltran had always lived in and around downtown Stout City.

It had started with her parents, who had little formal education and worked multiple crummy jobs just to reach upper poverty. The constant battle to survive economically led to marital fights in whatever cheap apartment they were occupying that month. The drinking, the broken furniture, and the evictions depleted their meager resources and pushed them deeper and deeper until it all disintegrated. Broke and depressed, Emma's mother had remarried the first man who would propose, an odd but seemingly safe man eighteen years her senior. It turned out that he'd been in one of his better cycles during their courtship, and over the next few years he went back and forth between terrorizing rants and sickening passivity.

It was hard to say what Emma had learned from this upbringing. Her three husbands were not as dangerous, but each proved to be just as hopeless financially and emotionally. Looking back on her choices, Emma could never point to a common reason for accepting each, but she knew instinctively that love was never truly part of the equation. Perhaps her start in life had left her with skewed standards, or maybe she'd just gotten stuck in the quagmire. Whatever the reasons, she had always known downtown Stout City as home.

Even after being single for so long (her third husband had died twenty-two years before), she still remained downtown in part because of her career. The center of the city was where the action was, and it gave her the advantage of being nearby and available for any assignment.

On the other hand, downtown was a young person's habitat. It was so full of extremes. Downtown was where you walked next to the wealthiest and the sorriest humans the city had to offer. It was the gathering place for anyone seeking attention or seeking anonymity. At any moment you might see a purse stolen, a man swallowing glass as entertainment, or a threadbare orator describing the riches of Heaven. Visitors feared the place and longed to see it at the same time.

Emma had been a part of the scene her entire life, but she was growing weary of it. The urban circus, which had once been intriguing, now felt like turmoil, and a dangerous brand at that. This was only natural, as growing older meant growing vulnerable. Maneuvering safely through the chaos took a special brand of hyperawareness that Emma didn't possess anymore. Her experience made up for much of it, but not enough to counteract a mind that was prone to drifting these days.

Mostly her mind was occupied with issues related to work. And why not? Her career as a newspaperwoman was the single rewarding constant in her life. So cherished was her career that she had always used Beltran (her half-Mexican mother's maiden name) as her professional name, never wanting the turmoil of her real life to soil the steady, honest progression of her work life.

Beyond that, Emma's work had grown in significance by default. Her husbands were gone, her son was grown, and her dreams at this stage in life were just that—dreams. And to top it all off, her elderly years were no longer something hazy in the distance. She could make out details now, and it scared her. Now was the time to make the most of her working days.

Related to this was her concern about the *Sun's* survival. It had grown into a special place to her—a second home, if one were to get saccharine about it. It's where she worked with Deacon, and if the *Sun* failed, what other paper would accept them as a pair—and they were most definitely a pair in her mind. For seven years now they had been of one ink-stained mind, working in unison to make the *Sun* all it could be despite the odds. Where he was neglectful she was strong, and vice versa. Their mutual understanding was so instinctual it was darn near spooky. Reporters had long commented on it.

Those same reporters had also commented on whether the two shared more than just work. There had been no evidence suggesting romance, but the two of them got along famously and were widowed, so it seemed logical.

It seemed logical to Emma, as well. She understood grieving when one lost a spouse, having endured it herself. But Abigail had been gone almost three years now, and Deacon had not shown the slightest interest in turning to Emma for ... more. He treated her with respect and admiration and would probably declare her his closest friend if asked, but it stopped abruptly there.

She hated to think it, but she often wondered if he simply found her unattractive. Emma had never looked like Miss Redding, and she was now pushing sixty, but she was not unattractive either. A couple of Jerry's friends had even made passes at her. Yet Deacon never seemed to look at her in that way.

Or maybe it had something to do with her being a thrice-married career woman who'd hung tough in a tough business. Abigail had been a librarian. She'd dabbled in art and worked in her garden. The four or five times Emma had visited the Lowes' house in Arden Heights, she had been struck by the gentleness of their home, partly because of its idyllic suburban location and partly because Abigail made everything feel simple and easy and calm. It seemed unthinkable that Abigail could comment on murder or mayhem in an offhand, jaded way.

Emma always felt out of place at the Lowes'. She found herself sitting forward on their chairs like a hobo trying to leave the fewest downtown germs possible. If she were married to Deacon, would she measure up against the easy gentility of Abigail? Or did she belong downtown with all the other curious cases? Perhaps Deacon had already come to a conclusion, and perhaps that was why he never looked at her in that way.

She arrived at the office just in time to grab a cup of coffee (Gold Monocle, one cream, two sugars) and enter Deacon's office. Her chair was in place, but he was busy reading something and didn't look up.

"Good morning," she greeted him.

"Morning," he returned, still reading.

Emma sipped her coffee and waited. She wasn't about to talk if she'd have to repeat everything.

"This is the report from Koenig," he finally shared. "Dropped it off last night. Not a whole lot of information, but there is one nugget. He claims Wagster—the husband—has a big plan involving a large corporation and that he'll be rolling in the dough if it works. That's pretty heavy stuff. Not exactly the full confession we needed, but enough to keep us on his tail."

"Strong as far as circumstantial goes."

"Yes, now here's the troubling part. He says the plan wasn't his idea, that someone else brought it to him thinking he was the right kind of fella. Now tell me that doesn't sound like we're dealing with a crooked scheme?"

"He didn't say any more than that, I take it?"

"Said it involved 'stuff' happening in his life but wouldn't go into detail."

"Just like we figured, if he was really the one then he's been coached to play coy."

"Koenig also says that Miss Redding wasn't feeling well near the end, so perhaps her chat was a short one."

"Yes, I've been on dates like that. I always claimed vertigo. Very disabling and wholly unprovable. Of course, it's been many years since I went on a date. Not that I haven't been asked, just that I haven't accepted, although I would accept for the right person if that person asked, but he hasn't, which is no big deal," she rambled.

"Do you have that right person in mind?" he asked.

His direct response caught her off guard. She assumed he was only half-listening to her rhetorical rant, and she wasn't prepared for an in-depth discussion.

"Do I have a person in mind?" she repeated, stalling.

"Yes. Do you have the right person in mind? You mentioned a right person."

"Well, I guess there could be. I mean, there is probably a person who I would wait for."

She cringed internally about the waiting part, even though it was true. It made her sound helpless, and she hated being helpless.

"I just figured after your bad luck with husbands, maybe you didn't care to revisit that, um ... aspect."

"It does make me want to be careful, but everyone wants to share their life with someone, right? It's human nature."

"You're probably right," he agreed before changing the subject he'd pursued. "I guess you saw the latest piece foisted on us by Exlee."

"Yes, that husband and wife are starting to get a little testy with each other in a public sort of way. The way everything is unfolding, though, you can't help but wonder if it's real. Only Exlee knows, I'm sure."

"And I'm tired of all of it," Deacon complained, shaking his head. "Especially with the *Mercury* mocking us daily."

"Which they did again today."

"Yes, and apparently the story is growing nationally by the minute. I feel like we are the victim of some giant hoax, and *yet* ... it could be nothing at all," he fretted.

"*Or* Pinwheel is truly guilty of concocting an addictive drink, and somebody—or more than one somebody—has figured a way to profit from it through a lawsuit."

They lapsed into silence. How many times had they engaged in shades of this same conversation with the same empty results?

"I'm not sure if this helps," Emma began, breaking the silence, "but I've been thinking about Vivian Wagster since yesterday morning when we got Sanderson's report on their background. The husband's past fits with being a wannabe charlatan, but Vivian's seemed incomplete. Actually, I don't know if that's the right word. There are holes in her background, but what we did learn gave me the impression of someone a little on the sweet side, maybe someone drawn to an imp even if he were really more poseur than gangster."

"Yep, I kinda got that impression myself," Deacon agreed.

"What I'm trying to say is that she's more likely to reveal her knowledge of this scheme than the husband."

"Only we don't know where she is," Deacon interrupted.

"That's what I'm getting at, Mr. Patience. I was about to say I have an idea of where she might be."

"Well, why didn't you just start with that?"

"Because my idea still requires some research, and I wanted to convince you of its value before blurting it out and having you dismiss it because it wasn't your idea."

Emma said this with such comfortable irreverence that Deacon couldn't help but smile. She was right, and there was something wonderful about the way she knew him well enough for open derision.

"Yes, smile at me like a goof all you want, but it's true," she insisted. "Now, do you want to hear my idea or not?"

"My God, your eyes get dark brown when you're cross," he added, unable to stop himself from teasing her ire.

"Well, your eyes are gonna be black and blue in a minute if you don't shut up and let me tell you my idea," Emma threatened. She liked his comment, though, and happiness seemed to wash over her face.

"All right, already, tell me your idea. We could have followed through on it by now if you'd just led with it."

"I was thinking about where I'd go if I were her—after separating from my husband. It doesn't sound like they're wealthy, so a hotel or apartment seems unlikely for several weeks."

"Unless somebody like the *Mercury* is funding it."

"True, that's a possibility, but one that would be impossible for us to follow up on. I'm talking about an option we have a shot at exploiting. If I were her, I would stay with my parents. It's cheap, its local—you want to stay somewhat near your husband if it's a fake separation—and what was the other thing ... oh yeah, the folks can help with errands and expenses and so forth. They'd also be willing to believe her separation story, since they probably never liked her husband in the first place."

"They'd probably congratulate her on leaving."

"Exactly. I'm just saying that of all the possible places she could be *and* that we could locate, her parents' home seems the most logical."

"Assuming they still live in Stout City."

"Yes, assuming that."

Deacon looked at the clock on the wall while he considered her hypothesis.

"Tell you what," he said. "Check with Sanderson and see what he knows about her folks. If he thinks they might still be local or has no reason to believe otherwise, have him work on finding their address. If he comes up with something, we can have Koenig scout it. He should be in later—he's been working long hours, and I told him and Miss Redding to sleep in today if they were able to corner the husband last night. Sound like a plan?"

"What'll we do if we confirm Vivian's presence at the address?"

"Let's confirm it first, then we can decide. That'll give us time to think it through, anyhow."

"Okay, I'm gonna get some more coffee, then find Sanderson."

When he was alone again, Deacon looked at the little calendar propped on his desk. Tomorrow was Saturday, so he was sure resolution would have to wait until Monday or later. Maybe then he'd have the lab results so he could get *some* indication of Pinwheel's guilt or innocence. He was also anxious to hear from Addie, who had promised to call him that afternoon with an update on her inspection. After four days she should know something, good or bad, and he was dying for some definite news.

22

By the time Exlee bought his morning papers each day it was usually afternoon, but that was all right. Being out of step wasn't a sin. As a matter of fact, Exlee had always found that it gave him unique insight. That was his excuse for late-night cavorting, anyhow.

It was past noon on Friday when Exlee purchased his papers and retired to his office above the wig shop. Stretched out on the couch, he'd barely begun reading the obituaries in the *Stout City Herald* when his office door opened and Kate Roth entered.

This was highly unexpected, as was the arrival of any guest, but Exlee showed no expression and made no effort to get up. He laid the paper down on his stomach and watched as she walked in and sat in his desk chair.

"You look good in that chair," Exlee said. "Of course, you'd look good anywhere."

"I wanted to see what it felt like sitting on the throne—running a press agent empire," she explained, ignoring his compliment.

"So, how does it feel?"

"A little unfulfilling, really, and my expectations were very low when I arrived. Is there a reason you have so many unopened envelopes?"

"It's not the nineteenth yet. That's the day each month that I open envelopes."

She smiled softly. "I honestly have no idea if you're serious or teasing me or telling me to mind my own business. No idea at all, and I'm not kidding."

"Let's keep it that way. It may serve a purpose one day."

"So 'one day' and I are related in your mind?"

"I think about you, so yeah, that sounds reasonable."

"Oh, really? Do you daydream about me, Exlee?" she asked sarcastically. "Do you rue the day you let me walk way? Or does it just make you want me more now that you can't have me?"

"You won't believe me, no matter what I say, and I've earned that. I will tell you that I knew you were special on our second date. You remember that? It was at the zoo."

"I remember you bumped into that little girl and made her drop her cotton candy."

"That was awful, wasn't it? The look her mom gave me—made me feel like the clumsiest Neanderthal that ever lived. I couldn't give her a quarter fast enough."

"You'd have been a more impressive date if you'd stopped there. Trying to make the little girl laugh by picking that cotton candy off the ground and taking a bite was disgusting."

"It was a bite off the top side. And she did seem amused."

"She was horrified, you nincompoop. She laughed hoping it would put the lunatic at ease. Now let's get back to the part about me being special."

"We were sitting on a bench near the tortoises and I asked you what you'd wish for if you could have anything in the world. And you said 'a good view.' "

"I did?"

"Uh, huh. That was your total answer, and I kinda fell for you right then. It was just so brilliant, no matter how you looked at it. A good view could mean anything. A view from somewhere like the Eiffel Tower or an opinion-like view on some subject or being above the fray watching opposing sides battle it out or on a street corner watching someone beautiful walk past. It fascinated me, and I couldn't quit thinking about it the rest of the day. I still think about it sometimes, and I'm prepared to use it as my own if asked one day."

"Who says you have permission?"

"You don't even remember saying it."

"I was probably just being flippant, anyhow. I'm sure I never intended it to be a philosophical touchstone."

"I thought about the flippant angle, too, and I still thought it was clever as an off-the-cuff answer. That's how I knew you were special."

"And yet you let me walk away."

"That doesn't change the fact you're special."

"But why wouldn't you want to spend your life with that person, especially if they also think *you're* special? Isn't that what we strive for as humans, finding someone who satisfies us in a way that no one else can?"

"You're implying that living together every day is the only response to finding that someone. And frankly, I think if a person had nothing to do but sort through potential mates all day, they'd find that there are hundreds, if not thousands, of good matches."

"So, basically, you just don't believe in true love?"

"Sure I do. I believe everyone's true love is themselves," he said, sitting up on the couch. "Other people only enhance or dilute that true love of self."

"Believe it or not, I get what you're saying, and there is some dark truth to it, but you just admitted another person can enhance your life, and I know I'd have been the best. I'd have enhanced the heck out of your life, Exlee. Why would you not want that? Is being alone and unaccountable really better than being married to someone who adores you?"

"You're not being realistic, Kate. You might have adored me, but do you really believe it would have been that easy—you striving to please me without ever wanting to be pleased on that same level? That's the part of the bargain always ignored when love is new and illogical. There will come a time when the effort outweighs the reward."

"God forbid you have to give anything for being enhanced. The problem is you'll never know, because that dynamic between two people who adore each other takes real risk—not risking five bucks to see if Purdue wins or if you can get two drunk strangers to dance with each other. You can talk logic all you want, but the truth is you're scared to share yourself, and it cost you a damn good life with me."

"I'd forgotten about getting the drunks to dance. It sounds like a simple bet, but ... "

"Yes, I know you'd like to change the subject. I told you the truth, and you don't like it."

"Is that why you stopped by today—to explain to me what I've lost?"

"I doubt I could make you fully understand, although I think deep down inside, you know—like when you first saw me at Troscanza's the other night. Tell me your heart didn't ache for a second."

"You're pretty sure of yourself."

"No, I'm just angry because that's what I feel every time you appear out of the blue, and I don't want to feel that. I don't want to forever be in love with you, and yet that's exactly what you want. You want to own my heart for the selfish joy of it."

There was silence as Exlee smiled at her. "Maybe I am an idiot. I probably should have married you and had six children and worn a cardigan to supper every evening."

"I like a man in a cardigan," she said suggestively.

"Really? Does Theo wear them?"

"Why, are you a little jealous? You wish it were your cardigan I was snuggled up to after a long day?"

Exlee and Kate stared at each other. They had renewed their old impasse, only in different words.

"Listen, the only reason I'm here is because of Theo," she continued. "He's worried about you."

"That's what he told me yesterday, although I'm wondering if he isn't really worried about protecting Stout City's biggest employer."

"You make that sound like a bad thing. It's part of his job to worry about what's best for the city."

"Then he should concern himself with that instead of acting like he's worried about me."

"He's not acting. He really likes you, Exlee, but he thinks you're wading into waters you don't belong in."

"So he sent you over here to tell me to stay in the shallow end?"

Kate laughed. "He doesn't *send* me anywhere."

"But does he know you're here?"

"He might guess that I am. We just had lunch together and one of the topics was you, and since I'm already downtown, he might put two and two together."

"So you both worry and want me to be careful— just like you were my parents. Your care is insulting, Kate. I can swim in the deep end as easy as I can the shallow end, so you and Daddy don't need to worry."

"He's not saying you're incapable, just that it's not your style. And I agree."

"I'll worry about my style, and right now I need to get busy," he said, rising from the couch.

Exlee walked toward the door, and Kate got up from the desk chair and followed him. When they reached the door, Exlee paused with his hand on the doorknob, then turned around. He was right on top of Kate, who'd assumed they were exiting. A look of fear came into her eyes, and she wanted to back away almost as much as she wanted to step forward. She breathed heavily as he looked down into her eyes.

"I know you care," he said softly.

"I do," she whispered, touching his arm.

"And you're probably right about me."

She tried to answer him, but words wouldn't form.

Exlee desperately wanted to kiss her one time just to validate the feeling between them, but he couldn't do that to her or to Roth. He pulled her up against him, and she turned her head so that it rested on his chest. Her hair smelled sweet, and he let his lips graze its softness.

Then he released her and looked into her eyes one more time before turning and opening the door.

"You go ahead," he said. "I'll see you around some time."

Kate stared at him with a sad smile, and then she was gone without a word.

Exlee listened to her heels descending the stairway. He heard her first two steps on the sidewalk, and after that any sound she made was swallowed by the city going about its business. After a few moments of feeling sorry for himself, he joined it.

23

This was Addie's fourth day of inspection at Pinwheel, and the chance of finding any significant shenanigans was dwindling. It wasn't that Addie desired to find some heinous crime, she just feared that unearthing nothing might be perceived as a mark against her.

It looked like it would all come down to one solitary item of interest: Drutoa. An invoice from someone or something named Drutoa had mistakenly ended up in the accounts receivable pile the previous day, causing a silent but definite reaction from the department head. Addie needed to know why.

Because of this, Addie had spent the morning poking into Pinwheel's financial sector. She'd been allowed access to reams of financial papers but very few key employees. Hazel Kellison, under orders from the owners, had been doggedly evasive about granting permissions, unleashing more of her skillful doubletalk when pressed into a corner. It was a latent talent which Hazel had had no previous occasion to employ, but one she wielded with ease now.

Before lunch, Addie made specific requests to meet with Pinwheel's chief financial officer, comptroller, and head of bookkeeping. Hazel rebuffed them all. The reasons given were "family issue" for one and "project deadline" for another, and then legal mumbo jumbo was implemented for the third.

Upon returning from lunch, Addie made the same requests and received the same answers, only this time the answers and the employees had been inadvertently rearranged. Addie thought about pointing this out as proof of stonewalling, but figured it would do no good to alienate Hazel, the gatekeeper. With grim politeness, they instead went back and forth on alternate choices for whom Addie *could* have access to.

Aware that her reticence was beginning to look downright hostile, Hazel feigned surrender by allowing Addie to interview one Quinn Delahanty, a minor official in charge of the company pension fund. He was also a second cousin of owner Farrell O'Bryant. Because of this relationship, and because his role lay safely outside of any mainstream financial activity, Hazel considered Delahanty a safe haven for Addie's prying.

Delahanty was not aware he'd drawn the short straw, and would have been irritated at the appearance of a bothersome stranger had it not been a willowy young woman. At the sight of Addie his countenance briefly livened, only to return to its normal sullen state after hearing she was there for business reasons. Like most dames, she seemed to maintain a lofty work ethic, which ran counter to his subsidized reading of hunting and fishing magazines. This interview was destined for failure, but not before each took a stab at success. Addie tried first, asking a series of basic questions that elicited savvy responses like "I'm not sure" and "Maybe." Thwarted, she surrendered the floor to Delahanty, and he attempted to save the acquaintanceship by asking if she enjoyed fishing. It was a longshot, but he asked with eyes brightened, imagining them frolicking in a stream for trout and then on a bearskin rug by a fire in the lodge. When Addie responded that she didn't fish, Delahanty was crestfallen and made no attempt to hide it. All hope was lost. Neither party would be victorious, and their future held nothing but tedious dialogue.

Addie stubbornly poked a little deeper but was finally forced to admit that Delahanty not only had no desire to discuss finances, he genuinely knew nothing of importance. He was merely the custodian of a virtually self-sufficient pension plan. Any specialized work that was required from his tiny department he left to his underling, John Zwirzs.

Anxious for a return to the *Sports Afield* magazine that lay open in front of him, Delahanty conveniently remembered a phone call he had scheduled and sent her down the hall to Zwirzs's office, where he would "fix her up."

Addie was only too glad to leave. And though she figured John Zwirzs couldn't be any worse, Addie was still miffed that she was trapped in this pension cul-de-sac. It was highly unlikely that the question of Drutoa would be resolved here.

So when she spied the name of another employee named John on one of the hallway doors, Addie saw an opportunity for a beneficial, yet plausible, mistake. She would accidently visit Mr. John Ballantyne.

Not wanting to call attention to her "error," Addie chose to forgo knocking on Ballantyne's door in favor of getting inside quickly. She swung his door open suddenly and jumped into his office. To say Mr. Ballantyne was startled would be an understatement. Previously bent over his desk working on a ledger in dead silence, he found himself bolt upright, wondering if his high-pitched yelp had been as audible as he feared. It had.

Addie tried to cover a laugh with her hand, but it was no use and she surrendered, openly enjoying his fright. She felt bad and tried to explain, but the giggles would not allow it.

What saved Addie was that she was a stranger and she was a woman. To the male way of thinking, this meant she was an amorous possibility and therefore worthy of polite behavior until proven otherwise.

"Wow, you about gave me a heart attack." He laughed, trying to create good will.

"I am so sorry," Addie earnestly confessed. "I got a little lost and opened the wrong door."

"No, it's quite all right; I probably needed a break from these numbers, and who knows, maybe you opened the right door after all."

"Well, I was supposed to interview John Zwirzs, and then I saw the name John on your door and swung it open at the same time that I realized the last name was different, but it was too late," she explained before catching her breath. "I blame it on the three cups of Tingle I had at lunch."

"You were looking to interview Zwirzs?" He laughed. "I never thought I'd hear that one. You must be from *Flat Tire Magazine* or something. What were you going to ask him about?"

"That's a good question, although I'm not from a magazine. Maybe you've heard, but I've been given the job of inspecting your company ... "

"Ah, so you're the one, huh?"

"Yep, that's me. Anyhow, I'm trying to get to the bottom of a financial matter and was referred to Mr. Zwirzs by his boss, Mr. Delahanty."

"Holy Toledo, you're really scouting the cream of the crop. I'm not joking one bit when I say that giving you directions was probably the first productive thing Delahanty has done all day. And trust me, it's by the grace of God that you missed out on Zwirzs. He's a smart fella, all right, but only if you speak in numbers. On second thought, you interviewing him would be highly entertaining. I might pay to see that one."

"Unfortunately, that probably won't happen. It's doubtful he'd have the kind of answer I need anyhow."

"Probably not."

"But now that I'm here, perhaps you'll be of some assistance," she continued. "Um, I didn't catch your title on the door."

"Officially, it's the junior assistant to the assistant bookkeeper. Screwy, huh? On this floor it's just called the 'under book'—as in so low on the totem pole I'm underground."

"At least you have your own office," Addie reasoned.

"There used to be four of us in here before the economy croaked. The only reason I'm still around is that I was out sick the day they fired the other under books. I keep thinking they'll note their oversight one of these days. Why do you think I jumped so high when you blasted in here?"

Addie giggled like she was on a first date. He had a certain something about him, and the fact that he was about her age and not bad to look at didn't hurt, either.

"You think I'm joking, don't you?" he continued, aware that he was achieving the desired effect on Addie and wanting more. "A hermit on the moon gets more visitors than me."

"Well, it's not all bad," Addie offered. "At least you have a steady job."

"Yeah, that's true. It could be worse. Hopefully I can keep it long enough for my music career to take off."

"Ah, that's what it is. I knew there was something about you that didn't fit a ... an under book. Of course, most men don't try to impress me with their *real* purpose in life this quickly."

"Which is either an insult to me or an admission that your men have no ambition."

"They're not *my* men, first of all, and secondly, I was just trying to say that most guys want to be something other than whatever it is that wins their bread, and sooner or later they make it clear what that something is."

"I bet for a lot of 'em that something involves you."

"Gracious, you've been stuck in this closet too long. Anyhow, you might as well tell me all about your music so we can get that out of the way and move on to business. What instrument do you play, and so forth?"

"I'm glad you asked, it saves me from looking like a shameless promoter." He grinned. "I play a lot of instruments but my specialty is the trumpet. Right now, I'm working with a swing outfit called Baby Sam's Tornadoes. Ever heard of us?"

"Uh uh."

"Didn't figure you had. We're pretty new, been playin' those little clubs near the delta while we work on our sound. There's a few of us in the band that compose, and we all have different styles so it takes time to sorta find a common sound. I can already tell a couple of 'em won't last, they wanna play it too safe for the wingdings we like. It's a pretty swell group of guys overall, though, so I'm hopin' we find our sound and hit it big enough to go on the road full time. And that is my true purpose in life, Miss ... You never told me your name, did you?"

"It's Addie Sumner," she informed him. "And I have to say that I never really thought about all the background churning that occurs in a band. Guess I always thought there was some sort of organic magic that happened and the notes just came together."

"There's some of that, too," he acknowledged. "Bands fail all the time because they never find their magic. I've been part of my share of 'em. But you just keep arguing and playing until you succeed or fall apart, one or the other. Either way, I'll be working the trumpet forever."

"Well, I may just have to come hear you sometime, but first you have to help me with *my* purpose."

"Which is?"

"Figuring out the implication of Drutoa."

"Oh."

"That's it? Oh? Does that mean you're familiar?"

John answered by scrunching his face. He knew something, but was in no hurry to discuss it. Additionally, he was being put on the spot by a woman he wanted to impress.

"I take it you don't want to say?" she asked.

"That and I don't really want to be connected to your finding out. I'd rather remain forgotten in this closet than gain notoriety as the fella who stirred up a hornet's nest."

"Hmm. So it's enough to stir up a hornet's nest?"

"Now, now," he warned with a wag of his finger. "This is just the sort of thing that leads to trouble."

"Maybe I just assumed a swing musician enjoyed a little trouble."

"Unbelievable. I'm minding my own business one minute, and on the hot seat the next—put there by a woman I've just met. Listen, I can point you in the right direction, but you have to take the heat for what you might discover and how you use it."

"I'm willing to take the heat, but I fear that any direction you send me will have a roadblock waiting, courtesy of Miss Kellison."

"Hazel? What's she got to do with anything?" He laughed.

"You really are out of the loop in this closet. ... Wait, how did you know about my inspection, then?"

"Read about it in the paper."

"Oh yeah, I forgot about that." A look of contemplation passed over her face before she continued.

"Anyhow, Hazel has been designated as my tour guide and warden rolled into one. She seems particularly jittery about my being footloose anywhere near the financial floor."

"Well, I'm sure she has her marching orders from the top. And as it turns out, she should be jittery, what with you nosing around about Drutoa and God knows what else."

"I'm just trying to do my job like she's trying to do hers. I started out in politics so I'm used to games where everyone wears a fake smile while trying to undermine one another."

"So tell me, what do you think about our Miss Kellison?"

"You know, it's funny how often I've been asked that during my stay. I always give the same answer but get no enlightenment in return."

"Maybe you should give a new answer. Less political, maybe."

John had amused himself with this dig, as evidenced by his Cheshire Cat grin. Addie rolled her eyes, amused that he would think it was a dig of any note. She decided to set him straight anyhow.

"Keep in mind, I'm a visitor with a reputation at stake and no context for my surroundings," Addie reminded him. "I can't just go around sharing every impression only to discover later in a conversation that I've shared with precisely the wrong person. Maybe she's your girlfriend, for all I know."

"She isn't, but not because she hasn't tried. You know how every company has its serial daters?"

"I've gathered it to be common."

"Well, it is, and she's Pinwheel's. During your tour, has it seemed like she and every male employee are familiar?"

"Yeah, there's a friendliness—sometimes a frostiness. Not every man, of course, but enough to fascinate me. It's a big company."

"You are a true professional." He laughed.

"Coming from you, I doubt that's a compliment. But let's get back to the original task at hand. I need to know about Drutoa, Mr. John Ballantyne."

"If I remember correctly, a little while ago you said you'd come see my band if I helped you ..."

"Uh huh."

"Well, that might be a fair bargain, but only if you deliver the goods first. In other words, you should come see us tonight at Bailey's Comet. We go on about nine."

Addie smiled lightly. It was fun being flirted with, even though she was sure that no male inspector would receive a request this blatant. It was amazing the choices women were always encountering.

"And if I don't go?" she asked, testing the waters for her own satisfaction.

"You'll miss the greatest swing band yet to be discovered."

"What about Drutoa?"

"Well, to be honest, I don't exactly know all the details," he admitted. "There was a fella that worked here—an older man—and we got along real well for whatever reason. He's retired now, but at the time he sort of hinted that he knew the whole story of Drutoa. He shared the basic concept with me but that was it. I still talk to him every now and then and could probably find out if I wanted to."

"Would you?"

"That's not so simple either. There's a lot involved—my job, the well-being of the company, the success of your inspection—it's a lot to consider for a guy in a forgotten closet."

"That's the most honest thing I've heard in four days," she said, beaming. "Nine o'clock is past my bedtime—being the responsible girl that I am—but I might be there."

"You'll never be the same after you hear us," he bragged.

"Exactly what I fear," she said with a smirk before getting up to leave. "See ya."

"Hey. Don't tell Hazel you were ever here if you know what's good for your inspection."

"She'd just say, 'John who?' "

"Hey, that hurts," he called toward the closing door.

24

Exlee was lost in thought, walking along a sidewalk on the outskirts of Arraignment Alley, when he heard a small commotion. It was coming from inside the Downtown Auxiliary Library, a smaller version of the main library, used jointly by two nearby elementary schools, a junior high, and a senior high. Exlee had never paid attention to the place, but it was Friday and he was tired of thinking about Kate, so he entered to see what the minor fuss was all about.

He followed the noise to a far room in the back of the building, where there was a permanent stage and seating for educational performances. Today, this little venue was hosting a children's spelling bee. Exlee stood and watched for a few moments and was on the verge of departing when he spotted a familiar face in the back row: Willoughby Solberg, reporter for the *Stout City Daily Mercury*.

Now, *this* was interesting. Solberg was the *Daily Mercury's* top bloodhound and an ace reporter who typically worked the political beat. To find him at a grammar school spelling bee bordered on the absurd. Exlee had no choice but to slide into the empty seat next to him.

"You know this isn't an auction, right?" Exlee whispered. "These kids aren't for sale."

"Honest to God, I just knew I was gonna run into someone like you," Solberg complained. "Did Mealy tip you off?"

"No, I just happened to be nearby. What are you doin' here? And please tell me you don't have a child."

"Pity that poor kid if I did. Nah, I finished up my business downtown, and when I called in after lunch, they asked me to cover this since I was in the area. I think they're interested in showing this library as thriving since a couple of the council members— friends of the *Mercury*—were behind the funding of this place."

"You mean Roth and Mullinax?"

A mother two rows up turned and glared at the men, holding a finger to her lips to convey the need for silence. The two men dutifully shut up and watched as a girl in pigtails took her turn on the stage. She was probably ten and so skinny that the short sleeves on her little blouse didn't touch her arms despite the best efforts of the elastic edging. Her word to spell was "cathartic," and she asked the official pronouncer for its definition, then language of origin.

"She's stalling," Exlee concluded. "She doesn't know the word."

"She's being cautious," countered Solberg. "I like the look in her eye."

"A dollar bill says she misses."

"You're on."

They waited patiently as she requested and received an example of "cathartic" used in a sentence. Now, fully armed, she took her stab.

"C-A-T-H-A-R-T-I-C."

"That is correct," declared the lead judge, a severe looking woman with pince-nez glasses.

"Atta girl," cheered Solberg over the polite clapping of the others. A few eyes glanced at him, assuming that pride for his daughter was making him a little ebullient.

"She didn't even hesitate," Exlee had to admit. "You're up a buck and get first call on the next one."

It was another girl, a head taller, with one sock pulled to her knee and the other askew at her ankle. She wore a barrette and glasses. Solberg didn't even wait for her to speak.

"I think she does it," he declared. "Geniuses always wear glasses, right? And the sock thing is clearly a case of being too deep in thought."

"Or she's blind and clueless," Exlee argued. "I'll take that action."

Her word was "demagogue," and she asked for no clarifications, launching directly into her attempt. She spit out the letters hoping for the best, but her alacrity caught the judges off guard, and there was confusion about what they thought they'd heard. They leaned their heads together and whispered intensely.

"Looks like a steward's inquiry," Exlee joked, using horse racing parlance.

"Even in a spelling bee, fate finds a way to ruin my daily double," Solberg lamented.

Unable to resolve their dispute, the judges referred to a book of rules. The woman with the pince-nez glasses sternly flipped the pages.

"So what's the story on this Pinwheel mess?" Solberg asked Exlee as they waited. "I keep hearing whispers among the head honchos about you and the *Sun*, but nothing concrete."

"Can't tell you too much right now because I only know so much myself. I might have a surprise or two for you down the road, but right now I'm being paid to promote, and that's what I'm doing."

"I understand. Just like you get paid to promote, I get paid to gather information. What they do with it after that isn't part of my racket."

"That's right, your racket is covering spelling bees," Exlee ridiculed.

"I knew I was never going to live this down, especially since ... "

He stopped talking to hear the judges' decision. Using some fine-print rule which put the burden of clear speech on the contestant, the girl with the droopy sock was eliminated.

"Who's paying these judges?" Solberg complained a little too loudly. Several parents looked at him with disapproval, feeling he might be getting too enthusiastic on account of his daughter.

"Listen, I can't take your money on a disputed call," Exlee gallantly conceded. "Who's next?"

No answer was needed. A boy in a suit stepped forward. He was wearing a bow tie, and he kept licking his lips and fidgeting.

"Holy cow, that kid looks like he's about to bust a gear," Exlee whispered.

"And his momma dressed him awfully fancy. No way he passes."

"Agreed. They give him a word with more than four letters and he'll soil that suit."

The two men laughed, causing sidelong looks of exasperation from the parents.

"After this kid, I'm outta here, before *we* become the story in the paper," Exlee informed Solberg.

The bow tie boy received his word: "analogous." He chewed on his lip and looked as though he might cry as he awaited his public failure.

"I can't watch," Exlee said. "Tell me when it's over."

"You'll smell when it's over."

The boy bravely misspelled his word, and when he sat back down, his relief was so apparent that one might have mistaken him as having won the contest.

Exlee did not immediately depart as he'd promised. One more bet led to another, and at the end of the round he was up a dollar. When intermission was declared, Solberg stood up and fished a buck out of his pocket, which he then handed to Exlee. They began to share parting words when an elderly lady interrupted them.

"You two need to be kept after school and forced to clean erasers," she teased. The two men smiled sheepishly, but she wasn't done with Solberg. "In all seriousness, though, you don't want to make your daughter any more nervous than she is. How can she focus on spelling while worrying about her father's antics at the same time?"

Solberg started to explain that he didn't have a daughter, but Exlee interrupted.

"She's used to being nervous, ma'am. Her mom works three jobs to support the family, and this one spends half his day drinking and the other half chasing the babysitter."

Exlee wanted to stay and enjoy his handiwork, but it was more fun to imagine Solberg's red-faced mitigation.

He abruptly departed and smiled all the way to the sidewalk, a dollar richer and one hour closer to Friday night.

25

Frank Herrick, overseer of the *Sun's* society page, had been summoned to Deacon's office, where he now sat and faced the music.

"I'm gonna keep this short and sweet, Frank. You have *got* to stop favoring Mrs. Hollins."

"What are you talking about, Deacon?"

"Listen, I've mentioned it before, and I had someone warn you Tuesday ... "

"I don't remember any warning Tuesday."

"It's no use playing dumb about this. Did you really think I wasn't going to notice your column about the country club opening? You mentioned Mrs. Hollins three times, Frank. Three times. And one of them described her as looking 'delicious.' I actually had an old dowager call and complain about it this morning. You need to understand that I don't have time for a society flap, so out with it. Are you in love with Hollins? Is she blackmailing you? What is it?"

Frank thought about his answer and was about to speak when Deacon's phone rang.

"Mother of pearl," Deacon groused as he grabbed the receiver. "This is Deacon."

"Afternoon, Deacon," came the voice on the other end. "This is Jude Ostwald over at Pinwheel. How are you?"

"I've had better weeks, but I'm managing. What can I do for you, Jude?"

"Well, I'll tell ya, Deacon, it's been a difficult week for us as well, and for the same reasons, I'm sure, namely this business about the husband's lawsuit. We still think his claim is bogus and his threat of a lawsuit empty."

"I agree with you there," Deacon said while getting Herrick's attention and waving him out of the office.

"I know you agree, and we appreciate your help in managing this mess. The idea of an inspection was inspired, and I don't doubt that it will increase public confidence in the face of this ridiculous allegation."

"Uh huh."

"That said, we just finished talking to Miss Addie Sumner, and while we're pleased with her findings so far, well, that's just it: so far. Despite four full days of inspection, she insists she still needs Monday to complete her mission. I'm not sure what could be left to inspect, but so be it."

"Uh huh."

"So, I'll get directly to the point, Deacon. It's your newspaper, and you will run it as you see fit, but my recommendation is that we stop playing nice. Rumor has it that you've known the couple's identity for a good portion of the week."

"Actually, we're still working on confirming a connection between names and parties."

"So I've heard."

"Heard from whom?"

"Listen, we've been patient while our Tingle brand has been dragged through the mud without confirmed identities. Now it's time to even things out, don't you think? I'm not one to change horses in midstream, and I'm not making a firm threat here, but if you respect the loyalty we've shown over the years, it might be a good idea to take all of your information on this couple and shoot the works this weekend."

"Well, we're sort of working toward that end anyhow," Deacon hedged.

"I was sure of it. And just in case you think I'm only worried about Pinwheel, I should also mention that I got a phone call this afternoon from Chad Mealy at the *Daily Mercury*."

"Oh, yeah?"

"Yes. He gets some of our advertising money just like a lot of other papers, but not as much as the *Sun* gets, and he'd dearly love to change that, as you can imagine. The point is that he called to tell me he's been promised the couple's names and address on Monday. The husband's lawyer wants to double down, I guess. Whatever the reason, Mealy assured me he would attack this couple in print, 'unlike the *Sun*'—his words, not mine. See where I'm coming from?"

"Yeah, I see, all right. And like I said, we're working hard at it. You just have to trust me, Jude."

"Of course I trust you—Farrell does, too. I wouldn't be calling otherwise. You gave us great advice with the inspection gimmick, and I'm just returning the favor. These are hard times, Deacon, and we want nothing more than for both of us—Pinwheel and the *Sun*—to thrive. We just have to keep that a priority, that's all."

"Sure," Deacon agreed.

"All right, I don't want to keep you from your work. Hope it's a great weekend, and I'll talk to you Monday. Thanks again, Deacon."

"My pleasure, Jude. Say hello to Farrell for me."

"Will do, and the same to Emma. Bye, now."

"Uh huh, bye."

Deacon hung up the phone and leaned back in his chair for a few moments, tapping his fingers on his stomach as he thought. Then he stood up decisively, went to his door, and hollered out to the general office.

"Somebody find Emma, please, and send her in here."

Deacon hadn't been seated long when she entered the room. He began without any preamble.

"So I just got off the phone with Jude Ostwald, and they're really puttin' the screws to us. Sounds like the *Daily Mercury* gets the couple's names Monday and they're promising to expose them."

"Ha. They probably paid this couple off to begin with."

"Be that as it may, Jude also believes we are sitting on information about the couple and we need to expose them this weekend if we want to keep his loyalty."

"He really said that?"

"More or less, but mostly more."

"Where did he hear that we know so much about the couple?"

"I'm sure you're thinking of the same person as I am, but let's leave that alone for now. We've got bigger issues and not much time to solve them. Koenig hasn't called to confirm the wife bein' at her parents' house, but I'm darn well counting on it. The next step—and the one that this all hinges on—is getting the wife to talk, if she's indeed there. Any ideas other than knocking on the door and getting a 'No comment' or a 'She isn't here'?"

"I haven't thought of anything better than me going out there myself," Emma said.

"And what's *your* slant? Going down the chimney and threatening a confession out of her?"

"Very funny. Actually, I'm just thinking that if there's any way she'll confide, it would be with me. I'm a woman and old enough to be her mother. I know how to listen well, and I've had a lot of practice at convincing people that they're the victims in various situations over the years. How many times have these wives tried to stay silent about their high-profile divorces and how many times have they blabbed once they were made to believe they were wronged?"

"I've seen it any number of times."

"Back when I was strictly a reporter—before I came here—I was assigned all the feminine stuff. Luncheons, engagement parties, weddings, you name it. And when it came to notable divorces, they always figured it was the wife who'd crack and spill the beans, and they were right. That was my job, and I can still do it. This isn't a divorce—yet—but it's the same principle, and I just can't see anyone having a better chance than me. I've been thinking about it since this morning."

Deacon crossed his arms and studied Emma. He saw before him the perfect combination of tenacity and tenderness, a special kind of woman. He'd observed over the years that Emma didn't try to rub shoulders with men. She wanted to reinvent womanhood and help it to its own higher plane, enlightening one person at a time through steadfast form. Only at this moment did Deacon realize just how impressed he'd always been. Maybe it was because he was in need—that's when most people have epiphanies—and maybe he was seeing with his heart, thanks to Exlee's recent prodding. Either way, he needed her more than ever, and it felt good knowing he had a teammate who was so exceptional.

"When would you go?" he asked.

"As soon as Koenig believes the daughter is at that location."

"Good, I'll make sure we're prepared. I've already got them polishing up all the background goods that Sanderson uncovered. Whatever we have, we'll need to dump into the Sunday edition like a Wagster casserole."

"Funny," she mused, "this is when Exlee could provide that extra ingredient or two in exchange for a favor and a little cash. Instead, we're sitting here wondering if he's behind the entire four-alarm response in the first place."

"I know, but let's not get distracted. We have too much to do between now and the Sunday edition."

"You're right. I'm going to find that address on a map, just to be ready," Emma said, preparing to leave.

"Thanks, Em."

"Thanks for what?" she asked. They had dispensed with these sorts of workplace pleasantries long ago.

"I don't really know," he chuckled. "Just thanks."

She didn't understand, but it didn't matter. The way he looked at her was enough.

26

Emma took a taxi for her early evening trip to Mouton Springs, a suburb southwest of Stout City. She arrived at Tess Garrison's house just after five and asked the driver to wait, explaining that her visit might last thirty seconds or thirty minutes.

Emma knocked on the front door and waited, checking her outfit out of habit rather than because she expected any problem with it. When the door opened, it revealed a woman about her age wearing a housedress.

"Can I help you?" the woman asked.

"Yes, I'm here to see Vivian, she's expecting me." It was a half-truth, but delivered politely.

The woman hesitated, just as Emma had hoped. This was the right house, all right.

"Um, I'm pretty sure she wasn't expecting any visitors," the woman hedged.

"You must be her mother. I'm Emma Beltran, and I work for the *Stout City Sun*."

"Oh, nice to meet you. What's this about?"

"There's going to be a special in Sunday's paper, and I might be able to alter it in your daughter's favor if I can speak with her."

"I don't like the sound of this. Is it bad?"

"It doesn't have to be. It involves a lawsuit that your son-in-law is threatening to file."

"She hasn't done anything illegal." Tess resisted, her motherly instincts overriding her lack of knowledge.

"If you have a problem with ... with whatever it is, then maybe you should talk to her husband."

Tess began to close the door, indicating there was no more to say on the subject.

"Mrs. Garrison," Emma pleaded quickly, "I'm not here to harm your daughter. I'm here to help her. Certain things will come out in the paper Sunday, and that's just the way it is. However, if I can speak to Vivian, there are other things that need not end up in the paper. My guess is that she is more or less innocent of anything more than being a supportive wife to a husband who dreams a little too big for his skills."

The last part was eerily close to what Vivian and her mother had just discussed the day before. So close, in fact, that Mom realized she was just getting in the way of a conversation that needed to happen.

"You might as well come inside," Tess admitted with defeat. "If you want to wait here in the living room, I'll get her. Oh, here, let me grab these clothes I was folding. I wasn't expecting company, and sometimes I'll fold them while I sit and listen to the radio."

"I do the same thing."

Left alone, sitting on the living room couch, Emma spent a minute gazing at the room without really looking. She had waited in hundreds of living rooms during her newspaper career and found few of them nearly as noteworthy as the owner imagined. Today, for some reason, she found herself more focused on the smell. It was funny how every house gave off an undefined scent, a mixture of who knows what. The poorer houses leaned toward food odors, and the mansions toward flowers and fragrance. Sometimes a pet could be identified or dirty diapers if the place housed a baby, but mostly the smell was just unique, like a fingerprint. The odd part was that she'd have sworn her own apartment had no smell whatsoever. She knew better, though, and hoped it wasn't unpleasant in any way.

The silence was finally interrupted by two females talking softly but urgently in the hallway. Then a younger woman walked into the living room alone. She wore a dress but no shoes. She took a seat on the other side of the room and waited without speaking, like a teenager expecting punishment.

"Hello, Vivian, my name is Emma Beltran, and I work for the *Stout City Sun*."

"Hello."

"I'm sure you know why I'm here."

"Probably." Vivian nodded, unsure whether to cooperate or be difficult.

"As I told your mother, I'm really here to help you, if I can. On Sunday, our paper is running a special story about your husband's potential lawsuit concerning Tingle, and I wanted to get your side of things so I can tell them what not to include—if, for example, you are just sort of included in Mr. Wagster's lawsuit but not really behind it. Make sense?"

"I guess so."

"I also want you to know that I understand your hesitation in talking about this. It's one thing to have a few sentences in the paper without your name connected to them and another to sit here and talk about it face to face with someone who knows that it's maybe a little on the fraudulent side."

"What makes you say it's fraudulent?" Vivian asked with mild defiance.

"I only meant that there are some questionable elements, none of your doing, I'm sure. Your husband has engaged in risky schemes before. Minor ones. My first husband once fenced stolen guns, so I know a daredevil when I see one. Usually there isn't much you can do about it, right? Boys will be boys, and when they want to make extra money, sometimes a wife doesn't want to know too much. She's just pleased to see him show a little gumption and hopes it helps their living situation; a better place to live and better clothes to make her friends jealous. But deep down we know when something is questionable."

Emma paused in the hope that Vivian would speak, but she didn't, and that was to be expected. Vivian was scared, and scared people either flail for survival or clam up and hope the accuser doesn't know the whole picture.

"You probably think I'm the enemy," Emma surmised, "working for the paper that ran those stories that were less than flattering for you."

"That was not my fault," Vivian insisted. "That man Exlee got me to say things I normally wouldn't."

"Oh, honey," Emma confided, "that's the man's hobby—getting women to do things they normally wouldn't. Thanks to him, there's probably some gal in Stout City this very minute wondering where she left her virtue. And her stockings."

"Well, he didn't get that far with me," Vivian boasted.

"You've been separated, and presumably chaste, for a month. It would have been beneath him to even try. Trust me, he got what he wanted, and that was some good copy. And admit it, if it wasn't your life you were reading about, you'd look forward to the next installment every morning. But here's the bottom line: He may have charmed it out of you, but it was there to begin with. These problems you have with your husband—and I'm guessing there are plenty that didn't make the paper— they're real, and they're what have you behind the eight ball right now. You've been trying to fix him and please him and attach your dreams to him, but deep down you know who he is and always will be."

"You talk like you know him."

"I know he got sacked for a timecard scam once. I know he's bounced from job to job, and I know he got this Tingle idea from someone else who thought him capable of playing fast and loose with the truth. Those are just the surface facts. The rest of it—the part where I know how you feel—comes from me being married three times to three idiots. I've always thought I was reasonably intelligent, and I still do, yet somewhere along the line I surrendered a part of myself to three dopes, and I can't even defend it. That's the problem with being a woman. We can see a man's potential when he can't, and then there's something in us that thinks we can be the positive difference between his being a drugstore rebel and a rich maverick. And maybe it actually works out for some gal, somewhere. The odds almost dictate it. There's probably some woman in Georgia who succeeded in turning her frog into a president, but I'm here to tell you, I'm a three-time failure in the man fixing department."

"So what are you saying? That I'm supposed to give up on all men or just mine?"

"I'm not telling you anything, I'm just giving you a nice long look at a woman who's made mistakes with men but is still chugging along. I wake up reasonably happy every day and have a nice home and a great job. And between you and me, there's this man I think could end my husband jinx. One chapter doesn't make a book."

"Well, I think I still love Paul. ... It's just that I don't know what to make of everything. I mean, he still makes me happy most of the time, but ... I don't really know how to describe what I'm feeling."

"At least you're thinking about it, so maybe some good has come out of this separation already. I can't tell you where it's all headed, but I do know that there will be a large article Sunday morning, and I don't want to see you get caught up in a messy game if you already had one foot out the door."

"What if this isn't a game?"

"That's possible, I suppose. Are you really addicted to Tingle?"

"I'm dying for some right now."

"Would you rather have it than sleep with your husband?"

"Like you said, we've been separated a month, so that's not a fair question."

"Well, your love for Tingle is what this claim is all about, and that love is either troublesome—which means a lawsuit—or it just means you found a really good product. I know I *really* like my Tingle. So which is it?"

"Nothing feels troublesome when I drink Tingle, which in itself may be troublesome." Vivian smiled.

"All right, fair enough. You don't owe me a straight answer on that one, and it doesn't make any difference anyway, I'm no lawyer. Where it *does* get dicey for you is how this thing started. We both know the idea came from someone else, but who?"

"I honestly don't know," Vivian insisted. "Paul just said a friend, but he didn't say his name or why he didn't use the idea himself, and I'm not even saying it's a bad idea. You yourself said you loved Tingle."

"That I do, but a lawsuit because I like it so much? That's a bold premise. Does this friend have a connection to anyone that you know about?"

"Like a mobster or something?"

"Or a newspaper."

"I'm confused, but I guess it doesn't matter since I don't know of any connections."

"Is he a lawyer or does he work in that field?"

"Honestly, I have no more information on this person."

"When does Paul plan to file a lawsuit?"

"Not sure on that one, either. Last I heard, it's up to his lawyer."

"Which reminds me. Why do *you* have a separate lawyer if he's planning on suing Pinwheel?"

"Paul arranged one for me. Said that's what a separated wife oughta have. The lawyer isn't charging me anything yet, just enjoying the publicity, apparently."

"So let me ask you this: Why are you two *really* separated?"

Vivian started to answer but stopped and shrugged instead. "It just happens."

"It definitely happens when you're married to a con man."

"You should know from your four marriages."

"It was three, and you know it," Emma corrected. "I must have been a little too hard on Paul because now you're turning defensive. Maybe you really do love him. Then again, maybe you just need to defend your choice."

"I was being honest when I said I wasn't sure."

"What about the rest of the stuff? Have you been honest about that?"

"I think so."

"I hope so," Emma said as she stood up. "It's been a pleasure meeting you, and please tell your mother I said good-bye."

"I will. And thanks for being nice about this."

"Oh, this is the easy part. Don't forget to look for your name in the paper; you won't be able to miss it. Bye, Vivian."

"Bye."

After the front door shut softly, Vivian stood up and walked straight toward the kitchen. The smell of Tingle brewing had been driving her crazy.

27

Jude Ostwald was at peace with life as he sat, legs outstretched, in his large boat. It was still tied to the dock in front of his lake house, where it bobbed ever so slightly. His eyes were closed as he appreciated the sounds of the lake on a lazy Sunday morning—the gentle lapping of water, the distant buzz of another boat slicing the water, the faint sound of children laughing. It was moments like this that made all of his hard work worthwhile, and he was relishing every second of it, knowing it was about to end.

Already, he'd heard the crunch of gravel up by the house, signaling the arrival of Farrell O'Bryant's black Packard. He pictured the whole O'Bryant family exiting the car and making their way into the house, where they'd mingle with his family. The two wives would be busy preparing the children for their transfer to the nannies, then finalizing the food items to be carried to the boat. Farrell would be pacing around, awaiting his instructions while he drank a cold beer from the ice chest.

Jude opened his eyes when he heard a boat fast approaching, and he watched as it roared past with a skier in tow. A few moments later the wake arrived, causing his boat to rock gently, and he'd started to close his eyes again when he spied Farrell and the wives nearing the dock, their arms full in preparation for a boat outing. Despite the impressive collection of items, Jude already knew something would be missing—sunglasses, towels, maybe a different pair of shoes. He was already preparing himself to be the gracious volunteer who would fetch the forgotten piece.

"Ahoy," he called as they moved along the dock, their steps causing the planks to creak.

"We come bearing gifts," Farrell answered.

When he arrived, he handed the ice chest over the side of the boat to Jude, and when the women caught up, he unburdened them of their loads and passed them to Jude in the same manner. Then they all climbed aboard, and the wives began unpacking and stowing the provisions while the men moved aside to keep out of the way.

"How was your trip in?" Jude asked his business partner.

"Oh, about the usual forty minutes or so—not including our stops on the way out of the city. We picked up some of those raspberry tarts from the Mainz Bakery that you liked so much last time."

"What's the story on those, anyhow?" Helen Ostwald asked. "I stopped in the other day and couldn't find them on their menu. Thought maybe I'd remembered the wrong place."

"I thought I'd told you about that," Jude answered. "They're not on the menu. It's really a brilliant piece of marketing that we heard about from the fella who thought up the idea. Because they're not on the menu, the tarts have become a word-of-mouth secret, and everyone thinks they're part of some select, in-the-know minority. It gives them a sense of metropolitan exclusivity. Apparently, they sell like crazy."

"Very interesting *and* rather backward—playing hard to get with your best item," Farrell added.

"But as you can see, it works like magic when it gets going."

Farrell interrupted. "Look out behind you, honey," he called to his wife, Maggie.

She'd set a bag on the edge of the boat and nearly bumped it during the hubbub of unpacking.

"That could have been bad," she acknowledged with a laugh. "My necklace and bracelet were in there—the ones you bought me on our honeymoon."

"Maybe we should leave those at home if we're going on a lake trip," Farrell suggested.

"I know, but then I think, what if we stop somewhere nice to eat on the way back, or if we get invited somewhere. It's happened before; remember when we ran into the Oliphants that time?"

"Yes, but standards are more relaxed at the lake. Nobody would think less of you."

"And nobody would think more of her, either," Helen chimed in. Her logic meant little to the husbands, but they were no longer interested in the debate anyhow and gladly let it go. There was silence until Farrell remembered something.

"Maggie, did you bring that newspaper down?"

"I think so. Look in that bag, right over there." She pointed.

Farrell poked around in the tote before extracting the Sunday edition of the *Sun* and moving to the stern, where Jude was now sitting and sunning himself.

"Thought you'd enjoy seeing this," Farrell said, handing it over.

"I was hoping you would bring it." Jude beamed. "Let's have a look."

Jude had barely begun reading the front page story about the Wagsters, but Farrell couldn't contain himself and began verbally summarizing.

"Pretty good stuff, huh? I guess this Wagster fella has been involved in some other shady dealings before. Works at a tire store, where his pay was cut, so I'm sure he needed the money. There isn't as much about the wife, although she's admitted she has to have her Tingle. Sounds like the paper even talked to her directly."

"I knew they were separated," Jude added without looking up, "but I was still surprised at how they talked about each other in those articles during the week. Got the feeling that maybe there was some simmering dislike that boiled over once this went public."

"They reprinted those articles in the back of that section, including a new one from him. Some really funny stuff between those two. Anyhow, I'm not sure how much credibility they'll have after today."

"Jude," his wife called, "can we stop in at Heron Bay?"

"Hadn't planned on it, but we can. Whatcha need there?"

"I thought we could get some of those yummy milkshakes at that little café ... what's it called?"

"I forget, but I know which one you mean. We already have some tarts, though."

"Hey, watch what you call us," Maggie joked, to everyone's amusement.

"If the shoe fits," Jude teased back.

"We're almost ready," Helen decided. "I just want to finish cleaning this a bit. I thought we cleaned everything well last time."

Jude started to answer but decided it was a rhetorical complaint. The women resumed their efforts, and Farrell leaned toward Jude.

"You do remember that Heron Bay is where Betty and her husband stay, right?"

"Who?"

"Betty. The one who kept calling me at the office last fall after I broke it off."

"Oh, *that* one. Yeah, you need to run into her like you need a kick in the groin."

230

"And she might do it, too—she was a little on the batty side. Husband seems nice, though. I met him once and he seemed afraid of his own shadow."

"Yeah, well, those men are the kind that snap and visit you with a pistol shaking in their hands. I'll see if I can avoid Heron this time, but you've gotta straighten that out by springtime because I can't avoid that place every time we get together."

Farrell nodded and looked out on the lake before changing the subject.

"Hey, what do you think about this Addie Sumner gal?"

"I think there are some muffins best left alone, and she's one of 'em. She's a tall looker, but not one who'd go in for being a side girl."

"No, no, no. I mean from a business standpoint—the inspection. You think she has a real reason for returning Monday?"

"I don't know," Jude reflected. "She strikes me as one of those schoolgirls who sit in the front row and remind the teacher about giving out homework. She probably wouldn't notice something important if it was in front of her, but she'll still issue a forty-three-page report with big words about nothing."

"I say we tell her no more after Monday, and I also think ... well, we'll talk about it later. Looks like they're ready."

Jude moved toward the captain's seat, and Farrell hopped out of the boat and began untying a bumper in preparation for launch.

"What are you looking for?" Jude asked Helen.

"I can't seem to find my sunglasses. Would it be possible ... ?"

28

Addie Sumner knew she'd created an air of curiosity by insisting that she needed to return to Pinwheel on Monday. She'd offered no clue as to what she had missed or what she was pursuing, but she knew that her every move would be watched.

Therefore, Addie decided not to report to Hazel first thing. Instead, she began the day by getting off the elevator at the third floor and proceeding directly to John Ballantyne's office.

It was tempting to burst into John's office as she had done the first time, but Addie decided that scaring him nearly to death again might sabotage his cooperation. So she knocked and waited. Then she knocked again.

"Come in," John finally called from his desk.

"You must have been deep in thought," Addie speculated as she entered and closed the door.

"I never answer the first knock. If it's someone who's lost, they'll usually give up and go away after one knock. And anyone who's above me wouldn't bother to knock," he explained, lifting a mug of coffee to his lips (Pinwheel original with a splash of scotch from his flask).

"For a man working in a closet you're very choosy about the company you keep. Mind if I sit down?"

"Please do. I just assumed we were old friends and it went without saying."

"Old friends because you saw me in the audience Friday night?"

"I guess." He smiled. "Thanks for coming out and listening to us. It wasn't the greatest we've ever sounded, but it was all right. What did you think?"

"Well ... I'm no expert on jazz and I've only seen a few jazz bands in person, but I thought your band sounded wonderful. And I wasn't the only one; there was some spirited dancing happening on the floor. Seemed like everyone was having a good time."

"Yes, all twelve people. Like I warned you, it's one of the smaller clubs and we're still polishing our sound. It takes time to build a following, but those who do like us *really* seem to like us. Anyway, thanks for coming. Sorry we couldn't talk, but it felt good to see you out there, and the fellas were impressed when I told them you were there on account of me."

"I doubt that it's an unusual occurrence for you."

"No, but they all agreed you were the prettiest occurrence."

"Ah, can't say that I don't enjoy the flattery, although it really should be me doing the flattering, since I'm the one who needs information from you."

"Well, I guess I should be happy I got two minutes of fun before you turned to business."

"Sorry about that, but the clock is tickin' for me."

"I know, and let me start by saying I've been thinking about this off and on all weekend. It's a strange situation for me. I've always felt like a musician trapped in the corporate world, meaning I hate to take this job too seriously even though I get paid to do just that. This is the first time my loyalty toward the Pinwheel world has really been put to the test."

"I'm sorry if I've placed you at a crossroads," Addie apologized.

"More like you're sorry for my angst at being placed there."

"Yeah, that's probably truer."

"Well, either way, you don't need to feel sorry. It's actually been helpful, I guess you'd say, having to really assess what's important to me. Not that I've discovered anything earth-shattering about my ethics or whatever it is that I'm battling. Most people, if they're being honest with themselves, will admit they can't in good conscience take the paycheck and at the same time scoff at being loyal to the company. Then again, maybe you could argue that your time and effort are enough to satisfy the bargain and the loyalty is earned extra. See what I mean about battling?"

"I do, and normally I'd let it go, but I have a job of my own ... "

"And that job is to get me to share a company secret."

"Yes, but I'm not saying whether I would share it with anyone. I just need to know if it involves something connected specifically to the purpose of my mission."

"And if it is, what then? You've found the prize but can't tell anyone about it? That's my dilemma, deciding whether to open Pandora's box for you."

"Perhaps I could tell you what I'm looking for, and you could tell me if I'm hot or cold."

"I read the papers, and I already know what you're looking for, and this secret is both hot *and* cold. It would give you an answer, but not the one you expect, and then I'd have to trust you wouldn't use your answer to harm the company just so you can show off your inspection skills."

Addie was silent, so he continued.

"I went as far as actually talking to my retired friend last night. He filled me in on some of the story. I didn't tell him why I was asking, and part of the reason was because I wasn't sure if I would share the information with you or not."

"I don't know if this will affect your decision," she conceded, "but I spent several hours at the library Saturday and found a single mention of Drutoa. It was by luck; I was looking through the index of an old book that led me to an old version of a map. So actually it was two mentions of Drutoa, the second being on the old map of Kamerun when it was a German colony. When I looked at more modern maps of what is now British Cameroon, I didn't find Drutoa in the same spot."

"That's because it's a very small place," John explained. "And today it's considered more of a nickname for a part of that small area."

"So your Drutoa—the company's, I should say—really is a place in the Cameroons?"

"It really is."

"And what is its significance, or is that the part you're not going to tell me?"

"Let me put it this way: It's not my fault that you overheard mention of Drutoa or that you spent the weekend in the library, but it would be my fault if you went back to the *Sun* and let them use their resources to discover the truth and print it. I'll just have to trust that you don't destroy my attempt at loyalty."

Addie didn't answer. She wanted to promise him she would not share the secret, but this was the moment in the game when you had to act like you held the better cards. The final call was his.

"I don't know every detail," he began, "but here is how I heard it: Near the end of the war Farrell O'Bryant became friends with a British soldier who at one time had been stationed at a prison camp that held German soldiers. Somehow the British fella learned from one of the prisoners about a place deep in the western part of Kamerun where his German patrol had stopped before the war. It was barely a town, really, more a collection of farms with a shared meeting area. Anyhow, this meeting area included a café of sorts that served coffee using the local beans, and the men in the patrol were amazed at what they drank. Apparently, through decades of experimenting and cross-breeding, these little farms along this one area had developed a strain of Robusta beans that not only contained large amounts of natural caffeine but had a taste rivaling Arabica beans. In other words, a bean that yielded the best of both properties without any trade-off."

"Ah ha."

" 'Ah ha' is right. O'Bryant was already looking for a postwar business he could start, and coffee was one of the products he was considering. When he heard about these perfect beans, he had his angle: good-tasting coffee that would knock your socks off. After the war he traveled to Drutoa and made a deal for exclusive rights to their beans."

"Why the secret then, if he has the rights?"

"Because it's the cornerstone of this company and he wants to minimize the odds of funny business from the competition. I'm no expert on international rights or patenting bean species or what have you, but if someone like Blue Checkered worked hard enough they could find a way. Maybe they already know something through corporate espionage."

"Darn, I should have paid more attention to those bags in the offload warehouse. I can vaguely remember them having things stamped on them, but I didn't think to study them."

"I don't think they say Drutoa exactly, but they may offer a clue of some sort. Like I said, I don't know all the details, but there's a small Pinwheel office down there—operating under a nondescript name—and their whole purpose is to muddy the waters. They bribe officials, mislabel things, and keep an eye out for visitors. It's like a coffee spy ring from what I've heard. I've also heard that those beans are being grown somewhere else on a much bigger scale, and *that* operation is even more clandestine. For all I know Drutoa is nothing but a red herring now—or always was. Something designed to confuse the competition."

"How does he know the other soldiers won't talk, or any of the people who have heard their story?"

"Maybe he doesn't. All he can do is limit what he can limit."

"It seems like it would be common knowledge by now if every employee knew."

"Exactly. Only a very few are supposed to know, and that's only so they're aware to stop it in its tracks if it were to leak or be questioned. The man who told me had his reasons, and even then he only gave me a hint while he was still working here. There may be others like me—nobodies at the bottom who know fragments—but I imagine it's awfully rare."

"So, in other words, I got lucky when I ducked into your closet on Friday."

"Somewhat. You were already curious about the word 'Drutoa' and you've gained a bit of knowledge on your own. Who knows where it would have led had you mentioned the name to O'Bryant or the *Sun*."

"You sound convinced that I won't."

"You kinda get to know a gal by the third un-date."

"Is that what we're calling our meetings now, un-dates?"

"I'm ready to change them to real dates when you are."

"Wow, you really are full of assumptions this morning."

"So, is that a yes?"

"It's an un-yes. I need to finish this inspection professionally, and then we'll see. Maybe I'll show up at another one of your performances some evening."

"They're called 'sets,' and we play them at night. If you're gonna get involved with a jazz musician you're gonna have to learn the lingo."

"Oh, so now it's getting involved?" She scolded him with a shake of her head. "Don't count your notes before they're played."

They both laughed.

I'll say this much," Addie continued. "You've really helped me today, and that means a lot. Of all the under book trumpet players in the world, you must be the best."

"You got that right, sister. And your next chance to catch me is at the Fatted Pig, we're playin' there all next week."

Addie stood up and gave John a single wave of the hand.

"See ya later," she said.

"Bye, Addie."

29

Deacon grumbled when the phone rang, and he laid down the paper he was reading.

"This is Deacon."

"Hi Deacon, it's Addie. I was hoping to catch you before lunch."

"And I was just wondering what you've learned on your end. I'm sitting here looking at some results that just arrived from that lab in Chicago—the one studying Pinwheel's coffee."

"Finally. What does it say?"

"Says there is nothing 'unnatural' added as far as they can tell. Really high levels of caffeine, though. They tested some other brands also—to get a feel for normal—and apparently Pinwheel blows the rest of 'em out of the water where it comes to caffeine. Says here that 'due to time constraint and scope of sample we are unable to explain the abnormally high doses of caffeine found in the Pinwheel product submitted, but because no other significant foreign trace items were revealed, it is our current assumption that the high dosage occurred naturally. Further studies involving different stages of bean growth as well as factors such as growing process, habitat, harvesting, separating, and shipping would be necessary to learn more.' From there it goes on and on with a bunch of scientific jargon trying to justify why they don't know everything on God's green earth. From what I can gather, which is about half of it, there is nothing chemically addictive, just a load of caffeine."

"Did they test all of Pinwheel's products or just Tingle?"

"All of 'em, and the result for each is similar."

"Well, that pretty well answers your question, doesn't it? That explains why people love the product."

"Not completely," Deacon argued. "That report is a big piece of the puzzle, but even the lab admits to some uncertainty, even if it's a shred. And beyond that question, we still don't know if the lawsuit is for real or not, or who is behind it. Well, anyhow, enough of that. You called me."

"I was just going to let you know that I finished my inspection," Addie informed him. "I haven't talked to the owners yet, and I'll be submitting an official report later, but I wanted to let you know where we stood unofficially."

"And?"

"I don't have much, really, at least in the way of something that would make Pinwheel look bad. Definitely no adding of chemicals or agents that I could find. Their process is efficient, and the cleanliness is unimpeachable in the places where it needs to be. The employees seem happy, the owners seem happy, and everyone is busy. I couldn't find one single item that gave me legitimate pause."

"Hmm, I can't say that I'm surprised to hear that. They've always seemed like a top notch outfit. I've only been there a couple of times, but what little I saw matches what you just described. Well, I guess that's a dead end as far as conspiracy is concerned. When do you think you'll have that final written report?"

"Sometime tomorrow. I've already been working on it in the evenings and there won't be much to add. I'll have a copy typed up and then I'll give one to the owners and one to you—with their permission, of course."

"That shouldn't be an issue. We had an understanding going into this. Give me a call ahead of time so we can meet up when you deliver it; I might have some more questions. Plus I'd like to spend a few minutes getting to know you better, and I'm positive Emma would too. We're both impressed with the way you conduct business."

"You're too kind, Deacon. But if anyone is impressive, it's you. I've been enjoying the *Sun* since I was a little girl."

"Now you're making me feel old," he groused good-naturedly. "Talk to you tomorrow, Addie."

"Thank you, Deacon. Bye now."

"Uh, huh. Bye."

Deacon folded his arms and considered what he'd learned so far that morning. Earlier, Koenig had called and said that Paul Wagster hadn't left his house. On a hunch, Koenig checked with the tire shop and was told that Wagster had called in sick. That made sense. Yesterday's exposé in the Sunday edition had probably panicked Wagster, causing him to hunker down and regroup. Or maybe his lawyer or the *Daily Mercury* had instructed him to lie low. Or Exlee.

Deacon briefly thought about sending the lab results to the composing room but decided to wait for Addie's report. The two items would be more powerful as a team. Plus he had a feeling something more dramatic would emerge before the day was over.

30

Exlee usually started his work days in Arraignment Alley and then worked his way uptown, where he could deliver material to the non-*Sun* newspapers then leave himself positioned for the nightlife circuit. Today he was working in reverse. He needed to visit the *Daily Mercury* early and the *Sun* later, which meant having breakfast/lunch at Mud's, his uptown spot for starting the day. But when he got to Mud's, there was a sign on the door indicating they were closed due to a death in the family.

The sunlight was such that he had to squint to look inside, hoping against hope it was business as usual and they had forgotten to take the sign down. No such luck. The joint was empty, although Exlee suspected it was not without a mouse or two looking for crumbs. Mud wasn't exactly fastidious in his cleaning and counted on the power of his continual cigar smoke to dissuade the less ambitious pests.

Thwarted but still hungry, Exlee thought about heading west toward the uptown hub of eateries, but decided instead to expand his horizons. He chose the area east of the Hupmobile dealership at the corner of Twenty-First and Ulster. The first three blocks of exploring yielded nothing in the way of food, however. It was mostly drab little repair shops and secondhand stores squeezed between boarding houses that had been mansions at some point in the city's history. Exlee was about to give up on his misguided adventure when he spotted the Royale Hotel. He was fascinated by its faded majesty and drew closer for a better look. The hotel wasn't particularly large, but it was beautifully designed, with a dramatic front entrance. Exlee guessed that this had been an opulent establishment during the turn of the century. The fancy stone planters that lined its walkway were now cracked, and they held small plants in various stages of ill health, but he could imagine lush topiaries in the hotel's heyday.

He backed into the street for a fuller view, occasionally scanning the roadway for cars but half expecting to see horse-drawn carriages. During one of these safety scans, he took the additional step of looking directly behind him and was pleasantly surprised to discover a bar called the Haymaker.

Thinking he might have found food in some form, Exlee abandoned his wistful hotel viewing and crossed the street to a bar whose glory had also faded. Even the neon sign in the window struggled to declare her name properly, the letter M continually sputtering.

It was more of the same inside: Expensive fixtures were scratched and tarnished. The green leather seat covers each bore at least one strip of tape that someone had colored to match the original shade but had just barely failed in the attempt. Still, Exlee felt good about the place. Her appearance had slipped but her charm was still evident.

The bartender was nowhere to be seen, so Exlee took a seat on the nearest barstool and looked around as he waited. There was a definite boxing theme among the wall's adornments. There were photos of boxers in pugilistic poses—their expressions a curious mixture of fearsome and friendly—old placards promoting local fights, and even two sets of boxing gloves, which had been signed and hung on facing walls.

"Hi, there. I was doing some work in back and didn't hear you," the bartender said. He was close to sixty—short, wide, and balding, with a shock of graying chest hair at his open collar.

"Not to worry," Exlee returned, "I was just in the neighborhood and noticed this nice-looking establishment. Thought I'd stop in and see if you served food by chance."

"Not normally, no, especially this time of day, but I can fix you up with enough to keep you alive until supper. You like grapes?"

"Sure."

"My wife packs me a supper each day and always adds grapes no matter how many times I tell her I don't care for 'em. Says they're good for me, but so are a hundred other things I like better. Oh, well. I also have an extra hard-boiled egg and, of course, this being a bar, I have pretzels and Spanish peanuts."

"I hate to raid your lunch and all," Exlee said.

"Nah. Like I said, I don't want the grapes and the egg is extra. Plus I need the company. The first wave of drinkers won't start filtering in for another hour. They start off at Jim Stansbough's place a couple blocks over. He opens early because his kid closes for him. Except for some part-time help, I run this place by myself and focus my hours toward later, when you get a better clientele."

"Well, it really is a nice place. I can't believe I've never been here before."

"I'm in the wrong part of town by a few blocks, but those blocks make all the difference in the world."

"It looks to me like this area used to be a big deal in Stout City."

"It's been a big deal a couple of times. Long ago this is where the wealthy set up their homes. Those boarding houses were owned by some of the city's big names. The white one with the god-awful reddish-pinkish trim was built for Brock Traybur, who co-owned the old SC&E railroad. And the one right next to the hotel was owned by William Jenson Wedlord, the fella that started the department store."

The bartender placed the promised foods in front of Exlee along with a draft beer.

"I was noticing that hotel," Exlee said as he peeled his egg. "Rather pretty lines."

"Yep, that was during a period forty years ago when this area was sort of reborn. They built that hotel on the site of the old Holman home. Ever heard of him?"

"The name sounds familiar."

"Wilford Holman. He was a crooked politician. Crooked as hell. But not here. He did his dirty work in Kansas City, and when the people there finally wised up and decided he might oughta be hanged, he took all his money and moved up here. He was a scrawny fella and his wife was the toughest lookin' piece of beef jerky you can imagine. Anyhow, he eventually sold out to a fella named Florenstien who wanted to take advantage of the former reputation of this area and build a hotel on that site. By that time, the other mansions were falling apart because the seriously rich folks had moved farther out. But Florenstien figured the neighborhood was ripe for revitalizing and so did my uncles, who built this bar shortly after the hotel went up."

"So it's a family bar?"

"My two uncles started it—Eugene and Alexander. Everyone called 'em Gene and Alex. My mother is their youngest sister."

"Neither of the uncles had children interested in running this place?" Exlee asked while popping a grape in his mouth.

"Between them, they had six kids. Two died young and another was killed in the Spanish-American War. There were two girls who married fellas with no interest in the bar business—one was a preacher and the other did something with municipal bonds. That left one boy, but he was never fully engaged, shall we say. A nice fella and all, but not one that could handle any responsibility. He always lived with his folks."

"So you volunteered?"

"Not exactly. I was going to go to college and become a pharmacist, but my father died and we needed money, so my uncles suggested I work with them. They adored my mom, who was the baby of the family, plus they were getting older and needed someone they could trust. It wasn't long before they made me a minor partner, and then I claimed their shares after they each died, with the promise I'd take care of their widow wives—which I did. Been here ever since."

"Went from plans to serve one type of medication to serving another."

"You got it."

"So what's with all the boxing decoration? It's like a museum in here."

"That goes back to the Florenstien fella that built the hotel. Among other things, he was a fight impresario. He was really the one responsible for getting the game organized in Stout City, after the Queensberry rules took hold in the nineties. Naturally, he had a piece of every big card in town, and it was his notoriety that landed the famous heavyweight title fight here—the one between Sharkey and Rogan. Long story short, when Florenstien built his exclusive hotel as an investment, all the big name boxers stayed there on their travels. Their entourages, on the other hand, all stayed at the Stout, which is a couple blocks down Juniper Street and a lot cheaper. The Haymaker was their meeting place, and they'd all get together and raise hell here. Pretty soon anyone with any connection to boxing—or anyone interested in the sport—made this their headquarters for drinking."

"So this place was a real hotspot at one time. Not that it's not great now, it's just ... "

"Don't worry, you ain't offending me. Times change, and there's always a new generation looking to make their own mark. They don't want what their parents wanted, and those parents didn't want what their parents wanted. I still get some old timers from the boxing racket who stop in and I never get tired of their stories, but they're gettin' fewer all the time. I'm only a few blocks away from all the new, exciting joints, but it might as well be fifty miles. There isn't anything I can do about it short of moving, and I'm too old for that. So my wife keeps packing me a little food and I keep opening the doors at noon and making a living. When I die, she'll be the final widow to survive off the place when she sells it."

"I hate the thought of it being sold," Exlee said as he stood up. He moved to the nearest wall and studied a photo of a former bantamweight named Tim Csykanowski. "It just seems like such a jewel. How do you replace a bar with this sort of charm and unique history?"

"I'm not sayin' she'd sell it to the first person looking to demolish it and build a burlesque theatre. There might be some young fella who appreciates history the way you do, but he hasn't come knockin' yet. The wife and I don't have any children of our own and I'm 61, so the clock is tickin'."

As Exlee continued to peruse the walls, the owner began refilling pretzel bowls. In between bowls he sipped on a mug of coffee (Pinwheel original, black).

"Let me ask you something," Exlee said, turning around. "Do you have any sort of special drink you serve, something that your clientele associate with the Haymaker?"

"Well, they say I make a pretty good vodka martini. I can make one up for you if that's what you'd like."

"I'd be honored to try one, but actually what I'm driving at ... you know, I don't think we ever introduced ourselves. My name is Exlee, I'm a press agent."

"Nice to meet you. I'm Perry Hanigan and I own a bar called the Haymaker." They laughed and shook hands. Then Exlee continued.

"So the reason I ask about the drinks is that I have an angle that's succeeded before and thought maybe we could work a deal."

"I'm listening," Perry said as he prepared a vodka martini.

"The fundamentals of the deal are that I would place a good sized article in the paper pertaining to your establishment *and* I would provide you with a gimmick guaranteed to rejuvenate your business. It would be a one-two punch."

Exlee smiled in anticipation of Perry appreciating his boxing term, but Perry was busy absorbing the offer and making a martini all at once.

"What's in it for you?" he asked as he poured the drink and sat it on the bar for Exlee.

"I'm thinking a drink a day for life—yours or mine, whichever ends first—and then, if your business picks up as expected, maybe you could include the occasional monetary note with my visits."

"How big a note?"

"That would be up to you, Perry. I have a good feeling about you and believe you'd choose an honorable amount. In the meantime, I'd suggest that any spare cash should go toward a coat of paint outside and fixing the window sign."

Exlee stepped up to the bar and consumed half of his martini. He swirled it about in his mouth for dramatic effect and then ran his tongue along his teeth as a fabricated test. "That is indeed a good vodka martini, sir."

"Are you serious about what you're saying?" Perry asked. "Not that I don't trust you, but we just met."

"I am serious. And you have nothing to lose because I provide all the upfront goods in this arrangement. If anything, I'm the one who should be dubious, making a deal with a man who dislikes grapes."

Perry laughed. "You definitely talk like a press agent and your terms are more than fair."

"And in good faith, I hereby pay for my martini," Exlee declared, placing a quarter on the bar.

"Forget it," Perry objected as he slid the coin back. "You're the first person who's given me hope in ages, and I'll be damned if there is anything more lovely than hope."

They smiled and shook hands to seal their venture.

"All right, I'll start gathering information for the article in a bit," Exlee said, "but let's start by getting back to the special drink. What I'm looking for is something rare. Something you don't usually make. Maybe it's a request you get from a certain person. It could even be one from years ago."

Perry thought about it as he took the empty martini glass and washed it without looking. "There was a drink that I made years ago for Jasper Kline. He managed a boxer named Otto Gust—a burly son of a gun who could take a beating like you or I would take a nap. It was his one skill, and it's a terrible one to rely on. You aren't good enough to contend at the upper levels and nobody really wants to fight you. What opponent wants to wear themselves out slugging a wall all night only to have it slug you good one time when you have nothing left? Now, what did I start to say?"

"Something about Jasper somebody."

"That's right, Jasper Kline. He was a bit of a dandy, and whenever he was in here he'd order a champagne drink. I can't for the life of me remember what he called it, but it was excellent, especially when the champagne was chilled. The basic ingredients beside champagne were … "

"Whoa, hold on. I don't want to know the specifics, and you don't want to say. Ever. To anyone. Can you make up one right now?"

"Well, I don't remember the exact ratio of ingredients, but I do have a bottle of champagne in the back. Not much call for it with my current crop of boozers. Probably been there for three years and it's not chilled, nor is it a top brand."

Exlee went back to studying the walls—and taking notes this time—while Perry fiddled with his champagne concoction. After a couple misfires, he declared that he had recreated a version of the original and maybe even topped it by accidently adding another ingredient. Exlee tried a portion, closing his eyes to eliminate obtrusive senses. He took a second drink, then a third.

"You know what? That is a seriously good drink," Exlee announced. "If the champagne were chilled, like you said, and if it were a better brand, you'd have a showstopper on your hands. And I already have a name for it: Sharkey's Punch, in honor of the famous bout you mentioned earlier."

"Sounds good to me. Matter of fact, I really like it. The only problem is this isn't the champagne part of town. How are we going to get people in here to order a Sharkey's Punch?"

"By making no mention of it anywhere in this bar and by never suggesting it. It will gain its reputation by word of mouth only."

"Again, I don't mean to doubt you … "

PINWHEEL

"You'll have to trust me on this one. I pulled off the same maneuver using a raspberry tart at a bakery and it's been a huge success. People share the secret of those tarts like they're disclosing the location of the queen's jewels. I'll take care of the word of mouth, and you make sure the outside is painted, the sign fixed, and you have plenty of chilled champagne. And make sure it's good stuff."

"I do have a little money put away, but those dollars were wrung out of this business. I'm not gonna lie when I say it makes me mighty nervous throwing it all at this venture."

"That's the thing with a good gamble, though; being really nervous means the stakes are high, and when those bets work out there is nothing like it. It's even better than hope. What's today, Monday? Okay, starting Friday you will receive customers asking for a Sharkey's Punch. That gives you four days until your hope turns into reality, and all you have to do is fix a couple things and buy some cases of champagne. I'll do the rest. And when I walk in here next Monday morning, I will not bring up how nervous you were. We'll simply smile at each other and then you can make my free Sharkey's Punch."

"You win," Perry conceded happily.

"And you will too. Oh, and look for the newspaper article this weekend, although I'm not sure which paper yet. I'll bring a copy Monday just in case."

The two men shook hands one more time and then Exlee was gone.

31

Deacon walked into Emma's office and sat down. It was 4:05 in the afternoon.

"Whatcha working on?" he asked.

"That ironworkers strike—it just took a turn for the strange. Apparently the half who voted against the strike are now picketing their own union headquarters. Frazone called it in and Yun just gave me the rewrite."

"That reminds me. I just sent Alsop down to the Metro Exchange Bank in Tuttle Heights. Got a tip saying they'd closed their doors."

"Another one?"

"Yeah, there won't be any left if this keeps up."

"Heard any more about the Pinwheel episode? Seems awfully quiet the day after running such a big piece on it. I was expecting just the opposite reaction—thought there'd be some fireworks or at least Exlee rushing in here trying to put a new spin on things."

Deacon chuckled. "I like that—putting a new spin on Pinwheel."

"Clever, huh? Wish I could take credit, but my mind doesn't work that way."

"I don't know. I've always found your humor to be rather clever. It was one of the first things that made me realize we'd work well together. There were some other things that can't be easily defined, but you had all of them."

She smiled but didn't answer.

"You never like compliments, do you?" he asked.

"I don't know what to do with them. I got used to not needing them when I was growing up ... "

"Wait. That's funny that you would say you didn't need them. Everybody needs them. What you really mean is you got used to doing without them."

"Don't you start analyzing me, mister. I'm a content person and I ask for nothing, whether you think that's a strength or a weakness."

"Hold on just a minute, Emma. I never said there was anything wrong with you. I was just making an observation about you not liking compliments the same way I'd mention you hating tomatoes."

"Yes, but you'd like to change the first one. You think if I accept compliments then maybe I'd feel better about myself, which is making the assumption that I don't already. We both know you're wrong about such an assumption. It smacks of pity, and I can't stand pity."

"Listen, I don't know what in the world I have stepped into, but please take note that I am now stepping back out, all right? Let's just leave it at you having a clever sense of humor."

"Thank you."

"See, that's all you had to say."

"From now on I will consult you on proper reaction to things involving me."

"See, now that's funny. And clever."

Emma's phone rang but she hesitated, wondering if Deacon had anything else to say. He didn't, so she answered the phone and he left.

Ten minutes later he was back, holding an opened envelope and a letter.

"Exlee dropped this off downstairs," he announced. "Says the Wagsters have left town and the Pinwheel lawsuit appears to be dead for now."

"Unbelievable, and yet, why am I not surprised?"

"Oh, and you'll like this. He enclosed a final statement from Vivian Wagster."

"Let's hear it."

"I'll read it to you word for word: 'I wish to ask the great citizens of Stout City for their forgiveness. Paul and I have foolishly aired our dirty laundry over the past week and brought shame on this fair city. Couples have difficulties from time to time, and we are no different. Sadly, our silly debate about how much I love Tingle coffee was used as the reason for our troubles, and you, the readers, had to hear a lot more after that. The truth is I love Tingle but we love each other more and have decided that in order to keep that love alive, we must start over. That means we have moved away. It would be swell if we could come back here someday to this fair city, but only time will tell. Please forgive us for our public argument and please don't hold any grudge against Pinwheel. It's true that Tingle is almost as good as whoopee, but that's a good thing, and I'm not ashamed to admit it. I'll drink it wherever we go. Good-bye, Stout City, I hope to see you again someday.' "

Emma chuckled. "Almost as good as whoopee, huh? I guess that'll be the new slogan on every can."

"If they're smart it will be."

They smiled at each other, sharing the same unspoken thought about the whimsical nature of life.

"Well, I guess it's back to the standard civic nonsense for us," Deacon said.

"Don't be sad. It won't be long until the next thing comes along and threatens the *Sun*'s survival."

"Thanks, I feel so much better." He laughed.

"My pleasure."

"By the way, you like how Exlee finds a way to meet us face to face when he needs something, but does a hit and run when the game is over?" Deacon asked.

"He probably wants to devote his valuable time to gambling and skirt chasing now that he's done with such a taxing job."

"You've got a good point there. Say, I'm gonna run this Vivian letter over to Melton and have him write up a nice companion piece outlining the Wagsters' tiff and then let Timmerman know both items need to be in tomorrow's bulldog edition."

"Sounds good."

"And after that I'm gonna go down the street and have an ice cold beer to celebrate surviving this mess."

"Sounds even better."

"And I'm thinking maybe you should join me since we rode out the storm together."

She smiled a contented smile. "I'll be here when you're ready."

32

A week went by, and Deacon had almost forgotten about the Pinwheel situation when he ran into Exlee at Aronoff's.

"I thought maybe you took off with the Wagsters," Deacon said as he sat down and ordered an orangeade.

"Nah, I didn't feel like spending a whole trip in the backseat."

"Hotel situation might have gotten awkward, as well."

"For who?" He laughed.

Deacon's orangeade arrived, and he took his time with the first sip then chewed on an ice cube.

"So, you doing all your business with the other papers now?" Deacon asked.

"I have to spread the love after giving you the exclusive on the Pinwheel lawsuit. Can't afford to alienate anyone who might throw me a dollar."

"I suppose so. And I should add that despite the hell you put us through last week, we'd still be willing to throw you a dollar for good material."

"Oh, so now it has to be good material."

The two men laughed again, and Exlee watched out of the corner of his eye as the editor enjoyed some more of his refreshment.

"Listen, Deacon, the reason I've been waiting for you is that I wanted to explain something about last week."

"You don't owe me any explanations, you know that. It's the business we're in, and tomorrow I'll try to leverage you for my own purposes."

"It's not necessarily my part I was going to explain.... Actually, it'd be better if we did this at the dry cleaners."

Deacon sighed at this news and left Exlee standing and waiting while he slowly finished his orangeade. He didn't like to be hustled into hideaways, and he didn't like being the one catching up on the news.

"I can never decide if I love or hate that sweet smell," Deacon confided as they walked past the rows of clothes hanging in the back of the dry cleaners.

"That's the perchloroethylene. They call it perc for short, and it's the main solvent used for the cleaning."

"Maybe you should change your career and become a tour guide for the downtown businesses."

"That's not a bad idea," Exlee agreed. "People are curious about how things work, and I bet the stores would pay a little to be included for promotional purposes. You could even double up by collecting a tour fee from the customers. The cherry on top might be merchants offering coupons for discounts that would equal the customer's tour fee. Everybody wins."

"Especially you. And that doesn't even include collecting phone numbers from the customers and circling those belonging to the women you fancy."

"I hadn't even thought of that, you old dog."

"The heck you hadn't. Now tell me what you have to say so I can get back to slingin' the real news."

Their seating arrangement was identical to that of the last visit—Deacon in a chair and Exlee on the edge of the desk. To Deacon's surprise, the young press agent seemed ill at ease, maybe even embarrassed as he looked around the room trying to choose his words.

"So, this whole Pinwheel deal ... " Exlee started. Then he stopped and thought some more. "Okay, I don't know how to properly frame this discussion, so I'll just come right out and say that technically ... no, that's not right either ... "

"If it was you who caused the stock market crash in '29, then just say so," Deacon kidded.

"That's for another day," Exlee returned half-heartedly. "What I'm trying to say is that Pinwheel was basically threating to sue themselves."

"What did you say?"

"You heard me right. Pinwheel was going to sue themselves—for the publicity. I don't mean that the public would have ever known, but that's the fundamental concept behind last week's shenanigans."

Deacon smiled and shook his head. "I should have seen that one as it unfolded. It was right in front of me the whole time, and the worst part is I heard about a stunt like this one. Back around 1850 or so, P.T. Barnum, of circus fame, supposedly arranged to have his sideshow bearded lady sued on the grounds that she wasn't really a female. The case was ultimately dismissed, but you can imagine the interest in the bearded lady after that."

"Maybe that was the inspiration for the Pinwheel idea."

"Could be. It was a long time ago, but people in the news business or history buffs like me know about it. And I'm both, dangit. That's what makes it so embarrassing. So tell me some of the details. Did Pinwheel contact the Wagsters directly?"

"No, an underhanded scheme this big requires any number of lawyers. And before I say any more, I should point out that I can only tell you what I've been told—and I only got that much as a courtesy for doing my part well."

"And now you are extending that same courtesy to me."

"You sound a little cynical about it."

"No, the shoe just feels funny on the other foot. Anyhow, you were telling me about lawyers."

"I don't know if Pinwheel maneuvered it through their legal department or if they used one of their outside firms, but someone from the upper layer contacted someone from Arraignment Alley. I was brought in by Wickenstaff, who brought in Spencer, but they may have been chosen by another of the dubious attorneys I represent or directly by a Pinwheel lawyer. For enough money those guys would set aside any differences and conspire to bilk a church out of its communion wine."

"What about the Wagsters? How'd they get involved?"

"I actually know part of that answer. It was through a bankruptcy meeting between them and one of my lowbrow lawyers. That was how they pegged the couple for needing money, anyhow. Not sure how they knew Paul would play ball, except that he's known in some small circles for a willingness to misbehave."

"What about the coffee part? Emma seemed to think that the wife really was devoted to her Tingle."

"You got me there. Don't know if it came up in conversation or if Paul started buying it for her or if she was actively involved in twisting things. For all I know, she really does love the stuff in a big way. Matter of fact, I recall her saying so, but she might be a good actress."

"You should know, you've auditioned enough of 'em."

"I appreciate the sentiment, but actresses are too exhausting," Exlee confided.

"So you were responsible for those items we ran—you actually spent time with the Wagsters and wrote the pieces?"

"That was my slice of the pie, yes. Started off, I was supposed to get quotes from each of them mentioning how much she loved Tingle since that was the main angle—promoting Tingle. But those two opened up so easily and had so much to say about each other I couldn't help but package the pieces a little different and create sort of a humorous little saga, if you will."

"Well, you certainly accomplished that feat." Deacon smiled. "I think it was half the reason the wire services played it up and got it spread across the country. Pinwheel must be mighty pleased with you."

"Yes and no, I guess. It sounds like this thing was supposed to be strung out longer, but Pinwheel got cold feet when the Wagsters started bickering in such a public fashion. All of a sudden Pinwheel started imagining those two splitting up and confessing their role in the lawsuit scheme just as publicly."

"When you say 'strung out,' do you mean an actual lawsuit was part of the plan?"

"Yeah, I think that was the original plan. Not sure if they were banking on a dismissal like the Barnum suit you mentioned, but it would have added a huge measure of publicity—a court case about a woman wanting coffee more than sex. Again, I'm guessing, but if the case had made it to trial it wouldn't have lasted too long until an out-of-court settlement was reached, if you know what I mean. In a sense, that's what happened anyhow. The Wagsters left town a little richer."

"What I can't get over is that Ostwald and O'Brien played me on the phone," Deacon lamented. "I'm not sure they've ever done that before, and I don't know what to think. I'm used to some madness—you and I just finished some, with no hurt feelings—but this is coming from the firm that I helped get on its feet."

"Ah, I'm sure they were having fun. Not every day an executive gets to join in the madness, as you call it.

Whether they actually confess their role is a good question, but either way you have to feel pleased that you and the *Sun* got exclusive coverage. And as a bonus, those chiselers at the *Daily Mercury* made themselves look foolish for mocking the *Sun*."

"I assume, by the way, that this is all off the record."

"I'm afraid so. There's nothing to stop you from talking—and I'm sure rumors will surface—but if you're smart you'll just let it go and enjoy the rewards: new readers and new respect from a major advertiser."

"Listen to you lecturing me. I've been in this racket long enough to know when I see something and when I don't. I'm not saying you couldn't teach me a trick or two, but don't ever forget you need me more than I need you."

"Shoot, Deacon, I know that. The reason I'm telling you what I know is because I trust you and I always want you to trust me. You know how much I admire you."

"Well, now you're making me feel bad," Deacon admitted. "The truth is I wasn't trusting you much last week. I'll even go so far as to confess that Emma and I had a strong suspicion that you'd joined forces with the *Daily Mercury* in order to damage the *Sun*."

"First of all, that's not a bad plan. Make the *Sun* easier to buy when it toppled, eh?"

"Mm hm."

"Second of all, I'd never cozy up to those jelly beans. They might rule the roost as far as size, but you and Emma are family—or close to family as it gets in a job where you're always pushing agendas and chasing rumors."

"That, my boy, is the definition of family."

Exlee laughed. "Now let me add one last point. I spent extra time at the *Daily Mercury* that week, trying to hold them off from joining the Pinwheel hunt. I convinced them I was only following orders, and that I thought the lawsuit was bogus and the *Sun* was making a fool of itself. That's why they got so cocky with their little editorials against you. It's taken me the week since to assure them I knew nothing."

"You didn't owe me an explanation, but I thank you. Emma will be relieved to hear it."

"Speaking of Emma, didn't you say something about taking her out on a real date once the Pinwheel scare went away?"

"I did not say 'date,' and for your information we had a beer after work last week. So you can stop playin' Cupid now."

"A beer after work? Nope, I'm sorry, but Cupid still has some work to do. Tell me one thing honestly, then I'll leave you alone. What is holding you back from getting serious about Emma?"

Deacon was silent as he decided whether to answer the question directly. The line between mentor and friend was already feeling blurry enough.

"I can't do it to Emma," he finally confessed. "If she and I were in a romantic relationship, it would wreck the dynamic we have at the *Sun*. We'd lose respect in the newsroom, *if* management didn't act first. And Emma would take the brunt of it. That's just the way it would unfold, and I can't do that do her."

"Yeah, I see what you're saying. I hadn't fully considered it from that angle. There is a big difference between seeming married and being married. But listen, you really should talk about this with her first; give her an equal opinion, like you do with everything at work. Not saying it would change anything, but you need to explore the whole package together since it's not fair that you assume things for her."

"There you go lecturing me again ... only this time I needed to hear it. You know what? You win. I'll come into the city Sunday night and take her to dinner if she agrees. How about that?"

"Sunday night is a nice touch; making a special effort instead of tacking it on to work."

"Good. Now that you approve, I can get back to work. Thanks for letting me in on the Pinwheel story, though. I still can't believe I missed that old P.T. Barnum trick—even played my role in it like a trained animal."

"Sometimes a gamble works and sometimes it doesn't. In this case, everybody won."

"We did sell more papers, I can't deny that," Deacon admitted as he moved toward the door. "See you later, Exlee."

"See ya."

33

After stopping outside to chat with Ed the doorman, Exlee strolled into The Golden Goose nightclub. He paused at the coat check room and waited for the girl to finish with two customers.

"It's a little cold out tonight," Exlee said after the customers had left. "You might be busier than usual."

"Maybe." The coat check girl agreed without expression.

"Whoa, it's a little cold inside, too. But I guess that's my own fault."

She turned away and hung up a coat, then returned and scribbled a number in her claim book.

"Can we talk for a minute, Dora?"

"Sure, I've got a minute."

"Listen, I just wanted to apologize about the other night. I'm not usually a big drinker, but I'd had a lot that evening—started early and it just snowballed."

"I didn't mind that so much," she admitted. "You were actually very funny. And believe me, I see a lot of drunks while doing this job. It's a miracle if I go fifteen minutes without being propositioned. Sometimes it's with the fella's girl standing right next to him. But I never go in for that sorta thing. I'm not the prettiest girl in the city but I'm pretty enough, and young. And available."

"That you are, and that's part ... "

"Hold on, I'm not finished yet. A fella has some drinks and he's feeling good, it's only natural to want a girl like me who seems available. I don't take no offense, its part of the job and this ain't my first such job. I did this at a couple clubs in Chicago for over a year. Anyhow, I thought you'd be different. The first night we met you helped that poor gal home and after that we had some nice conversations whenever you came in. You always smell nice, and I can tell you're smarter than most of the crumbs I meet in here. I wasn't sure if you wanted me, but I kind of hoped you did; only I was hoping it would be in a more romantic way."

Two more customers stopped on their way inside. A husband and wife. He handed over his overcoat and she surrendered her full-length mink. Dora handed them tickets, scribbled in her book, and hung up the coats.

"I apologize for pushing so fast the other night, I really do," Exlee said. "Like I said, I was a little drunk, and that cute nose of yours ... "

"Do you remember what you told me? You said that of the seventeen girls you'd known who worked coat check here, I was the second most desirable. But then you never told me who number one was."

"Well, since I'm already confessing to being a rat, I'll just tell you that there is no real number one. It's just a line I use to get a girl curious, and then some of them get this weird competitive streak where they want to prove they are the most desirable, and naturally that sort of effort suits my purposes. The key, of course, is the ambiguity of the term 'desirable.' I leave that to their imagination for faster results."

"That's terrible."

"It absolutely is, and where it comes to you specifically, I was being a dope who wanted to forget about something and I chose you, and that wasn't fair. I was completely in the wrong and you deserve better."

"What did you want to forget about? A girlfriend?"

"She used to be a girlfriend. We hadn't really spent time together since it ended, and then that Friday we talked, and I guess it played tricks with my head. I don't know if I was trying to forget her or punish her or punish myself or what. Either way, I ended up trying to use you, and I feel bad about that."

Curious as to why Dora kept glancing over his shoulder, Exlee turned to see a foursome waiting to leave their coats.

"I better let you get back to business," Exlee said in a lowered voice. "Again, I apologize and hope we can still be friends."

"Thank you for being so honest about everything. And for your information, of all the men I've met in this nightclub, you are the fourth most desirable."

"Fourth? See, that seems too far back in the rankings, possibly insurmountable. You gotta stick with second or third if you want someone to make an effort toward changing your mind."

"Who said I was playing your game?"

Exlee chuckled. "You're not just a cute nose. See you later."

She smiled at him for an instant then turned her attention to the patient foursome.

Exlee continued inside and took a seat at the end of the bar, where he could observe the crowd. He was still scanning the far side when Billy appeared with a glass of beer.

"Exlee Ellis, you're a little early, aren't you?"

"I couldn't wait to see you, Billy. There's just something about you."

"It's the way I deliver you beer and help with your gambling transactions."

"Transactions you take a cut from."

"Possibly. Here's what's left of a bet you won from Charlie G."

PINWHEEL

Billy pulled out a small roll of bills from his pocket, and after pausing to think, he peeled off three five dollar bills and laid them on the bar.

Exlee gave the bartender a wry smile. "I'd feel like you weren't cheating me so bad if you'd at least keep something written or if you kept my winnings separate."

"It's no use trying to keep exact track. Even my wife steals a couple bills every morning while I'm sleeping."

"It never ends, does it? I wonder who skims off of her dough."

"Probably the grocer, but I'm just glad he's satisfied with money if you know what I mean."

"Be careful. If the depression gets any worse, you may have to do the honorable thing by stepping in and satisfying the grocer."

"You flatter me, Exlee."

Billy departed to take care of other customers, and Exlee resumed his people watching. His gaze fell on a couple near the wall, and he laughed softly. It was Deacon and Emma.

Just as Deacon had promised, he'd talked Emma into their first date. And as expected from two people who hadn't dated in decades, they were dressed quite formally, as though they'd stopped off following a funeral. And the way they sat there silently, watching other couples swing dance, made it seem like the funeral had killed their spirit.

Exlee knew better, though. He knew they were fish out of water, trying too hard to avoid newspaper talk and not remembering how to do date talk. Had he not cared for them, he'd have sat back and enjoyed their awkward show to the bitter end, but Exlee adored them, and that required action.

"You two going undercover to expose some corrupt Lindy Hoppers?" he asked upon arriving at their table.

"What are you doing here, Exlee?" Emma exclaimed.

"I told you there was no club safe from him," Deacon said to his date.

"And why would you want to be safe from me? I thought I added spice to your lives," Exlee argued.

"Too much spice, if you ask me," Emma teased. "Deacon shared the details of that Pinwheel mess you foisted on us."

"A mess that made everyone happy," Exlee declared. "He's just upset because he already knew the Madame Clofullia backstory but didn't connect the two."

"Madame who?" Emma asked.

"Madame Clofullia," Deacon interjected. "She was the bearded lady I was telling you about. The one Barnum arranged to have sued for publicity."

"Oh, that one," she said before turning back to Exlee. "And yes, he has complained multiple times about missing the connection between her and the Pinwheel story. But I keep telling him it's probably coincidence—the two episodes are separated by ... how many years?"

"Eighty. It happened in 1850 something," Deacon answered.

"That is a very long time, and I know you pride yourself on knowing history, Deacon, but nobody can connect every dot, especially when they are so far apart timewise."

"The time part is immaterial. It's the brazenness of the ploy that should make it stand out," Deacon explained.

"Hold on," Exlee interrupted. "For one thing, you don't know how this Pinwheel thing started. It may be coincidence, just like Emma said. Second of all, you two don't need to be debating news items. You do that every day. You need to spend this, uh, date getting to know each other—learning stuff you don't talk about at work. And for starters, you need to be drinking something better than Tingle and ... what is that, ice water? Unbelievable. I'll be right back."

Exlee left them and headed straight to the bar.

"He's right, we shouldn't talk about news if we can help it," Emma said when they were alone.

"We weren't, until he came along and started it. And frankly I'm tired of agreeing with him on things. I used to be like a father to him when he first started; I showed him the ropes and kept him from making mistakes with the other papers. We bonded, and even though I have never figured him out completely, I still feel like I should be the father in this arrangement, but lately he seems to have assumed the role. How did this happen?"

"Not on purpose, I'm sure. The Pinwheel episode just knocked you two out of balance, that's all. And I'm sure you're seeing things differently now that you've started looking for it. That's how it always works. You buy a blue car and suddenly there are more blue cars on the street than you remember."

"But it's bigger than just Exlee. There was a time when Jude Ostwald and Farrell O'Bryant needed my help. They were so grateful when I helped them early on, you'd have thought I was one of the twelve disciples. But now they're using me like a roulette wheel. Let's spin old Deacon around and see where the ball lands. They even had the nerve to play me along on the phone. It was like a big Broadway play and everyone had a script but us. I'm not mad at anyone—heck, you and I have pulled off some pretty impressive stunts—but maybe I'm getting tired of the stunt business, especially now that I'm the one who's older and stunted."

"Very clever, but not true. You don't give us enough credit for still running a top notch local desk."

"You still do, but not me. I'm telling you, I've been feeling ... I don't know ... less sharp lately, and this Pinwheel deal has shone a light on my faltering ways. The father is losing ground to his adopted sons."

"That's bound to happen, and you should be proud of them not only for flourishing with your lessons but for continuing to include you. Both Pinwheel and Exlee gave all the action to the *Sun,* and that was out of respect and admiration for you, Deacon. In a way, those men were honoring you."

"And you too, Emma. We're a team, and when I talk to those fellas they tell me how much they admire you. You can't imagine how proud that makes me feel and how important it is to have your loyalty while I feel my edge slipping away. The truth of the matter is, if there's one thing that really keeps me going, it's trying to show off for you."

Emma fought a wave of emotion. Deacon didn't make it any easier, extending his hand across the table to hers and gently holding the tips of her fingers with his.

"I like when you show off," she said tenderly. "And I bet if you wanted to, you could show those adopted sons some angles they never even dreamed about."

"I don't know about that," he said. "They're a formidable combination of clever and devious. But I will let you in on something; I wasn't going to tell you until later, but now you've inspired me to show off a little, so I will. You know how Exlee just mentioned Madame Clofullia?"

"Uh huh."

"Well, I never mentioned that name to him. Just called her the bearded lady, same as I did when I told you the story. It was a conscious decision on both counts because I didn't wanna muddle the simple story with unneeded facts. You know better than anyone that I can get a little carried away when talking history. I know for a fact I didn't mention Madame Clofullia by name, and it has me curious."

"Perhaps he looked up details at the library after you talked or even asked someone about it," Emma said. "Although, now that I think about it, the few people who could recall the bearded lady story probably wouldn't recall her name like you did. And her contemporaries are all dead."

"Exactly. I'd be willing to bet there are very few people in this city that could name her off the top of their head. You've probably already figured out what I'm thinking."

"That Exlee was already familiar with the story?"

"And?"

"And ... let me think." She paused. "Wait a minute, are you saying Exlee introduced the idea to Pinwheel—that he instigated the scheme *and* played a part in it?"

"That's pretty close, but I don't think you're giving Exlee enough credit. I think his full knowledge of the scheme really *is* limited, and he helped set it up that way. Neither he, nor those Pinwheel maniacs, nor the hired lawyers, nor even the Wagsters can ever admit to the portions they don't know about. What do you think about that?"

"I think you're sharper than ever and just a little proud of your devious boys."

"Or I'm just trying to show off."

"Well, it's working, and it has been for a long time."

"Shh. Here comes Exlee," Deacon warned. "It looks like he's bringing us drinks. Oh wait, he's stopped to talk to somebody."

"Is she wearing glasses?"

"It's a man. Two of them. Whoops, here he comes again."

Exlee arrived and set a cocktail in front of each of them.

"In my years of research, I have found that these specific beverages are unrivaled when it comes to livening up the conversation," he announced as he sat in the vacant chair.

Emma laughed. "By livening up the conversation, I assume you mean getting women to say the single word 'yes.' "

"Emma, you really are adorable. If Deacon doesn't pick up the pace with you ... "

"Don't bother," Deacon warned. "She's too smart for your tricks and too kind to leave me on my own."

"I hate to break your heart, Exlee, but it's true," Emma said. "Deacon and I work too well as a team."

"Don't make any bold declarations yet," Exlee cautioned Emma. "Let me show you what you'd be missing. Pick any woman in this joint, and I bet you I can get her to dance without me using a single word."

"No written notes or pointing to the dance floor?" Deacon asked.

"No tricks. Just me and my come hither face. Now pick a woman, any woman."

Emma was already sizing up female possibilities. "I'm leaning toward the one over there, straight across from the corner of the stage. The one in silver with two other women at her table."

"That one?" Exlee asked with pain in his voice. "She looks as drunk as a skunk. She's liable to scream or throw a drink at me, if she can even see straight."

"Exactly why I picked her."

Exlee stood up, staring across at the girl while he fixed his necktie. He began to leave, but Deacon reached up and grabbed him by the arm.

"Is there a time limit on this?"

"Oh yeah, I almost forgot. This particular stunt takes forty seconds from the moment I stop in front of her table until I have her on the dance floor. Any longer and you win the bet."

With that he walked away toward the girl.

"Did he ever say what the stakes were on this bet?" Deacon asked.

"I really don't think he cares."

Having previously failed at this stunt by employing a series of suggestive eyebrow wiggles, Exlee opted for a new strategy. He would stand before the drunken girl and play shy, complete with sagging shoulders and what he thought was a peaceful, heartwarming expression of passivity.

It didn't work.

"What are you doing?" asked the girl in silver.

"Yeah, what's the matter with you?" asked her friend.

"Can't you talk?"

"Oh my God, Lizzie, I think he's deaf."

"Deaf means you can't hear. Mute is when you can't talk."

"Hey, cute guy, are you mute?"

Exlee knew he was running out of time, so he decided to cheat just a little. He began humming loudly to the orchestra's beat. He stared deep into the eyes of the drunken girl in silver, hoping she would read his mind.

"Oh my God, I think he's in love with you, Lizzie."

"He's crazy."

"What's wrong with him?"

"Why won't you talk?"

"What do you want?"

Deacon, meanwhile, was trying to keep track of the time limit on his wristwatch, but the laughter made his arm shake. He glanced at Emma. She was chewing on her finger and watching Exlee with wide eyes. He looked back at Exlee and was surprised to see one of the friends tugging on his arm. For the girls, the game had become about getting Exlee to talk, and he smiled to let them know he was in on it.

"I know how to make men talk."

"Do you like girls, mute guy?"

"Yeah, you can kiss me, but you have to talk first."

Exlee couldn't resist. "I'd only kiss you if you promised to never talk."

The three girls looked at each other in dramatic shock and dissolved into ugly, drunken laughter. Exlee walked away. He could hear them calling, asking where he was going, but half the fun was leaving confusion in his wake.

He stopped at Deacon and Emma's table but didn't sit down.

"That was the funniest thing I've seen in a long time." Deacon beamed.

"It's my gift to you, commemorating your first date," Exlee explained.

"I'd hate to see what kind of gift you give at a wedding," Emma said.

"There's only one way to find out, and that's by inviting me."

"Don't you ever stop?" Deacon asked.

"Actually, I'm leaving right now. Have fun, talk about something besides the news. Talk about sports or the Roman Empire or what kind of carpet you like."

Exlee grinned and departed.

Then he returned a moment later.

PINWHEEL

"I forgot to mention one last thing ... for when you're done here. You ever had a champagne drink called a Sharkey's Punch?"